Praise for *The Mystery of the Lost Cézanne*

﹏

"Art theft is a hot topic on the mystery scene, and no one's heist is livelier than Longworth's." —*Kirkus Reviews*

"A sure thing for fans of art-themed mysteries." —*Booklist*

"Enchanting . . . the charming local citizens of Aix-en-Provence provide the true delights in this colorful story." —*Library Journal*

Praise for *Murder on the Île Sordou*

﹏

"Charming."

—Marilyn Stasio, *The New York Times Book Review*

"[T]horoughly delightful. . . . Longworth deftly handles what is in effect a locked-room mystery, but the book's real strength lies in the backstories she creates for each of the distinctive characters. The puzzle's answer, buried in the past, is well prepared by what has come before."

—*Publishers Weekly* (starred review)

"Longworth once again immerses readers in French culture with this whodunit, which will delight Francophiles and fans of Donna Leon and Andrea Camilleri. The setting will also appeal to readers who enjoy trapped-on-the-island mysteries in the tradition of Agatha Christie's *And Then There Were None*."

—*Library Journal*

"Longworth's novels, set in the south of France, are mysteries for foodies, with the plot providing a table upon which the enchanting meals and accompanyin

paints such a loving picture of Provence that it's likely you'll start planning a vacation trip to France the moment you set the book down." —*The Denver Post*

"This is an intelligently written police procedural with the warm comfort of a baguette with banon cheese."
—*Ellery Queen Mystery Magazine*

"Enjoyable . . . the book's real strength is its evocation of place."
—*Publishers Weekly*

Praise for *Murder in the Rue Dumas*

"Fans of European sleuths with a taste for good food . . . will have fun." —*Publishers Weekly*

"What really makes Longworth's writing special is her deep knowledge of French history, landscape, cuisine, and even contemporary cafés and restaurants. This is that rare atmospheric mystery that is street-wise and café-canny."
—*Booklist* (starred review)

"Longworth's gentle procedural succeeds on several levels, whether it's for academic and literary allusions, police work, or armchair travel. With deftly shifting points of view, Longworth creates a beguiling read that will appeal to Louise Penny and Donna Leon fans." —*Library Journal*

"French-set mysteries have never been more popular [and] among the very best is a series set in Provence featuring Monsieur Verlaque, an examining magistrate, and his sometime girlfriend, law professor Marine Bonnet." —*The Denver Post*

Praise for *Death at the Château Bremont*

"This first novel in a projected series has charm, wit, and Aix-en-Provence all going for it. Longworth's voice is like a rich vintage of sparkling Dorothy Sayers and grounded Donna Leon . . . Longworth has lived in Aix since 1997, and her knowledge of the region is apparent on every page. Bon appétit."   —*Booklist*

"A promising debut for Longworth, who shows there's more to France than Paris and more to mystery than Maigret."

—*Kirkus Reviews*

"Mystery and romance served up with a hearty dose of French cuisine. I relished every word. Longworth does for Aix-en-Provence what Frances Mayes does for Tuscany: You want to be there—now!"   —Barbara Fairchild, former editor in chief, *Bon Appétit*

"*Death at the Château Bremont* is replete with romance, mystery, and a rich atmosphere that makes the south of France spring off the page in a manner reminiscent of Donna Leon's Venice. A wonderful start to a series sure to gain a legion of fans."

—Tasha Alexander, author of the Lady Emily mysteries

"Longworth has a good eye and a sharp wit, and this introduction to Verlaque and Bonnet holds promise for a terrific series."

—*The Globe and Mail*

"*Death at the Château Bremont* offers charming French locales, vivid characters, and an intriguing whodunit."

—Kevin R. Kosar, author of *Whiskey: A Global History*

"Here's hoping the series lasts for years."   —*RT Book Reviews*

"Your readers will eat this one up."   —*Library Journal*

A PENGUIN MYSTERY

The Curse of La Fontaine

M. L. LONGWORTH has lived in Aix-en-Provence since 1997. She has written about the region for the *Washington Post,* the *Times* (UK), the *Independent,* and *Bon Appétit* magazine. In addition to the Verlaque and Bonnet mystery series, she is the author of a bilingual collection of essays, *Une Américaine en Provence,* published by Éditions de La Martinière in 2004. She divides her time between Aix, where she writes, and Paris, where she teaches writing at New York University.

The Curse of La Fontaine

A VERLAQUE AND BONNET MYSTERY

· M. L. LONGWORTH ·

PENGUIN BOOKS

PENGUIN BOOKS

An imprint of Penguin Random House LLC
375 Hudson Street
New York, New York 10014
penguin.com

ISBN 9780143110941

Printed in the United States of America

Set in Adobe Caslon Pro   •   Designed by Elke Sigal

For Laurence and Jacques

Author's Note

There are many fountains, and restaurants, in Aix-en-Provence, but the two in this story have been invented by the author.

The Curse of La Fontaine

Prologue

≈

Dei Corallini

Antoine Verlaque liked dei Corallini so much he almost
regretted that his wedding was going to be so small. The Baroque beauty had been built in the seventeenth century with
money earned from coral fished out of the Mediterranean. The
local fishermen, thankful for their riches, funded the church's
construction, and the artisans who worked on it had been just
as proud, elaborately sculpting every bit of stone they could get
their hands on. But the end result wasn't overdone or kitsch.
The color of the stone was a subtle ivory, its elegance matched
by the remaining smooth spaces of the façade that were painted
in pale shades of yellow, pink, and green.

He imagined that Marine's parents would have preferred a
large wedding at their parish church, Saint-Jean de Malte, but
Verlaque felt that he was too old for such a traditional wedding.
He had insisted on Italy because it was a love that he shared

with Marine, but he knew, deep down, that he had wanted to avoid a wedding in Aix-en-Provence. Aix was where he lived and worked, and although it was a stunning city he didn't think it suited the occasion. He wanted their marriage to be a secret affair, hidden away in a small Ligurian village, away from the prying eyes of his fellow Aixois. It was almost as if he couldn't believe his good luck and didn't want to risk having someone run up the aisle loudly objecting to their union. Until he met Marine—at a dinner party arranged by a fellow lawyer friend who had since moved to Paris—he had never thought of himself as a marrying man. Other people got married, other people were happy, never him.

The pastel-colored church was slightly curved, looming over the cobbled square, facing out toward the sea as if protecting it. Sailors would have been able to see dei Corallini from far away, perched on its hill. Verlaque looked up, trying to focus on the various statues that sat in niches carved into the façade and not on what would be happening inside the church later that morning. Cars and scooters whizzed by down below on the road that joined all of the seaside towns leading to and from Imperia. Someone in the village called "Dario! Dario!" and a door slammed. Verlaque thought it extraordinary that it was just another Saturday for the villager and Dario but such an enormous day for him.

He smiled and walked on, continuing toward the restaurant, planning the seating arrangement in his head as he walked. They had invited Marine's parents, Anatole Bonnet, a general practitioner, and Florence Bonnet, a retired professor of theology; Sylvie, Marine's best friend, and her eleven-year-old daughter, Charlotte; Jean-Marc Sauvat, a mutual friend; Bruno Paulik, the police commissioner of Aix, and his wife, Hélène, and their daughter, Léa, also eleven years old; Verlaque's father, Gabriel, and his girlfriend, Rebecca Schultz; and Sébastien, Verlaque's brother. Marine had Sylvie as her maid of honor and he had Sébastien, for whatever good that would do—he and his brother were seldom in contact. Sébastien found Parisian real estate as exciting as Verlaque found it dull.

After the legal—and obligatory—wedding at Aix's Hôtel de Ville two weeks previously, Marine and Verlaque had arranged with the manager of their favorite café on the Cours Mirabeau to have an outdoor aperitif, an occasion where they could invite friends and colleagues from Aix. Flutes of champagne and plates of cold cuts were passed around, and locals and tourists alike walked down the narrow street smiling at what looked like an impromptu party.

They both hated the idea of a destination wedding, but the Ligurian village was only a three-hour drive from Aix, where most of the guests lived. And it wasn't as if they were making the whole wedding party travel to a Caribbean island; a colleague of Marine's had described a cousin's wedding at a resort in Barbados, which had forced the guests, including two elderly grandmothers, to take a fourteen-hour flight to a place that had no meaning for them or the bride and groom. Besides, Marine and her parents had been coming to Paradiso—her nickname for the village—since she was small, staying in a small rented apartment in the lower section of the village, near the beach, and she had brought Antoine there when she knew she loved him. She and Antoine always stayed in the old upper village and walked down hundreds of steps each morning to the sea, where they would dive into the water off the flat rocks that extended out beyond the sandy beach.

It was already warm, despite it being early April, and still early in the morning. The village was always humid and Verlaque hoped he wouldn't get too hot. He had almost gone barefoot in his black Weston loafers, and Marine had laughed when he walked out of the bathroom of their hotel earlier, dressed in a cobalt-blue suit but minus socks. "Don't you think you should wear socks?" she asked. "That's kind of a Guido look, and I'm not sure it's your style."

He looked down at his bare ankles. "Maybe you're right. Aren't you getting dressed?" he asked, seeing that she was still in her bathrobe.

"In Sylvie and Charlotte's room," Marine answered. "You're to have breakfast downstairs with my parents. I want my dress to be a surprise."

Verlaque rubbed his hands together. "Does it have cleavage? A bare back?"

Marine smiled, got up, and held the door open for him. "See you later." She kissed him and said, "You look wonderful, by the way. I love that color on you."

"Are you nervous?"

"Yes. I'm nervous and happy but oddly calm, as if I'm floating. And you?"

"I'm nervous about the pasta tonight," Verlaque replied. "I

hope they use a thick-enough noodle. One that will really pick up the sauce."

Marine stared at her husband and gave a wry laugh. "To think that in a few hours I'm going to be married to you."

"We're so lucky," he said, kissing her. "I'll go down and have breakfast with your adorable father and surly mother, and then I'm popping over to the restaurant to make sure I like the wine-glasses."

She stared at him, knowing that he was serious. "Good luck, then."

"See you at the church!"

Marine closed the door and walked over to the dresser, where she had put her dress, wrapped in tissue paper, in the bottom drawer. She took it out and laid it on the bed and went to the bathroom to shower. Sylvie had promised to do Marine's hair, and since Charlotte would be present Marine had invited Léa, knowing that inviting one eleven-year-old girl but excluding the other would have been unfair, even cruel. For the same reason she had decided not to have a flower girl.

The priest, Piero, was an easygoing fifty-year-old who obviously loved his job and wore his happiness on his smiling round face. They had known Piero for two years, thanks to one summer evening when their favorite restaurant had been overbooked and they had been placed at his table. He spoke excellent French and was impressed by Marine's Italian. They sent him a handwritten letter asking him to perform the marriage, in French if possible, and had included a photograph in case he hadn't remembered them. But he remembered his tablemates and was proud to be asked to preside over the wedding of such a charming *Giudice* and *Professoressa*. The priest's only stipulation was that the wedding would have to be in the morning, as Saturday afternoons were booked eighteen months ahead. They immediately agreed, knowing that their wedding would be small. Without late-night dancing and a DJ, a morning wedding followed by lunch would suit them fine. Piero had delicately suggested that, given their small wedding party, the ceremony take place in one of the church's chapels.

Verlaque walked through the medieval streets that were about two meters wide and paved with round, smooth river stones, the center of the street lined with red bricks. Despite their love of Paradiso they had never found the villagers overtly friendly—except for Piero and the restaurant team—and the villagers, who this morning seemed to be mostly old women, watched him now, their narrow gazes fixed on him, then looked away, unsmiling. Their unfriendliness sent a shiver up his back despite the heat. For the first time in months he felt uneasy about the wedding. Was it the wedding or the marriage? Marine Bonnet was perfect, and he knew it. But he was far from perfect. He was arrogant and bossy—looking back on it, he guiltily remembered insisting that they marry here in Liguria and not in Aix. Marine had quickly agreed, but had he even given her a choice? Their friends and family all seemed thrilled by the engagement, but now he heard their voices saying "You are so lucky, Antoine," and not the other way around. He was lucky to have Marine's hand in marriage, but perhaps she was getting the short end of the stick.

He looked up at a palazzo—a round ceramic plaque proudly

gave the building's date of construction as 1578—that had bright pink bougainvillea cascading down its pale yellow façade. He loved the pink and yellow with the dark green of the shutters. Whoever had chosen the colors had an eye for beauty, and yet the cautious villagers hardly smiled. Perhaps good design taste and general happiness did not go hand in hand. As if on cue an old woman opened the door of the palazzo, looked at him, and then quickly closed the door. He hadn't even had the chance to say *buongiorno*. Could these old women see into his soul? Did they, too, think Antoine Verlaque unworthy of Marine Bonnet?

He sighed and walked on, ducking his head to pass under a low stone arch. It was dark and he kept his eyes on the beam of sun at the end of the cramped tunnel, about twenty feet ahead. As he walked, his footsteps got louder and louder, echoing off the ancient stone walls that dripped in the humidity. He quickened his pace. He thought of his parents' long, unhappy, and dishonest marriage, his own philandering before he met Marine, his snobbishness and rudeness. Was that what the old villagers could see in him and so they turned away in disgust? Marine had made him a softer and better man; even his best friend, Jean-Marc, had once admitted that to Verlaque. And what had he given to Marine? How did he complete her? He ran out of the tunnel, into a square drowned in sunlight. Blinking because of the sun, he saw the bulk of someone wearing black walking through the square toward him. "Signore Verlaque! Il Giudice!" It was Padre Piero. Verlaque shook the priest's hand and said hello. "Are you all right?" Piero asked in slightly accented French. "Did you see a ghost in the tunnel?"

"My own," Verlaque said.

The priest smiled and took Verlaque's hands in his. "You are going to be married today. It's normal that you are feeling . . . uneasy."

"Back in the tunnel," Verlaque said, trying to catch his breath, "it was as if all my demons were following me."

"We do not want demons around on your wedding day."

Verlaque smiled. "What can I do?"

"Well, dear judge," Piero said, putting his arm around Verlaque's shoulders and leading him out of the square in the opposite direction, "we have two choices. One, you can go to confession—"

Verlaque stopped and laughed. "I haven't been to confession since—"

"Your confirmation?"

"Yeah, about then."

Piero said nothing and they walked on.

"What's the second option?" Verlaque asked, turning to the priest.

"*Un caffè corretto.*"

"Coffee and grappa? I'd prefer that."

"I thought you would. Come, let's go to the café, sit on the terrace, and look down at the sea. You are a good man, Antoine. I meet with many couples who are about to get married; you've seen how beautiful this village, and its church, is. It's a popular place to get married. These couples marry for all kinds of reasons, sometimes good, sometimes bad. All I can do is offer my advice, my compassion, and then perform the ceremony and hope for the best. They are, of course, nervous on the wedding day, as you are now. The men worry about the money, the end of their wild days. Maybe I'm being old-fashioned; per-haps the women worry about that, too." He laughed, and they turned down a narrow street that led to the café. "But most of the women, they are worried about the ceremony. The flowers. Their dress. And then the reception. The food. The guests. But your Professoressa is—how should I say it?—Zen. She has an inner happiness; she is glowing. You have made her happy."

Chapter One

✢

A Duke and His Garden

*L*e Duc de Pradet (Michel Xavier to his friends) was a lucky man, and he knew it. He was born in Paris in 1946 and so had missed the war and the German occupation. He was too young to have felt the hardships and rationing that continued well into the 1950s, having been protected by his parents. As a teen, he studied the subject he loved—not law, as many of his cousins were forced to—but history. His father was not very practical. At twenty-five he married Marguerite—again for love, not prestige or land (although Marguerite was rich).

Of course, not all of his life had been easy. They hadn't been able to have children, and that had been, in the beginning, heartbreaking, but as the years passed, they got used to the idea of being a family unit of two. To forget their childless state they traveled widely, and whereas another couple might have adopted or become more involved in their nieces' and nephews' lives, the duke and duchess became closer as a couple. They were not withdrawn—they had many friends and social obligations—but were simply content with each other's company. And so they got on with things: tending to their house and garden in Aix-en-Provence, a small manor house in Burgundy, and an apartment on the Left Bank in Paris. It seemed to fill their days. And then Marguerite died of breast cancer when she was sixty-three.

The duke sat on a wooden bench in his garden. It had rained earlier in the week, and the late April sun was shining. The plants were at their greenest—they would fade as the dry Aix summer arrived—and it was still cool enough, even in direct sunlight, to sit outside. That ability, like the neon green of the leaves, would soon disappear, and the duke would escape to Burgundy until mid-September.

He got up, stretched his legs, then picked up his basket and clippers and kid-leather gardening gloves. The duke watered the plants religiously, especially the roses, and when he was in Paris or Burgundy, he generously paid the maid to do the watering for him. The pale yellow Lady Banks was in full bloom, its clusters of small, almost-feathery roses cascading down against the stone wall of his town house. He clipped, humming, setting the roses carefully in the basket. Marguerite had been a talented flower arranger, but that task had been taken over by Manuel, the duke's manservant and cook.

A neighbor's window opened and closed, a child laughed, someone coughed. There was always noise in the garden, as more than a dozen buildings shared it. But the birds made the most noise there, drowning out the foot traffic on the nearby rue d'Italie and the cars and buses that sped along the boulevard du

Roi René. The duke stopped and smiled, remembering a fine two weeks visiting his friends Lord and Lady Ashcroft, whose Kensington town house also gave onto a communal garden. His idea of buying a wooden bench came from that London garden, including ordering an inscription to be carved across its back. It read: *Pour Marguerite, qui adorait ce jardin.*

He heard the cough again and turned around. "Mme Dreyfus," he said, smiling. He used the formal *madame* when addressing her; he was quite sure she had never married, but she was of a certain age. She was a handsome woman, with thick white hair kept short, almost a pixie cut, which showed off her deep blue eyes. She wore tortoiseshell reading glasses permanently around her neck, on a chain, and seemed to wear only black and white. He guessed the antiques dealer to be close to his age, or perhaps a few years younger.

"Lovely roses," she said.

"Would you like some?" the duke asked, pointing to his basket. "You must have a small elegant vase, perhaps from Sèvres, in your shop."

"I have the perfect one," she answered. "Yes, I'd love a few roses, if you can spare them."

"Shall I run into the house and get Manuel to wrap these up for you?"

"No, no," she said.

"But the thorns . . ."

"I have a handkerchief," she replied, pulling an antique linen handkerchief out of her sweater pocket.

"Very enterprising," the duke replied, carefully wrapping the handkerchief around the stems. "Who's manning the shop?"

Mme Dreyfus pointed to her watch. "It's lunchtime."

"Oh, so it is," he answered, looking up at the sky. "I lost track of time."

"You can't hear the clients in the restaurant?" she asked, gesturing behind her. "They have the windows wide open."

"No, mercifully; although I can hear the fountain, especially at night." The duke realized that Gaëlle Dreyfus's shop and her apartment were only two buildings away from the new restaurant, whereas his house sat at the garden's opposite end. He never heard a peep from the restaurant, and, in fact, rarely had the opportunity to walk along the rue Mistral. It was as if it was worlds away.

"That's partly why I'm here," Mme Dreyfus said. "It's about the restaurant . . ."

"Please," the duke said, "sit down."

Gaëlle Dreyfus sat down on the very English-looking bench and looked at the duke, realizing for the first time that he resembled an English lord more than a French duke, from his Harris Tweed coat and woolen waistcoat to his thinning gray hair that he wore a little too long in the back. And yet she saw, from his high cheekbones, wide thin lips, and blue eyes (not unlike her own), that he would have been a handsome young man. "I have a client," she began, "an architect, who has informed me that the chef of the restaurant, who is also its owner, has applied to the city for permission to extend the dining room outside."

"He'll never get permission," the duke quickly replied, crossing his arms for emphasis. "There's not a single restaurant terrace in this *quartier*."

"Ah," Mme Dreyfus said. "But the new mayor, I'm told, is sympathetic to business owners and less to . . ."

"Residents."

"Yes," she answered, intentionally leaving out the words *privileged* and *nobility*.

"*Mais la fontaine*," he continued. "It's historically listed."

"Yes, but the fountain is, technically, on the restaurant's land, although we all share the greater garden."

"My parents used to get water out of it."

You mean they sent the servants off to fetch the water, Mme Dreyfus mused. "I still do," she answered.

"Is it safe?"

"Of course; it's tested every year," she said. "All natural springs have to be."

"Well, then. What can we do about this situation?"

"That's partly why I'm here," she answered. "I'm on the historical committee of Aix, and we'd like your help."

"Of course, of course," he replied, almost absently.

Mme Dreyfus smiled. "I've just begun to inform the other neighbors," she went on. "Bénédicte and Serge Tivolle, who live next door to the restaurant, already know of the chef's plans . . . Bénédicte is the treasurer of our historical committee. I've spoken to Thomas and Stéphanie Roche, who live near the restaurant, and Marine Bonnet. Professor Bonnet teaches law at the university and lives on the top floor over there." Mme Dreyfus pointed to a top-floor apartment about halfway down the garden, with a large terrace that had climbing roses, a jasmine plant that twisted its way around the terrace's railing, and two potted olive trees.

"A law professor . . . ," the duke mumbled. They had been at a dinner party together, years back. He remembered an interesting conversation and a great loud laugh.

"Yes, but she's recently married Aix's *juge d'instruction.*" The antiques dealer beamed, as if she had just delivered the winning answer on a quiz show. A door opened to the duke's house and the smell of cheese and eggs wafted outside. "I'm sorry," Mme Dreyfus said, seeing Manuel Arruda, who was wearing a starched apron, standing in the kitchen doorway. "I believe your lunch is ready."

The duke turned around and waved to Manuel. "*J'arrive!*" he called. He would have liked to invite Mme Dreyfus for lunch, but he had no idea how much omelet, or soufflé, Manuel had made.

"Montaigne had quotations carved into the beams of his library's ceiling," Frère Joël said after taking a sip of his strong hot coffee. "I used to visit his house all the time; my grandparents lived nearby."

"I remember the library and the carved beams," the duke replied, passing a tray of cookies to the brother. "But I can't remember what was written on them."

"Words of the Roman philosophers," the brother answered. "One was Seneca's advice on living well."

"A subject of great interest to Montaigne."

"Exactly," Frère Joël said. "It says if you get depressed or bored in your retirement, just interest yourself in the variety and sublimity of things around you . . ."

"Gardens, for example," the duke quickly said.

"Your roses," Frère Joël suggested, looking up at the Lady Banks. "Or our historic buildings in Aix."

"You could carefully study all the Cézanne paintings in the Musée Granet."

The men laughed and both took another cookie off the porcelain plate Manuel had brought out. Aix's museum owned only ten works, minor ones, of its most famous son.

The duke slowly chewed and then asked, "Are you saying I look depressed? Or bored?"

"No," Frère Joël replied after a moment's hesitation. "But I'm afraid something is bothering you."

It had been more than a year since Frère Joël and the duke began their coffee tradition, now almost daily, at 5:00 p.m. The half-Gothic, half-Romanesque church of Saint-Jean de Malte shared the same garden; its access was a small wooden door that opened on the rue Cardinale, across the street from the church. The duke wasn't an especially religious man, or even a believer, but he was so used to going to Mass that the thought of not going seemed impossible, like not eating breakfast or not stopping to wash oneself. Marguerite, a Bavarian, had been deeply religious, and a fine singer as well, and so if he went now it was more to listen to the choir and hear Père Jean-Luc's thought-provoking sermons than to be beaten over the head with the Scriptures. But no one was getting beaten over the head at Saint-Jean de Malte, and although the duke admired Père Jean-Luc, he had more in common with the young brother from Périgord who had arrived at the church two years previously, and who, like the duke, had studied history as an undergraduate.

The duke looked at his young friend and said, "I've had a rather disagreeable visit to my physician."

Frère Joël put his head down for a moment and then looked at the duke. "I'm sorry," he said. "Has the doctor made a prognosis?"

"Not yet," the duke replied. "More nasty tests are needed. And before you tell me not to worry, I'm not worrying about death. Like your fellow Périgourdin, Montaigne. I don't remember what's written on the carved beams, but I do know what he said about death: Don't give death a second's thought."

"So there's no use worrying about it," Frère Joël quickly said, trying to smile. "Is there something you'd like to talk about?"

"Get off my chest?" the duke asked. "Before—"

"I didn't mean that," Frère Joël quickly said.

"I haven't been to confession in years. Decades."

"We can do it here."

"In the garden?" the duke asked, looking around at his carefully pruned hedges. "All right. There is something I'd like to confess. But not today. I suppose I should prepare myself for the worst. Prepare to die, if needed."

"I wouldn't worry—"

The duke laughed. "Are you quoting Montaigne again? What was it that he wrote? 'If you don't know how to die, don't worry. Nature will show you. She'll do it beautifully.'"

Chapter Two

❧

The World According to Philomène Joubert

"M ay I congratulate you, Marine?" Philomène Joubert said. They were in the market, at the same stall, looking at bundles of local springtime asparagus.

"*Oui, merci beaucoup, Mme Joubert,*" Marine said, smiling and taking Mme Joubert's hand and squeezing it. "It was a small wedding," she quickly added, in case Philomène Joubert had the feeling that the entire choir of Saint-Jean de Malte should have been invited. "In Italy . . ."

"Your mother showed us photographs, just before Mass last Sunday," Philomène said.

"Really?" Marine asked, not hiding her surprise. Of her parents, a family doctor and a retired theology professor, it was her mother, the theologian, who was the least likely to show her emotions, or enthusiasm, especially over sentimental matters.

"Oh yes," Philomène replied. "You were beautiful." She selected a bundle of asparagus and examined it. "Mme Martin," she called out, holding the bundle up and waving it in the air, "*vous en avez des blanches?*"

Marine smiled, hoping that Mme Martin had white asparagus for her neighbor, and that way she could have more of the thin green ones for her dinner party that evening. She had been introduced to the green variety by an old woman selling her produce out of a small boat in Venice. "Risotto, risotto," the elderly Venetian insisted, and Marine had bought the whole lot.

Mme Martin handed her client a bundle of fat white asparagus. Philomène looked at the vegetables, nodded to Mme Martin, and set them into her cloth bag. She went on. "And that jewel of a pink church; it looked like candy or a wedding cake." She then laughed at her joke, and Marine joined in.

"Nice to hear laughing," Mme Martin said. "Lots of glum faces around here this morning."

"*Ah bon?*" Philomène asked. "In this lovely weather?"

"Boredom," Mme Martin replied flatly.

Marine picked up three bundles of the thinnest green asparagus she could find and put them into a basket. Philomène Joubert looked at Marine and frowned. "That doesn't have the same flavor as the white."

"I know," Marine answered, smiling.

"People are bored," Mme Martin went on, warming to her subject.

"Who's bored?" Philomène asked, now inspecting the artichokes, also in season.

"If you've nothing to do, then you're depressed," Mme

Martin said. "Look around you. I have at least seven or eight female friends who have every reason to be happy—health, a roof over their heads, a safe country to live in—and they're depressed. What's lacking?"

Philomène said, "Perhaps—"

"Well, I'll tell you," Mme Martin said, cutting Mme Joubert off. She held up her hand and began counting on her fingers. "Number one: children, or a child. Having to take care of another human means you can't worry about your own petty problems."

"I have three fine sons," Philomène said.

"Number two: if you don't have children, and there are lots of people who can't, you need to be happy in your work."

Philomène, who had helped her husband run his printing shop for more than forty years, had loved their work, but she kept quiet this time. She looked over at Marine, who was smiling and nodding. *Newlywed*, she thought. *She's in the clouds.*

"And if by chance you have neither of those, you need a hobby," Mme Martin said. "*Une passion!*"

"My passion right now is getting home to cook this asparagus!" Philomène said, handing Mme Martin a handful of coins.

Marine picked up a dozen small violet artichokes and decided to brave the preparing of them; they would be wonderful along with the leg of lamb she had planned for her dinner party. She quickly paid Mme Martin, who had turned her attention to another customer who had joined in on the conversation: she had read an article about the importance of keeping busy in a women's magazine.

"Well?" Philomène asked. "Are you going back to your apartment? We can walk together."

"I am, in fact," Marine said.

"Are you going to sell it?"

Marine smiled, not surprised by her neighbor's boldness. Philomène Joubert was known for it. "We can't decide," Marine answered. "We both love our apartments."

"A fortunate problem."

"A first-world problem, my students would say," Marine replied as they walked along the rue Thiers. "We are lucky, yes. And very happy."

Philomène clicked her teeth in agreement. "What a lot of hocus-pocus Mme Martin was on about. It's only common sense that if you keep busy you will be happy. Sure, I've had the blues now and then, especially when our François lost his first wife, or when we finally closed down the print shop, but I told myself, 'Philomène, do at least one productive thing with your day. Just one.' So I'd get up out of bed and bake a pie. Or do the ironing. The next day I'd do a little more, and then, voilà, the emptiness was gone."

Marine nodded. She liked the fact that Philomène had used the word *vide* instead of *triste*; "emptiness" was more apt, and more powerful, than "sadness." The nagging feeling in the pit of her stomach acted up again; it had been coming and going for two weeks, and she had told no one about it. It came at the oddest times, usually happy moments like this one, walking in the morning sunshine with a neighbor. She said, "Mme Martin is partly right in what she says. About having a passion. I have a good job, but I'm not sure how much I like it."

"You wouldn't call it a passion?" Philomène asked as she frowned at two high school students who passed by, both eating croissants while they walked. "*Bon appétit, les filles!*"

"There's nowhere for them to sit and eat," Marine said to defend the girls. "We need more benches and parks downtown." The pit gnawed at her stomach once more. It felt a little odd to be having this discussion with someone she didn't know that well, instead of Antoine, or Sylvie, or her parents. But perhaps Philomène might be the best person to talk to. She continued. "No, it's not a passion. It used to be. But I do have a hobby that I love."

"And what's that?" Philomène asked. She knew that Marine Bonnet was very educated and cultured, and that her husband was as well. She hoped she would understand Professor Bonnet's reply and that it wouldn't be something too odd.

"Writing," Marine said.

"But you have to do that as a professor, don't you?" Philomène picked up her stride, happy to have provided a response.

"Yes, but I don't want to write law articles anymore. I'd like to write about lives."

"Lives of famous people?" Philomène couldn't imagine Marine Bonnet writing about movie stars or soccer players.

"Yes, I'd like to be a biographer. I've started researching the lives of Simone de Beauvoir and Jean-Paul Sartre. I'd like to write about their relationship."

Philomène Joubert stopped in the middle of the sidewalk. She whistled and then said, "Do you want to sell a book on the bedroom life of those two? No one would buy it, Mme Verlaque! What smut!"

"Perhaps it wasn't as smutty as all that," Marine said.

"Tsk tsk," Philomène answered, shaking her finger. "*With* her *students*," she whispered, leaning into Marine. "Her *female* students."

Marine tried not to cringe. As much as she admired the couple's work ethic and open relationship (it worked for them, but never would for her), the fact that Simone de Beauvoir had slept with her students, be they male or female, appalled her. But perhaps making a moral pronouncement wasn't up to her; all she could do was to research and read as much as she could and then lay out the facts for her readers. Wasn't that the biographer's job? Even her beloved Montaigne admitted that he didn't know all the answers: he watched, questioned, and wrote, often ending his sentences with "though I don't know." The problem was, Marine Bonnet *wanted* to know. Admitting bewilderment went against her nature. It was one of the reasons why Antoine Verlaque was so good for her: he helped her to slow down, to be less perfect, to relax.

Bear Valets was running down the rue Thiers, his arms taut and extended from carrying two bags of various sizes and kinds of artichokes, when he saw the women ahead of him, strolling and chatting. He slowed down and stopped; then, putting one of the heavy bags down, he looked at his watch. It was almost 9:00 a.m. He picked the artichokes back up and walked on, watching them. The tall, younger woman was a client he was particularly fond of. He didn't know her name, but she came to his restaurant with a guy with a broken nose, who, despite his lack of classic good looks, intrigued Bear: He was at once authoritative and serious (especially when studying the wine menu, full of Italian stars), but when he looked across the table at *her*, he was someone very much in love.

Valets worked in an open kitchen—something he had first seen in London—and would watch his customers when he got the chance. After the last clients had finished their main course, Bear made the rounds of the small dining room: He had spoken to this couple more than once and had noted their bright gold wedding bands. She played with hers, as if still getting used to it; his looked like it had been on his hand forever. They had lots of questions about the food and, like everyone else, asked how he, a young French cook, had acquired the name Bear. "I moved to England after high school and my mates couldn't pronounce Sigisbert," he usually replied. "So I've been Bear ever since."

And he did have a bearlike quality to him, both Marine and Verlaque had commented while strolling back to Marine's apartment. The chef was short, with a thick build, a head of coarse, curly black hair, and sideburns that he grew intentionally long, trimming each end into a long, thin point that came to within about a half-inch of his wide smile. Antoine Verlaque took an instant liking to him.

Bear Valets, born and raised in Aix, had graduated from high school with an 18,5 Bac score in general sciences and, instead of applying to a French medical or pharmacy school, left France for a full scholarship to study biology at University College London. He had always enjoyed his English classes in high school and had spent summers with families in Wales, Wyoming, and Yorkshire, perfecting the language. He swam through his first year of studies, but halfway through his second year the recession hit and his father lost his job as the head of a small French pharmaceutical company. Bear tried stretching his scholarship money as much as he could, but it wasn't enough to live in central London or to pay for train trips back home. "Do what I do," a brilliant Indian friend in his dorm had told him. "Get a part-time restaurant job."

Bear realized why he was so intrigued by this customer and why he was making himself late at the restaurant by slowly following her down the rue Thiers: She reminded him of Jane. Jane Clark had been his inspirational boss at Cavolo Nero, a chic restaurant on the banks of the Thames. He had passed it on the bus, saw its name and the bright blue awnings that covered the big windows in what had once been a factory, rang the bus's stop bell, ran off the bus, and marched into the restaurant at 5:30 p.m., a folded CV in his back pocket. Jane and Judith were standing at the bar, drinking cups of strong espresso and going over the evening's menu with a pencil and an eraser. He recognized them from a *Guardian* article he had read: Jane and her business partner, Judith Hodges, were the only female chefs duo in London, and were vanguards, putting rustic Italian cuisine, the food of Jane's Italian mother-in-law, back on the city's once-stuffy, old-fashioned, men's-club-inspired menus. Bear Valets pretended to study his cell phone as he listened to their conversation.

"We'll use the Capri arugula in the artichoke salad. Do we have enough?" Jane had asked.

"Yes," Judith had replied. "Just." Where Jane was tall and slim, with curly auburn hair, Judith was short with spiky black hair and olive skin.

That day's lunch menu was sitting on the white marble counter. Bear put his phone away and read the one-page menu in fine detail. It was like taking a trip to Italy, something he and his family had done numerous times. The ridged zucchini for the soup came from a walled garden in Suffolk; the linguine with mussels was made with a rare wine from Liguria called Pigato; the pan-fried organic chicken was stuffed with mascarpone and rosemary. He thought mascarpone was a thick cream cheese, but he wasn't certain.

"Can we help you, young man?" Judith asked, setting down her white espresso cup.

The room smelled of herbs and olive oil, and there was a clatter and laughter coming from the kitchen. The view out the back windows, which he hadn't seen from the road, was of a garden and the rushing, churning Thames, which he knew flowed in both directions, being tidal.

"I'd like to work here," Bear blurted out. "Anything." He approached them, shaking their hands and pulling out the CV, then handing it to, he decided, the nicer of the two, Jane Clark. Jane quietly read it while Judith looked at Bear with a raised eyebrow. "Have you worked in a restaurant before?" she asked.

"No," Jane answered before Bear could.

"I'm a student at UCL," Bear said, his voice breaking. "I'm French, and got eighteen point five on the Bac. In science."

"Nobody gets that kind of grade on the French Bac," Judith replied. "Even I know that."

Jane pointed to Bear's CV.

"My dad lost his job," Bear went on, trying to look into Jane's sympathetic green eyes. "I need the money. I'm a good worker, I love Italian food, and I'll do anything."

He thought he saw a smirk forming at the corners of Judith's mouth, but Jane put her hand on her colleague's shoulder. "Can you give us a second . . . ? How do you pronounce your name?"

"See-jeez-bear. But everyone at school calls me Bear."

"Bear it is," Judith said. The women left the bar and walked into the kitchen together. It was partly open and he could see them speaking, while the kitchen staff, young, and most of them very good-looking, began pulling vegetables out of crates or cutting herbs. He saw Judith hold her hands up, then go speak to a young man who was doing something to a fish; Bear couldn't quite make out what. Jane came back out into the bar and smiled. "Can you work tonight? We're short one person. I was going to call my husband and get him to come down." She pointed to the ceiling. "He has his architecture practice upstairs."

Bear smiled widely. He liked her humor, as he knew of the famous, very famous, architect upstairs; that, too, had been in the newspaper article. "Yes, I can."

"You can bus tables," Jane answered. "Jamie over there—the guy with the messy blond hair—will show you the ropes. We do things unconventionally here; the waitstaff often helps in the kitchen. Are you in for that?"

"*Sì!*" said Bear, grinning.

"Okay, great," Jane answered. "Do you have any questions before Jamie finds you an apron that fits?"

Bear bit his upper lip, deciding not to ask if everyone who worked at the restaurant had a first name that began with *J*. He asked instead, "What's a cavolo nero?"

Chapter Three

≿

The Dinner Party

M arine wore a short white dress, fitted in the bust with a puffy and multilayered skirt falling to just above the knees. It was, Verlaque thought he remembered, made out of a fabric called dotted swiss. Much to his disappointment, Marine had not taken up his offer for a shopping spree in Paris or Rome but had bought the dress on sale on the Internet. It had a scoop neck and short sleeves that showed off her arms—thin, slightly tanned, and with thousands of freckles. He lifted the album to just below his nose and looked at his wife. She was holding a small bouquet of pink and white peonies, which they had bought just after crossing the border, at a roadside stand beside a gas station. Peonies were in season and Marine had forgotten to buy the flowers in Aix. They had cost fifteen euros, and she had snipped off the bottom of their stalks using a picnic knife that Verlaque kept in the glove compartment and then tied them together with one of her elastic hair bands. Once at the hotel, she stuck the flowers in the bathroom sink.

He turned a page in the thick white album—a gift from Sylvie—and took a puff of his Bolivar Super Corona. Sylvie, a renowned photographer, had suggested her best student, Régis, as the wedding photographer. Sylvie wanted to relax and enjoy the party, and she knew that she could follow Régis around, too, suggesting photo opportunities. They couldn't very well ask Sylvie to take the photos anyway. It would have been like asking a three-star Michelin chef to make hot dogs, mused Verlaque. And Régis had done well, mixing black-and-white photos with color and portraits with group shots, then stills: a silver bowl full of local cherries; a lone champagne glass sitting on a low stone wall, the sparkling sea below; Marine laughing, caught by Régis as she quickly reapplied her lipstick.

His father looked good. Tall and thin—so unlike Antoine. Rebecca smiled, her hand slipped through the elder Verlaque's arm. They looked happy, and much like they had been a couple for decades, not months. Rebecca Schultz was an art historian—a Cézanne specialist from Yale—whom Verlaque had met a few cases back: Schultz had helped (and got in the way of) the Aix police determining the authenticity of a nineteenth-century portrait, one that appeared to be a Cézanne. The case had taken them to Paris, and when Rebecca was followed by a menacing motorcyclist, Verlaque had put her into the one safe Parisian house he knew—his parent's—not ever imagining that his father and the art historian would fall in love. At the time his mother had been in a hospice, suffering from anorexia, and had since died.

He looked more closely at the photograph and saw something he hadn't seen the first time around: On the right, a few meters behind the couple, stood Marine's mother, arms crossed, frowning. Verlaque laughed out loud. He looked at Florence Bonnet's expression. Could her disapproval stem from the fact that Rebecca was thirty years younger than his father? Or that they had fallen in love while his mother was still alive? Or that Rebecca Schultz was an African American who had been adopted by a Jewish couple? Verlaque took a long puff of his cigar. Was Dr. Florence Bonnet anti-Semitic? Or racist? Not likely. Verlaque chose the most benign option and decided that Marine's mother disapproved of the couple's age difference. In fact, he did, too. Had Régis seen the disapproving theologian looking at the couple? Or had this excellent photograph been an accident? It was brilliantly composed, and Verlaque was still laughing when he heard the front door open and close. Marine came into the kitchen and then walked through the door, out onto the terrace. She leaned down and kissed his forehead. "What's so funny?" she asked.

Verlaque held up the book for her. "Look at your mother, behind Dad and Rebecca."

Marine rolled her eyes and laughed. "Maman isn't much good at hiding what she thinks."

"*Ah bon?*" Verlaque asked with heavy sarcasm in his voice. "We should hire her at the Palais de Justice," he added. "She'd scare the wits out of some of those young thugs."

"We could get Philomène Joubert to help, too," Marine suggested. "She was working her magic at the market this morning."

Verlaque laughed even harder and set the book down, motioning for Marine to sit on his lap. She sat down, wrapping her arms around his neck and resting her head on his shoulder. He picked up the book and his cigar.

"Antoine," she said, "you can hardly smoke and look at wedding photographs with someone sitting on your lap!"

"Sure I can. Look." He turned a page and Marine wobbled back and forth, losing her balance.

She stood up and pointed to her watch. "Guests are arriving in less than two hours. I'm going to start cooking."

"I'll come in and help," Verlaque said. "I just want to look at the photos one more time."

Marine laughed. "I'll give you five minutes and then I need you in here to trim the artichokes."

"May I—"

"No, you may not smoke your cigar at the same time."

Verlaque mumbled something and Marine laughed, putting on an apron. As she got the food out of the refrigerator, she glanced at her new husband, who was looking at their wedding photographs for the hundredth time, his reading glasses perched at the end of his once-broken and now-crooked nose. He had a huge smile on his face. How the examining magistrate of Aix-en-Provence had changed from the first time she met him, a ball of nerves thinly disguised with a glass of whiskey and a cigar.

Verlaque closed the book and set down his cigar in the oversize red Havana Club ashtray, a birthday gift from his brother, Sébastien. Going into the kitchen, he kissed Marine on the back of the neck and washed his hands at the kitchen sink.

"Remind me who's coming," he said, drying his hands with a tea towel.

"Sylvie; some neighbors, Thomas and Stéphanie Roche; and Gaëlle Dreyfus. We'll be six."

"Gaëlle is the antiques dealer on rue Cardinale, right? My father loves her shop."

"Yes," Marine answered, setting a bowl with a dozen artichokes in front of Verlaque. "And the Roches live in a garden apartment on our street, down a few buildings."

"The garden with the Portuguese tiles on the wall?" he asked. "You can see it from the terrace."

"That's the one," Marine answered.

"*Azulejos,*" Verlaque whispered, hugging his wife. Marine kissed him and whispered back "*Azulejos,*" but with a better Portuguese pronunciation. "Showoff," he said. "Okay, put me to work."

Marine opened a drawer, took out three different knives, and set them down. Verlaque looked at the knives and then at his wife, perplexed.

"The serrated knife is for cutting off the tip of the artichoke," she said. "Then you take off most of the outer leaves until you get to the pale yellow ones. With the big knife, you cut the artichoke into fourths lengthwise, and with the small paring knife you dig out the hairy middle and any other thorny bits."

"There will hardly be anything left," he said, frowning. "It's a lot of work for not much artichoke flesh."

"Yes, that's why they're so expensive when jarred in olive oil and sold in fancy shops." She set a bowl of cold water before him and squeezed a lemon into it. "Drop them in here. They need to soak a bit."

"Why lemon?"

"I have no idea," she quickly answered. "I had to look up the recipe today, between classes. Now stop asking questions or we'll be late."

Verlaque nodded, seeing that Marine was getting frazzled. Cooking was the only thing that he knew of that made her lose her composure—not lecturing, not writing law articles under unreasonably short deadlines, not meeting new people or shopping in the market on a busy Saturday, something that he avoided at all costs. Marine winced, rubbing her stomach. She had turned her back, but Verlaque had seen her discomfort. It was unlike her, too, to raise her voice and be short-tempered. He picked up an artichoke and the serrated knife, then said, "Lamb, artichokes, potatoes, and fresh asparagus. It's going to be fabulous."

Gaëlle Dreyfus was the first to arrive. When invited for dinner she sometimes selected a small object from her shop as a gift, as she did this evening. Marine had been going to Gaëlle's shop for years, ever since she was a teen. Marine had always loved antiques, and in particular silver and china for the table, perhaps because she hadn't grown up with it. Before closing her shop Gaëlle selected a set of six crystal knife rests. They were Baccarat, and she slowly wrapped them in lilac-colored tissue paper, as the 1940s box the set came in was long gone. It was an extravagant hostess gift, but it was a wedding gift, too, and she had bought them at a good price from someone who hadn't known their value.

Marine loved the knife rests, and Gaëlle was delighted. The professor's husband, introduced simply as Antoine, quickly took the existing knife rests off the table and replaced them with the Baccarat.

"I wish you both years of happiness," Gaëlle said.

"Thank you," Marine answered. "I feel like we should be toasting that with champagne, but—"

"No, no," Gaëlle said. "We should wait for the others."

Five minutes later the other guests, having arrived at the same time, were present, introductions were made, and Verlaque lifted the champagne out of its icy bucket.

"Thomas used to open champagne with a saber!" Stéphanie Roche exclaimed.

"Only outside in the garden," Thomas said. "It was for the kids, really."

"So that works?" Sylvie asked, giving a start as the cork made its usual popping sound. "I thought it was a myth."

"Clean as a whistle," Thomas replied.

"How long have you lived on our street?" Marine asked.

"We bought the apartment when we were still living in South Africa, where Thomas was an engineer." Stéphanie answered. "I grew up here, so we bought the apartment for our retirement. We moved in five years ago."

"Ah, retirement," Gaëlle said. "That's a magic word."

The aperitif passed smoothly. The guests enjoyed several rounds of champagne (a second bottle was opened), thinly sliced sausage laced with green peppers that Marine's butcher had recommended, fresh radishes with sea salt for dipping, almonds, and a small bowl of sweet pickled garlic. Despite the guests having little in common, the conversation flowed smoothly enough, and they all agreed that the mayor's new shopping mall built at the bottom of Aix's main street, the Cours Mirabeau, was a disaster. "I refuse to buy anything there," Stéphanie exclaimed, crossing her arms. Gaëlle kept the thought to herself that Mme Roche had never bought anything in her shop, either.

"I'm proud of our bookstores standing up to the mayor and big business," Marine said.

"Is that why the FNAC doesn't sell books?" Thomas asked of the huge Parisian franchise that sold electronics, DVDs, CDs, and, in Paris, books.

"Yes, they agreed to that when signing the lease," Marine explained. "They could sell music and electronics and such, but not books."

"You've been into the FNAC?" his wife asked, glaring. Thomas looked into his flute and muttered something about needing advice on fixing his computer.

"Hear, hear," Verlaque said, raising his glass. "To our booksellers."

"That Anglo-Saxon bookshop down the street is a heavenly spot for afternoon tea," Gaëlle said. "I sometimes go there before I open up my shop again at four-thirty. There's something wonderful about tea and scones and the smell of books."

The aperitif went on, the guests on their best behavior, avoiding subjects that can ruin a dinner party between neighbors, like politics. During a conversation about Aix's new dance theater, designed by a young Marseillais architect, Marine noted that Stéphanie Roche politely nodded up and down while her husband yawned.

"It's a jewel of a building," said Gaëlle Dreyfus. "It's basically a glass box, but what a brilliant move to frame it with those black concrete beams that crisscross, going every which way, like webs." She gestured with her hands quickly slicing the air in long diagonal movements. "And I don't even like contemporary art!"

"I love it, too," Sylvie agreed. "We need more black buildings."

Marine saw Thomas Roche flinch. "I stopped on my way home from the library one night," she said, passing the olives across the coffee table. "The rehearsal room was lit up and I could see the troupe dancing. It was mesmerizing. I must have stayed there for ten minutes."

Verlaque stood up to serve more champagne. "Plus the architect is a cigar aficionado. He was on the cover of *L'Amateur de Cigare* this month."

"Oh, shut up, Antoine," Sylvie said, winking. "Nobody cares about your stupid cigars."

An hour later they were sitting at the table. The leg of lamb was cooked perfectly—pink—and the potatoes and artichokes that had roasted under the meat were tangy and juicy. As Verlaque thinly sliced the meat, Marine served the wine, walking slowly around the table.

"Oh, a female wine steward," Thomas Roche said.

Sylvie looked across the table at Marine and mouthed "Moron."

"Marine chose the wine, too," Verlaque said, smiling. "I wanted a red Bordeaux, but Marine quite rightly pointed out that the acidity of the artichokes called for a floral white." When they had begun dating Marine had been a novice wine drinker. But she learned to appreciate and understand wines by doing what she usually did when setting out to learn about a new subject: She read. She pored over wine atlases, memorizing the many *appellations controlées* in France; then read in detail about wine in Bordeaux, Burgundy, and the Rhône; finally devoured biographies on winemakers and critics. The last one, a gift from Verlaque, was the memoir of Jancis Robinson, the eminent English wine critic. "It's in English," he had apologized. Marine had muttered thanks and grabbed the book, fluffed up the two pillows behind her head, and turned to the first page. "But I suppose it could be written in Russian and you'd still devour it," he'd joked, seeing Marine's excitement to begin yet another book about a life.

"Oh, it's a Châteauneuf-du-Pape!" Thomas exclaimed. "No problem with white, Antoine. The white ones are hard to find up there."

Verlaque smiled, hoping it looked genuine.

"I once dated a New Yorker," Gaëlle said. "He took me to his favorite restaurant in Manhattan—Veritable, Veritas, something like that—and introduced me to the owner, an American who has the keys to the village of Châteauneuf-du-Pape."

"A Yankee!" exclaimed Thomas, setting his napkin down with a theatrical thump. "Why on earth?"

"Because in his subterranean wine cellar," explained Gaëlle, "he has eighty thousand bottles of the stuff. All Châteauneuf-du-Pape." She quickly added, smiling at Verlaque, "Red *and* white, I would imagine."

"Not a very varied collection, I have to say," Thomas Roche said.

Who's asking you? thought Sylvie.

"Thomas," Verlaque said, reaching across the table to pour his guest more wine, "have you been to the new restaurant on the rue Mistral? The chef is really proud of his wine list. Mostly Italian . . ." He thought he should try to make conversation with Marine's neighbor, a man with whom he had nothing in common and a man he would unlikely ever share a table with again. But good breeding had trained him to engage others in conversation.

Marine, seeing Thomas Roche's face turn red, quickly added, "The chef is very charming and enthusiastic, and everyone calls him Bear, short for Sigisbert."

"You've *spoken* to him?" asked Stéphanie Roche.

Verlaque looked around the table, surprised. "Of course," he said. "We love eating there." He looked to Marine.

"Yes," Marine said. "He—Bear, I mean—has a really interesting CV. He studied science in London—"

"I don't care where he studied!" Thomas Roche said.

Stéphanie Roche set her knife and fork aside and said, "You all know, I presume, that the chef has been granted a license for outside seating. In our neighborhood!" The Mazarin was a privileged neighborhood in downtown Aix, filled with listed eighteenth-century manor homes, most of which had been cut up into apartments. The small *quartier* had very few shops, no bars, and only two or three restaurants. Bear's was the most discreet, hidden behind carved wooden doors save for one window on the street, with only a small brass plaque announcing its name: La Fontaine. Shopping was done on the rue d'Italie, technically in the Mazarin but not considered so by those residents lucky enough to live in the listed buildings on the rue Cardinale, the rue du 4 Septembre, or the rue Goyrand, where often the only sounds were birds and water gurgling from fountains. Stéphanie Roche looked around the table for support.

"Don't look at me," Sylvie said. "I live on the poor side of town." She held out her empty plate for seconds. Verlaque jumped up and served her.

"It's not the same for any of you," Stéphanie went on. "You don't live on the ground floor, two doors down from the restaurant, like we do."

"I agree," Marine said. "But have you spoken to him about it? I heard that he has promised not to play music and to only have a few tables out there."

"The duke is on our side," Thomas said, not replying to Marine's question.

"A real duke?" Sylvie asked, looking up from her plate.

Marine looked down at her lap, suppressing laughter.

"We've started a petition and I've brought it with me," Thomas continued, ignorant of Sylvie's teasing. "I was hoping you would all sign it, and that you, Antoine, might have some sway at the mayor's office." He gestured, poking the air with his elbow.

"The mayor hates me and I hate her," Verlaque replied, shrugging. "What can I say? We got off to a bad start."

Gaëlle Dreyfus stayed quiet; she had hoped that Thomas Roche would abandon his silly petition, which in her mind, like all petitions, wouldn't be of any use. She could do better work at the historical society, where they would accumulate facts about the fountain and the garden, hopefully enough to sway the city planners. She changed the conversation, bringing up the neighborhood's long-standing debate over speed bumps. The Mazarin had two schools, an elementary school and a junior high, where Cézanne and Zola had been inseparable friends. Residents had been trying for years to get the city to install one or even two speed bumps on their streets, or close the Mazarin off altogether to traffic other than badge-carrying residents. Sylvie tried to suppress a yawn, and Verlaque suggested that she help him with the dessert in the kitchen.

"What a barrel of laughs in there," Sylvie whispered as she got six dessert plates out of the cupboard.

"An experiment," Verlaque answered. "Not to be soon repeated. But the antiques dealer is quite sympathetic. Say, that photo album you gave us is fantastic. Did you see the picture of my dad and his . . ." What was Rebecca? He finished his sentence with "His girlfriend?"

Sylvie laughed. "The one with Dr. Florence Bonnet scowling in the background?"

"So you noticed that detail."

"Régis was really proud of that shot," Sylvie replied. "That's one of the signs of a great photograph, and it's something I tell my students over and over. An A-plus photograph is—"

"In focus," Verlaque said, grinning.

"Yes, you dork. It's also perfectly composed, the subject matter is interesting, but what puts it into the A-plus zone are the hidden surprises. Each time you look at it, something new appears."

"Well, tell Régis he did a great job." Verlaque lifted the cake, an *Opéra*, which he had bought earlier at Michaud's, and

Sylvie followed with the dessert plates. They heard laughter coming from the dining room and Verlaque was relieved.

"That's not the only thing my crazy colleague did when we were young and foolish," Thomas Roche said, pouring himself a glass of wine, then setting the bottle back down in front of him without offering any to the other guests. Marine looked at her husband and winked. "Pierre also stranded his young bride at the altar up in Brittany . . ."

"Not quite," Stéphanie Roche cut in. "He gave her a few weeks' warning, although the invitations had been sent."

"And then Pierre went and married a local!" her husband went on.

Sylvie looked at Verlaque in puzzlement. They had obviously missed something when they were in the kitchen. A local of which country?

"A South African beauty!" Thomas said, answering the question for Sylvie.

"As black as coal," Stéphanie said, pursing her lips.

Sylvie put the plates down on the table with an intentional thud.

"And they had two children, and you'll never guess what happened," Thomas continued.

The others looked at one another and shrugged. Verlaque carefully began cutting the cake and said, looking up, "I guess you'd better tell us."

"The first child, a boy, was black!" Thomas roared. "And the other, a girl born two years later—"

"*Elle était impeccable!*" his wife cut in, waving her hands in the air.

"Perfect?" Marine asked, her hands gripping the edge of the table.

"Well, white, of course!" Stéphanie exclaimed, beaming.

Verlaque sat on the edge of the bed, taking off his shoes. "That was a great dinner, Marine," he said. Marine was hanging up her blouse in the closet and she turned around. "I had no idea the Roches were like that," she said. "I'm embarrassed I invited them over."

"No worries," Verlaque answered. "You didn't know, and you were being neighborly. We can unfriend them, as my younger colleagues say. I think it has something to do with Facebook."

Marine laughed. "At least you didn't call it Bookface."

"I've never done that!"

"Yes, you did, once at the Pauliks'." She took off her slacks and hung them on a hanger, laughing.

"Well, if my technology handicap makes you laugh like that, it's all worth it," Verlaque said. "What's wrong, anyway? You looked worried, and tense."

Marine came and sat beside him, then sighed.

"Wow, that was a Florence Bonnet sigh," he said, taking Marine in his arms. "When she's overcooked something—"

Marine laughed. "Or is one word away from finishing the *Le Monde* crossword but is stuck."

"Is it work?"

"Not directly," she said, taking a breath before she continued. "I sent my manuscript in."

"You're finished?" he asked, drawing away from her for a second so that he could look at her face.

Marine nodded.

"That's amazing news! I'm so proud of you. You didn't tell me you had finished it!"

"Oh," Marine said, shrugging.

"Your modesty shrug."

She smiled. "I finished it weeks ago but was terrified to send it to a publisher."

"I understand that."

"You do?"

Verlaque said, "Absolutely. You've put so much time into this project—"

"At the expense of my teaching job."

"The students probably didn't even notice. What are you worried about? That the manuscript will be rejected?"

Marine paused before answering. "Not exactly," she replied. "I'm worried about what I'll do when it does get accepted."

"So much for Mme Modesty. I'm joking."

"Because I think it's good," Marine said, standing up and beginning to pace the room. "It's original, and some will even think it's shocking."

Verlaque beamed, happy to see his wife back, one hundred percent. He was also happy to see her walking around in the room in her bra and underwear. "So what's the problem?"

"That it will get published, and everyone will hate it. You. Sylvie. My parents and colleagues. The critics."

He wanted to tell her that she was jumping the gun a bit but didn't. They were her fears, and so were legitimate. "Somebody won't like it," he said. "That's only normal, and you'll have to be prepared for that."

Marine began picking perfume bottles off her dresser and moving them around. "I once had a friend who said that Sartre and Beauvoir lied to each other and everyone else," she said, "and my friend was right, too. Despite their great efforts at not being bourgeois, that's exactly the kind of life they were living . . . Sartre was a classic philanderer straight out of Molière and Beauvoir put up with it—"

Verlaque said, "Like so many before her."

Marine turned around. "Exactly. What if readers hate the book for that reason? How can I make their lives sound . . . worthy? Or even admirable?"

"You may not be able to do that," Verlaque said. "You're the biographer, not the judge." He smiled; his joke hadn't been intentional. "Just give your readers the facts and make it an enjoyable read."

Chapter Four

❧

Bear's Problems Begin

*Y*esterday's artichoke soup had been a hit, and he made it again today. Bear had used Jane and Judith's simple recipe, which called for large globe artichokes, Parmesan, and lemon, and served it with a garlic-rubbed crostini on top. To the crostini Bear added chopped sun-dried tomatoes. "It's kind of cheating," his apprentice, Florian Miotto said, watching Bear prepare the soup. "Anything tastes good with a sun-dried tomato crostini."

"Give the people what they want," Bear said, smiling. "Why make fussy food when we all crave simplicity? But to do that, we have to use the best possible ingredients." Bear knew that there was some truth in what Florian said. He had not gone through the rigorous French kitchen apprenticeship scheme, in which some people began as early as thirteen years of age. And Judith and Jane hadn't, either. But they had been daring and imaginative, and their timing had been right: When they had started the restaurant, people were making lots of money in London and after a day in the City clients wanted to sit down to what was, basically, stylish comfort food with Italian names. Judith and Jane became successful restaurateurs and had been generous with their staff in passing on their wisdom: Jamie was now a superstar with his own chain of restaurants, and Hugh, another sous chef, had his own television show, cooking from his cottage in Dorset.

When Bear finished his science degree at UCL, he joined the restaurant full-time. His parents thought that cooking was a passing phase and that their Sigisbert would come back to France and get a laboratory job. But when, after five years, Bear was still at Cavolo Nero, they began putting money aside for him to buy his own restaurant someday. (Bear's father had found work again, at a pharmaceutical start-up, which went public after four years. He made a fortune.) *And here I am*, thought Bear, looking out the windows onto the back garden. Back home, in Aix. His parents gave him the money to buy a ground-floor apartment on the rue Mistral, with access to a shared garden. The upstairs apartment was available for rent, and he took it. A small but efficient stainless-steel kitchen was installed, and like at Cavolo Nero, it was open to the twenty-five-seat dining room. It was the first of its kind in Aix. His splurges were a tall, glass-front side-by-side Liebherr wine fridge and white Cararra marble for the tabletops. The chairs were mismatched—all old and wood—bought with the advice of his mother at garage sales and off leboncoin.fr.

But it was the outside access that had sold Bear on the space: The garden was tiny, but if it was cleaned up and properly arranged, he could fit four or five tables there, with portable heaters in cool weather. A restaurant with a garden. It reminded him of that sloping garden at Cavolo Nero, where Jane and her assistants had planted herb and vegetable gardens that led down to the Thames. This garden was flat and didn't have a mighty river, no, but it did have water: a historically listed fountain, carved by an anonymous mason in the late seventeenth century.

"Your turn to clean the hood," Bear told Florian. It had been one of Bear's first jobs at Cavolo Nero, and he soon learned that everyone at the restaurant took a turn at climbing onto the range and scrubbing down the interior of the hood after every service, including the dining-room staff and Judith and Jane. Florian moaned, and Mamadou, their dishwasher, grinned. He had done it the day before.

Florian hopped up on the stove and stuck his head inside the hood, talking as he cleaned. "This is the icing on the cake," he called down, his voice echoing off the stainless steel. "When you sign up to become a cook, you know you're a freak, like everyone else in the restaurant world."

"Speak for yourself," Bear mumbled.

Florian went on, "You know that while all your friends are off having fun on the weekend and traveling around Europe during the holidays, you'll be working."

Bear nodded. "Don't forget evenings."

"You can burn yourself, cut yourself, and freeze your ass off walking into cold rooms," Florian said. "You need the strength of a rugby player to carry hundred-quart stockpots or half a cow, then the finesse of a ballerina to move around your busy coworkers in a kitchen that's smaller than your mom's."

Bear grinned and winked at Mamadou, who had set down his dish towel to listen.

"And you need fine motor control in your hands," Bear added, "when you're doing the final plate presentation, arranging flower petals or minuscule pieces of thyme with friggin' tweezers—"

"And all the tools you need!" Florian said, pausing to stick his head out of the hood for a second. "Your own set of ridiculously expensive Japanese knives, when all your buddies are buying cars or motorcycles . . ."

"Pots and pans, fancy stemware," Mamadou pitched in.

"Fine Italian cutlery," Bear said, having just bought some, "and you need to mortgage your ass off, if you're lucky enough to buy a place, and then you hope you've chosen a good neighborhood, the right street that's busy enough—" He paused and thought of his current difficulties with his terrace project. Florian and Mamadou saw their boss's face fall, so they got back to work.

Bear took off his apron and carefully folded it, even though it would be washed and he'd put on a clean one this evening. He left the kitchen and walked out into the garden. It had been abandoned, and it showed. The previous owner, Béatrice Germain, had lived there on her own for more than fifty years. She had no children and had never married, but had cats. *The crazy old woman with cats*, thought Bear. *What a cliché. But God bless her.* After she died, the apartment, and the garden, were left abandoned while her nieces and nephews argued over the succession. After four years of that Bear and his father finally signed the contract for the purchase, and it took another two years to renovate the interior and get approval to open a restaurant in Aix's chic Mazarin neighborhood. Opening night had been on the first weekend of September, and Judith and her husband had flown in from London. Jane was in New York—her husband had just renovated a wing of an uptown museum, and they were there for its opening—but she sent two dozen roses and a crate of Pol Roger champagne. The restaurant—called La Fontaine—was packed that night and two years later was still busy.

Bear looked around. He had quickly cleaned the garden for the opening and hadn't had time to touch it since. The fountain gurgled away; the water came from a source deep below ground and was drinkable and good. It had just been tested by a city worker and had passed with flying colors.

Mamadou came out and stood beside Bear. After a few moments of silence the dishwasher said, "You could plant herbs out here."

Bear nodded and smiled. "That would be perfect. Basil, rosemary, thyme, oregano, marjoram. Around an olive tree."

"I dreamed of olive trees before coming here," Mamadou said. He pounded the earth with his beat-up running shoe. "But this earth, Chef, it's bad. So bad. It's drier than in Togo."

"I know," Bear said. "I'll need to dig up this garden and start over. Bring in new earth and pave the bits where the tables will be."

"I'll help you, Chef," Mamadou said.

"Thank you! I'll pay you, of course," Bear said. "One of our clients is a stone mason and he suggested we lay the terrace with those colorful cement tiles they used in the nineteenth century. He offered to do it for a few free meals."

"The barter system," Mamadou suggested.

"Exactly."

"I prefer cash."

Bear laughed and punched Mamadou in the shoulder. In the April sunshine Mamadou's scar was even more pronounced. Usually Bear ignored it, but now, as Mamadou was looking around the courtyard, the chef took in the scar: It ran from the bottom corner of his employee's right eye, down across his cheek, where it veered off toward his ear, and then came back, following his jaw line, finally stopping at the corner of the mouth. Bear looked up at the sky, imagining an olive tree covered in hundreds of tiny blossoms, when loud voices coming from the dining room caused both men to turn around. La Fontaine's waiter and front-house man, Jacques Oller, quickly walked into the garden.

"What is it?" Bear asked, seeing the look of worry on Oller's face. Jacques Oller had come to La Fontaine after spending more than fifteen years working at a two-star Michelin restaurant north of the city. There, he had worked tirelessly and had helped the restaurant go from an unknown bistro to an elegant Michelin-starred restaurant. But fifteen years had been too much on his body; his right hip would soon need replacing, and the normally suave and coolheaded maître'd had become a nervous wreck. His doctor put him on disability and ordered him to stop working in the restaurant business or to find a much-smaller one. He had heard about Sigisbert Valets through colleagues and called him up, asking for an interview. Oller's knowledge of the business was outstanding, and in his career he had developed a passion for wine, especially Italian ones. "Follow your gut," Jane had once advised Bear. And so he did. Bear hired Oller that day, agreeing to give Oller, as he would with his other employees, a share of the profits.

Bear could see a tall, thin man in his sixties standing in the restaurant. Sensing that something was wrong, Oller and Mamadou stayed in the garden while Bear walked into the restaurant. He opened his mouth to speak but was cut off. "I'm your neighbor," the man said, holding out a long, thin arm. "Thomas Roche."

Bear nodded and shook his hand, noting to himself that he had more than one neighbor. He had dozens. But this man seemed to think he was the only one. If Jane had taught Bear how to trust his instincts—which herbs worked best with which pastas and soups; how to check if the fishmonger's fish was fresh, the flesh rigid when poked with a finger, the skin shiny and firm, the scales intact, the gills a deep red color and the eyes clear, not cloudy—it was Judith who gave him his business savvy and confidence. When he turned in his resignation at Cavolo Nero, Judith had poured two glasses of her favorite grappa, from Piedmont, flavored with chamomile. "Be as kind and innovative as Jane," she said, throwing back the grappa. "But be a bitch, too, when you have to be."

"Sigisbert Valets," Bear said, unsmiling. He saw Roche twitch slightly; Bear's posh medieval name usually surprised those who stared too long at the tattoos on his forearms.

"May we have a few words?" Roche asked.

"I can guess why you're here," Bear said.

"I have with me a petition," Roche said, patting the manila envelope that was in his hand. "It's been signed by seventy people so far, but I haven't finished my rounds of the neighborhood yet."

"It's about the garden, I assume."

"Nothing to do with the garden, young man. The terrace. A terrace with outdoor seating."

"When I was given the permit for the terrace"—Bear emphasized the word *permit*, Judith-style; he then smiled, Jane-style—"I promised the committee I would keep the seating to a maximum of five tables for two and never play music. The fountain will drown out any noise, and you may hear the chatter of people having fun, but we all hear that in this courtyard during the summer months." If he had to, he'd bring up the fact that most of the owners of Mazarin apartments had illegally built balconies and terraces.

"This is a copy of the petition for you," Roche said. He took a few pieces of paper out of the envelope, handing them to Bear, but kept the envelope for himself.

Now Bear smiled.

"Next week I'm meeting with the historical committee of Aix. That fountain," Roche said, pointing, "is listed—"

"I know," Bear cut in. "I'm very proud of it. And now I have to prepare for the dinner service. Goodbye, M. Roche." He held his hand toward the dining room, signaling to his neighbor the way out.

Roche left, giving Bear a wave of his hand.

Bear turned on the espresso machine and sat down at one of the small marble-topped tables. He put his head in his hands. What would Roche and his cronies do? Sit down in front of his restaurant in protest? Perhaps. This was France, after all.

Chapter Five

❧

L'Anchoïade

Gaëlle Dreyfus quickly crossed the Cours Mirabeau. She had closed her shop at 7:00 p.m. having had two customers that afternoon—one, a very amiable German tourist who fell in love with a rare, pale yellow porcelain set but who could in no way take it home on Ryanair. The second customer was a university student on vacation from Paris who had hemmed and hawed over buying a small linen tablecloth that morning and returned in the afternoon to buy it. Gaëlle took an immediate liking to the girl and offered a ten-percent student discount. "That's so kind!" said the girl. "Every little bit helps!"

"I agree," Gaëlle said. "What are you studying?"

"Art history at the Sorbonne."

"I'll give you twenty percent, then," Gaëlle announced. She kept her next thought to herself: *You've chosen a real money-maker.* She was touched when the girl promised to take a photograph of the tablecloth in her Parisian studio and email it to Gaëlle. That was one of the reasons she had gotten into antiques: She had a deep respect, and knowledge, of *le patrimoine*, of course, but she also loved the idea of recycling objects, giving them new homes, new lives.

Gaëlle looked at the time and hurried on, quickly stopping to say hello to friends who were having an aperitif on Le Mazarin Café's terrace. She gave the three of them the *bise*, apologizing that she couldn't stop. As she called out "*À bientôt*" she almost ran headfirst into Antoine Verlaque, who was walking out of the tiny tobacco shop on the rue Clemenceau. "*Bonsoir, M. Verlaque*," she said, reaching up to give him the *bise*.

Verlaque kissed both her cheeks and said, "Good evening. And you must call me Antoine, please."

"Likewise," she answered. "Please call me Gaëlle. Thank you so much for last evening. It was wonderful to get to know you, and the food and wine were fabulous."

"I'll pass that on to Marine."

"I did send her a text message this morning," she said. "I know she has classes today, so I didn't want to call."

Verlaque smiled and nodded. *A class act*, he thought, *not like Thomas Roche serving himself wine or his horrible* "elle était impéccable!" *racist wife.* As a way of apologizing for his neighbors' behavior he said, "We hope to repeat the evening sometime soon, with our neighbors on the second floor. They're . . ."

"Not racist bores?" Gaëlle suggested.

Verlaque laughed and Gaëlle covered her mouth. She said, "I'm a bit of a loudmouth. Sorry. It was a lovely evening, and tell Marine she's brave to have cut up all those artichokes! They still intimidate me, even after thirty years in Provence."

Verlaque smiled again. "I'll tell her."

Gaëlle patted his shoulder and gestured to her wristwatch. "I have a meeting in five minutes! Gotta run!"

Verlaque saluted and said goodbye, then took a cigar cutter out of his jacket pocket and snipped the end off a cigar. He began walking, going over in his head the dinner he had promised to make for Marine. It had been Emmeline's—his English grandmother's—favorite "cheating recipe," using leftover lamb and potatoes, to which she would add tomato paste and water and a few tablespoons of Patak's Vindaloo paste that she would bring back from London. Verlaque detested the globalization that seemed to be sweeping across the world, and especially in Europe, when it concerned food and wine, but he had been secretly relieved when he had found a jar of Patak's in Monoprix's *cuisine du monde* section. He had bought a Grand Cru Gewürztraminer from Alsace to accompany the curry, hoping the sweetness of the wine would marry well with the spices.

Gaëlle Dreyfus turned around to look at the judge and smiled when she saw that he was walking on, smoking a cigar, with a pink plastic Monoprix bag swinging in his left hand. *Married life*, she mused. *He's making dinner or at least doing the shopping.* She had been impressed by Antoine Verlaque the previous evening and liked him even more today. Mutual acquaintances had judged him harshly, she thought, calling him a Parisian snob, an epicurean snob, and a ladies' man. Her friends had told her of the family fortune, made from flour mills, but she hadn't found Verlaque at all pretentious. Perhaps he had once been but had softened due to Marine's influence? That was entirely possible.

She continued up the rue Clemenceau, avoiding looking in the shop windows. The sales were coming up in July, but even with discounts she wouldn't be buying clothes this season. At any rate, her weakness was for shoes and handbags, and she had enough of both. Five minutes later she was on the rue Granet, a street she had always liked as it contained no restaurants or bars but only small independently owned shops like her own. She rang at number 14 and a voice replied "*Montez!*" followed by a clicking sound as the red front door opened. They switched locations for meetings, and tonight's was in the apartment of Anthony Sauze, a history professor at the university. Sauze, a tall, thin, angular man, wore a distinctive thin black moustache matched by a small goatee and round John Lennon–style eyeglasses. He was also the history association's president and although she had been a board member of the Association Historique Aixoise, or AHA for short, for more than a year, Sauze was so discreet that Gaëlle had no idea if he was married, divorced, gay, or just a confirmed bachelor. When she got to the second floor, the door was open and she was about to say "Hello, Anthony" when the association's secretary, Robert San Martin, leaned forward and gave her the *bise,* his breath already smelling of garlic. "Anthony's in the kitchen," San Martin announced, brushing crumbs off his wrinkled and gray-looking white shirt. "He's made this divine anchoïade."

Gaëlle nodded. She hated anchovies. She walked into Anthony Sauze's living room, which could have been in a hotel for businesspeople, it was so devoid of character. The bones were good, though, Gaëlle noted with sadness: high ceiling, carved moldings, and, rare for Aix, wood-paneled floors. There were a few historical etchings on the walls—prints, not originals—in cheap frames, and the furniture was dull and from a catalog, most likely Camif, used by France's civil servants. Robert San Martin quickly sat back down and smothered a piece of baguette with more of Anthony's apparently delicious anchoïade. Bénédicte Tivolle, Gaëlle's neighbor in the Mazarin, looked up from a bowl of olives where she had been sorting through the black ones to find the green ones with a toothpick. Bénédicte taught philosophy at the Lycée Vauvenargues. "Oh, say, Gaëlle. Hello. Anthony's anchoïade is to die for."

"I heard," Gaëlle replied. "Anthony, are you going to spend all evening in the kitchen?" she hollered. Getting her fellow committee members to actually begin a meeting was always torturous.

"I'll be right there," Sauze called back. She heard a cork pop out of a bottle and leaned back on the vinyl chair, glad there would be wine at least. Sauze came out of the kitchen wearing a plastic apron with Michelangelo's *David* on it and Gaëlle laughed out loud. "People actually buy those things in Florence?" she asked.

Sauze passed the wine bottle to San Martin and looked down at his apron. "My students bought it for me."

"Oh, sorry, Anthony," Gaëlle mumbled.

Sauze said, "And I remembered that you don't care for anchovies, Gaëlle, so I have some salami in the kitchen. I'll be right back."

"I'll come and help you, since the anchoïade bowl *already* needs refilling," Bénédicte said, staring at San Martin.

Gaëlle sank guiltily into her chair and watched as San Martin filled their wineglasses to the brim. She opened her mouth to suggest that he only fill them three-quarters, but after the apron comment she decided to stay quiet. Bénédicte and Sauze came out of the kitchen and set down more food on the coffee table. Gaëlle was relieved when Sauze suggested they begin the meeting on time, while they eat, as he wanted to finish early.

"Hot date, Anthony?" San Martin asked, cutting another piece of bread.

"There's a special on Arte this evening about the Cold War," Sauze replied, looking as dejected as he had when Gaëlle insulted his apron.

Gaëlle sat forward and clapped her hands. "All right, then, let's get started. The president has spoken."

Robert San Martin fumbled in his man-bag and pulled out a pen and a notebook, which Gaëlle noticed had a photo of a clown blowing bubbles on the front cover. She rubbed her eyes with her fingers and sighed.

Sauze coughed as he usually did when beginning the meeting. "The meeting of the Association Historique Aixoise is about to begin."

Gaëlle glared at San Martin and held her breath. He hollered out, swinging his thick upper body back and forth, "The AHA! Ah-ha! Ah-ha! 'Knowing me, knowing—'"

"Robert, if you sing that stinking ABBA song, I'm leaving and taking the anchoïade with me," Gaëlle said.

"Our first topic is the hair salon on the rue Espariat," Sauze cut in. "I've just found out that thanks to our complaints, and

Bénédicte's excellent photos, the owner has been asked by the city to change her storefront."

The group applauded. "She should change the name, too," Bénédicte suggested. "*Epi-tête! C'est horrible!*"

"Yes," Sauze said, pulling at his goatee. "One wonders who would want to get their hair cut at a place called Spike Head."

"At any rate, a bubblegum-pink storefront has no place on the rue Espariat," Gaëlle said. "Especially next to a medieval church."

"Agreed. Item two," Sauze announced. "The restaurant on the rue Mistral." He looked at Bénédicte and Gaëlle, who both lived nearby.

"I'll begin this one," Bénédicte said. "The chef, who's from Aix, is a very nice young man. And we all know how difficult it is these days to own a small business."

"Hear, hear," Gaëlle said. She tried to smile but still felt outnumbered by the three civil servants (Robert San Martin had some post too high up in the Canal de Provence to ever be fired, despite being a nincompoop).

Bénédicte went on. "But there is no way that a restaurateur should be allowed to open outdoor seating in the Mazarin."

"The restaurants on this side of town have outdoor seating," Sauze reminded her. Aix-en-Provence was split down the middle by the elegant Cours Mirabeau. To the north was the *vieille ville*, whose twisting tiny streets revealed the city's medieval origins. To the south was the *ville neuve*, or new town—Le Mazarin—built on a grid in the seventeenth and eighteenth centuries. Even then the Mazarin had been the more expensive place to live, and it still was. Sauze added, careful not to insult his co–committee members, "But I understand that the neigh-borhood must be protected. That should have happened here, too, years ago."

Bénédicte put her forefinger in the air. "But there's even more reason not to disturb that garden."

"Other than the fact that both you and Gaëlle share it," San Martin suggested, wiping his mouth with the back of his hand. Gaëlle was about to jump to their defense when she saw that he had a look of concern on his face: His comment had not been judgmental.

"*Oui*," Bénédicte said, pursing her lips and nodding as she did when explaining a philosophical idea in detail to her students. "*La fontaine*."

"The spring itself is ancient," Gaëlle added. "And the fountain is listed, built by an anonymous sculptor in 1664. It was constructed in commemoration of a peasant's execution by hanging on the same spot."

"When was that?" San Martin asked.

"In 1660," Gaëlle answered. "The year Louis XIV rode into town."

"Ah, the Sun King," Sauze cut in. "He was a young man then, in Provence to cool down protests against the monarchy."

"He arrived on the seventeenth of January," Gaëlle quickly said.

"Good one, Gaëlle," Bénédicte said, winking. "How can you remember that date so well?"

"It's my birthday," Gaëlle replied.

"I knew you were a Capricorn," Bénédicte said, shaking her finger at Gaëlle.

Sauze coughed. "Back to the seventeenth century. Louis stayed two months in Aix. It was a harsh winter; the Rhône froze in Arles—"

"I can confirm that," San Martin said, choking slightly on the tapenade he had eaten too quickly.

Sauze grimaced and went on. "Louis reviewed his troops every morning and then went to Mass, and in the afternoon the hunt. The beginnings of a great king."

Gaëlle laughed. "I wouldn't go that far. He would later bleed the coffers dry. And it wasn't an entirely joyous visit. There was a hanging . . ."

"Ah, the peasant who refused to cry '*Vive le Roi!*' when Louis road into town," Sauze said.

"He had a name," Gaëlle said, her voice cracking. "Valère Maurin. He was twenty-three."

"Now I remember . . ." San Martin said. "He was killed in your garden." He looked at Bénédicte and then over at Gaëlle.

"That's right. I'm going to include his story in my walking tour," Gaëlle said.

"You can't take the group into the garden," Bénédicte quickly said.

Gaëlle started to protest, "I don't see what the problem—"

"Absolutely not," Bénédicte said.

Sauze said, "You could stop in front of your shop to tell them about Valère's murder."

"That way you may sell some antiques!" San Martin said, cutting himself a thick slice of salami.

"Thank you for the suggestion, Robert," Gaëlle said.

Sauze laughed and San Martin looked at him, perplexed. He leaned forward and asked, "And the curse? Is it true?"

"Béatrice Germain—she's the old woman who lived where the restaurant now is—told me quite a few stories, passed down by *her* grandparents who originally owned the house," Gaëlle said. "Valère was hanged from an elm tree that immediately died after his death, and nothing has grown there since. Bad luck seems to strike those who live there or, in Béatrice's opinion, those who tried to plant in that spot of the garden. Béatrice's parents tried growing a vegetable garden—"

"What happened to them?" San Martin asked.

Sauze rolled his eyes toward the ceiling.

"They lived into their seventies," Gaëlle replied, "but lost two sons in World War Two. They were *résistants* and were shot by the Gestapo, in the garden."

"Ah, the plaque on the rue Mistral . . . ," Sauze commented.

"Yes, it's for them. And Béatrice gave birth to a stillborn. Her only child. A few months later her husband walked out. She had no idea whatever happened to him."

"That explains the cats." San Martin slowly set his wineglass on the coffee table. "What a sad story," he mused.

"Some families are cursed . . . ," Sauze said.

"It wasn't only their family who had bad luck," Gaëlle went on. "Every fifty years or so tragedy would strike, and just before"—she paused, swirling the wine around in her glass—"there would be a warning."

Robert San Martin's eyes widened.

"The spring would stop flowing," Bénédicte answered.

Chapter Six

Lunch at La Fontaine

The next morning Bear Valets lay in bed, a freshly made cappuccino at his side, and went over the day's specials. It was his daily routine: A prep list would form—he could see the written list in his head, jotted down as it usually was, on the closest piece of scrap paper he could find. His was a small kitchen compared to Cavolo Nero's, and he never had the amount of leftovers that had to be reinvented as the London restaurant had. But still, he was careful with his stock; careful not to waste. The list began: mesclun, carrots, onions, garlic, and potatoes from an organic farmer who delivered; meat and bones from a butcher who drove down from the Drôme twice a week; seafood, also delivered, from Bandol, by a fisherman who hated driving into Aix and constantly complained about it; dairy goods that came with the above-mentioned organic farmer—her in-laws owned a dairy farm in the Savoie; and finally, various dry goods, including premium dried pasta from Italy, Arborio rice, organic polenta, and cases of Tuscan olive oil. Whatever else he was missing, or inspired him at the last minute, he would get at the market. Bear sometimes thought that he spent more time making lists than actually cooking.

Both Florian and Mamadou had keys to the restaurant, and Bear could hear them thrashing around downstairs—probably fighting over whose music would get played on the kitchen's cheap boom box. He threw off the covers and dragged himself into the shower. Not every chef could live upstairs above his own restaurant, and that kept Bear sane. Exhausted after the lunch rush he would climb the stairs, shower, and fall into bed, waking up to repeat it all over again for dinner. Florian and Jacques Oller had studios downtown near the Place des Cardeurs, but Bear was ashamed that he didn't know where Mamadou lived. Could his dishwasher get home over the afternoon break, or did he live too far away? Did he wander the streets of Aix or lie down in the Parc Jourdan? Bear had no idea.

After he had dressed, Bear walked slowly downstairs, irritated that because of the coffee in his right hand and his meal list in the other, he could not plug his ears. "Florian, turn down your music!"

Florian looked at his boss across the dining room and shrugged. "I can't hear you!"

Bear laughed and looked out of the dining room's back window. He could see Mamadou sitting on the edge of the fountain, washing leeks and talking to himself. Mamadou had walked in off the street after La Fontaine had first opened and was hired on the spot. He was enthusiastic, and when Bear asked him if he was interested in food and cooking, Mamadou's eyes lit up. He described in detail the meals he had prepared with his mother on holidays and feast days in Togo. A few days later, as they were chatting during a calm period toward the end of a lunch service, Bear mentioned that Mamadou must miss his family terribly. He thought about all his own family had done for him, and they lived in the same town. The African nodded and turned his back to Bear, picking up a pasta pan to wash it. They hadn't spoken of his family since.

"Your music is so loud you've chased our dishwasher outside," Bear said to Florian. He set his coffee cup on the stainless-steel work surface and, reaching around Florian, turned down the music.

"You'll never appreciate early nineties' grunge music," Florian complained.

"No," Bear answered, smiling. "But I do appreciate the way you get here every day on time and never complain about how many times you've had to do the same prep."

Florian saluted his boss. "Your wish is my command. By the way, I checked the fridge this morning and there's enough cod from last night to do a lunch special."

"Great minds think alike. Let's do the cod in a curry sauce."

Florian raised his eyebrows.

"Even Italians love curry," Bear answered. "I'll add some saffron as they do. It will be our one-dish meal, served with basmati rice. Use a ring for the presentation. How's our asparagus supply?"

"We used it all last night."

"Let's go to the market and get some more."

"Should we get some fresh cilantro, too? For the curry?" Florian asked.

"Good idea," Bear replied.

The back door opened and Mamadou walked in carrying a colander. "The leeks are cut and washed by pure spring water!" he announced, tilting the colander for Bear to inspect.

"Thanks," Bear said. "We have to wash the mussels and spinach next, dice tomatoes, and crush peppercorns . . ."

"I'll start on the mussels," Florian said, adjusting his apron.

"What should I do, boss?" Mamadou asked.

"Say, why don't you go to the market?"

Mamadou gave Bear a huge smile. "Just give me the list!"

Bear told him what to get and gave Mamadou some money out of his back pocket and a large wooden crate. "Just make sure you go to Mme Martin!" Bear hollered as Mamadou hurried out the front door. "Try to get most of the produce from her!"

Less than an hour later Mamadou was back. "I have a great idea, boss," he said, setting the crate down gently. "You should put the restaurant's name on the front of the crate. Free advertising!"

"Then people would see we buy fresh, too," Florian added, holding a large meat cleaver in his hand. Mamadou backed away.

"Florian," Bear said, pointing to the knife. "I've warned you about that a few times. Be careful. Let's see how you did, Mamadou," he continued, sorting through the crate. He pulled out a large bunch of fresh cilantro and sniffed it. "Perfect."

"And free," Mamadou said. "Mme Martin didn't have any, but the young couple across from her did."

"The organic kids from Pertuis?"

"Yes," Mamadou answered. "I bought the mint and these strawberries from them. Mme Martin had strawberries earlier this morning, but she was already sold out by the time I got there."

"Damn," Bear said. "But you did well to buy organic ones." He took the strawberries and tasted one, handing one to Florian.

"Roses," Florian said, chewing.

Bear closed his eyes and swallowed. "Yes, they taste more like flowers than fruit. It's what strawberries should taste like."

"I tasted one in the market to make sure," Mamadou said. "Will you serve them with Chantilly?"

Florian laughed. "He's catching on quick," he said, pointing to the dishwasher.

"Yes, all they need is a little Chantilly, and some ice cream I'll make using vino Santo from Tuscany," Bear agreed. "You can help me with the ice cream, Mamadou. Go and get twelve eggs and the double cream out of the fridge."

"And a bottle of your best vino Santo?" Mamadou asked.

"Two."

Marine arrived at the restaurant five minutes early. A table in the window had been reserved for her—her favorite spot—and she ordered a large bottle of sparkling water as she waited for Sylvie. From there, she could watch people walking down the street, but she also had a clear view to the open kitchen and out the back door onto the courtyard. She lowered her head, to almost tabletop level, and she could see her balcony across the garden.

"Is everything all right, madame?" Jacques Oller asked. He was standing beside her, opening a large bottle of San Pellegrino.

Marine quickly brought her head up. "Yes!" she said, laughing. "I can see my apartment, just barely, from here."

Oller said, "You don't have far to come, then."

"No," Marine agreed. "About two minutes on foot."

Oller poured her water and left. A thud then caused Marine to look up. Sylvie Grassi had just set her oversize Italian purse on the table. "I'm sorry I'm late," she said, giving her friend the *bise*.

"Would you like some water?" Marine asked, holding the bottle up.

"Yes, please," Sylvie said. "Have you ordered yet?"

"No, of course not. The two specials today are curry of cod and lamb chops with fresh mint"

Sylvie strained to read the blackboard that was posted on the far wall. "They both sound good."

"I agree," Marine said, frowning.

"What's wrong?"

"I had curried lamb last night for dinner."

Sylvie laughed. "*Pas de chance!*"

"Antoine's special recipe for using leftover lamb."

"So how is newly married life?" Sylvie asked. "Antoine seems to be in heaven."

"He is. We are."

Jacques Oller returned to take their order. "I'll have the cod," Sylvie said, folding her arms and sitting back.

"I will, too, please," Marine said.

"White wine?" Sylvie asked, winking.

"Do you have classes this afternoon?"

"Nope. All done for the day. I taught a three-hour photography class this morning."

Marine bit her upper lip. "Okay, let's have some wine. We haven't been together, alone, since the wedding."

"I'll bring you the wine list," Oller said. "Although I can tell you that our wine of the week is a Chardonnay from the Alto Adige mountains. It would be very good with the curry."

"Sold!" Sylvie said, looking across at Marine.

"Sounds perfect," she confirmed.

Oller smiled and left.

"We needed a restaurant like this in Aix," Sylvie said. She looked around and jabbed an olive with a toothpick. "It's elegant but not snobby."

"And it's not trendy, with house music playing over the restaurant speakers. With those all-gray interiors that seem to be the rage."

"And waiters with ponytails and necklaces," Sylvie added, shuddering.

Oller reappeared with an ice bucket, the wine, and two tall, delicate wineglasses. Marine leaned forward excitedly as he opened the wine. "Will you taste, madame?" he asked her.

"Yes, please."

Sylvie smiled as she watched her friend, who had gone from a wine neophyte to a burgeoning connoisseur in a matter of a year.

"It's perfect," Marine said, setting the glass down.

Oller smiled and poured the wine into their glasses. "Please, if you need anything at all, just ask," he said before leaving to occupy himself with the other tables, which were now all full for the lunch service.

Marine took her cell phone out of her purse and snapped a photo of the wine's label. "Alois Lageder," she mused, turning the bottle in her hands. "A Germanic name."

"Alto Adige is on the border of Italy and Austria," Sylvie said as she took a sip of wine. "I have a colleague whose parents grew up there during the war. They were Italian, and once a week they would walk into the Austrian side of the mountain and exchange their wine for milk and cream."

"*The Sound of Music*," Marine said.

"Yeah, with Nazis and all."

Marine laughed and held up her glass. "To life during peacetime. At least for us. In so many other countries war is still a part of daily life. This morning another boat full of African refugees was saved by the Italians. There were more than four hundred of them . . . terrified . . ."

"Your neighbors the Roches would be at the seaside, using long poles to turn away the refugee boats. I can just see it."

Marine buried her head in her hands. "Don't remind me of them," she said. "What a mistake that evening was."

"Ah, it's good to mix it up now and again," Sylvie said. "Invite a few racists for dinner, see what happens."

"Oh, speak of the devil," Marine said, sliding down in her seat. "It's M. Roche, coming toward the restaurant. With some guy who looks like he's military. I've never liked brush cuts."

"But he hates this place," Sylvie said, turning around to look out the window. "Maybe he's gonna spray-paint the front door."

"Oh no! He *is* coming in."

Sylvie swung around to face Marine. "Pretend you didn't see him."

But Thomas Roche and his friend, who was slightly younger, walked straight toward the kitchen, where Marine and Sylvie could see Bear Valets leaning over the stove. "M. Valets!" Roche stormed. "I have something for you!"

Jacques Oller was immediately at his side. "May I help you, sir?"

Roche brushed off the waiter with a wave of his hand. "It's the eminent chef we'd like to speak to!"

"What an arse," Marine whispered.

Bear rolled his eyes and put down the wooden spoon he had been using.

Roche went on, not waiting for Bear to be at his side. "Here, in my hand, is the petition, now with more than two hundred names on it!"

Marine looked at Sylvie, astonished. "How did he get two hundred signatures? I didn't sign it, nor did Antoine."

Bear nodded and was about to lift the petition off the bar when Mamadou came forward, stretching and twisting a tea towel between his hands. "Problem, Chef?"

Roche saw the six-foot-four African and took a step back. But his friend pointed at the dishwasher with a shaky hand and quickly turned away, then almost ran out the front door. Roche was left standing alone. "Have a good look at that petition," he said, slowly walking toward the door backward. He raised a finger in the air for effect. "This is far from over! You can be sure I'll be back!" He turned around and with some difficulty managed to open the door and leave.

"I'll be back!" Florian hollered from the kitchen, in his best Arnold Schwarzenegger voice.

Sylvie and Marine burst out laughing, and some of the other patrons applauded.

Marine set her napkin down, got up, and walked over to the bar. "Are you okay?" she asked Bear.

Bear smiled and shook his head back and forth. "Thank you—I'm sorry, I've forgotten your name."

"Marine," Marine said, holding out her hand. "Marine Bonnet."

"Thanks," Bear said, shaking her hand. "I'm fine. M. Roche has been here before and warned me he would come again. I recognize his friend, too; he lives around the corner. I just didn't expect grief during the lunch service." He turned to Mamadou and said, "You sure frightened them."

But Mamadou had disappeared. He was already back at the sink, in a small room off the open kitchen, washing pots and pans.

Chapter Seven

❧

A Toss of the Dice

Marine and Verlaque had agreed to meet at his apartment, around the corner from Aix's cathedral Saint-Sauveur. When her class finished at 5:30 p.m. she had called Verlaque, offering to stop by her butcher on the rue d'Italie to buy sirloin steak for dinner. "Sounds great," he said. "Make sure he cuts it nice and thick, and then we can share it. Better that than two thin ones. We'll eat at my house, then, if you don't mind."

Marine smiled. "I have a gas stovetop, too, you know."

"I know. But I have a wine cellar. And this kind of steak needs a Grand Cru."

"Burgundy?" she asked while walking through the Parc Jourdan on her way home from the university.

"Exactly. I have one from a village south of Beaune, not as expensive as a Côte du Beaune or a Côte de Nuits. It's a village that has mostly pinot noir grapes, and its neighboring village, only three or so kilometers away, has mostly white—"

Marine smiled, enjoying the quiz. She stopped to watch a young mother push her daughter on a swing. "Mercurey," she answered. "And Rully is the village next to it, with Chardonnay grapes."

"*Merde.*"

"You have to give me harder questions next time," Marine scolded, walking on. "Do you have salad fixings in your fridge?"

"No, you'd better get some arugula. Do you mind?"

"It's no trouble," she answered. "We can serve the steaks on a bed of arugula with olive oil, as they do in which famous Italian city?"

"Rome?"

"No, Florence, you dolt!"

Verlaque laughed and she could hear the flame of his lighter lighting a cigar. He asked, "Will you speak to me in Italian when you get home?"

"Yes, if you stop yakking and let me get off the phone to do the shopping."

"See you soon," he said. "I'll take the long trip downstairs to the cellar to look for that Mercurey."

"Watch out for the boogeyman," she teased.

"Thanks." Verlaque said. The apartment building's shared cellar had a dirt floor and five or six rat traps scattered around. Every time he went down to get a bottle he dreaded finding a dead rodent in a trap. He quickly added, "I think I'm going to buy a wine fridge for the kitchen, with a glass door—"

"Your kitchen is too small."

"I'll take out the dishwasher."

Marine laughed, knowing he was only half joking, and said, "The *périphérique* is up ahead, so I'm hanging up."

"Yes, don't get run over."

"Thanks." She hung up and slid her cell phone into her coat pocket—she had been married only a few weeks but she already knew that Verlaque would call with more food for her to buy—cheese, cherry tomatoes, a fresh baguette. She'd buy all of that anyway, and an extra treat for Verlaque.

Forty minutes later Marine was in front of Verlaque's apartment, on a tiny street off the Place des Archevêches. She set her briefcase, purse, and cloth shopping bag down and put her key in the carved wooden door. Holding the door open with her right shoulder, she reached down and picked up the bags and then set them inside the foyer on its white-and-black marble floor.

"*S'il vous plait, mademoiselle,*" said a voice from behind her. Still bent over, Marine looked up and smiled as a man in his mid-thirties reached over her head and held the door open for her.

"*Merci!*" she said, pushing the bags farther into the entryway and straightening up. "That was very kind of you."

"*De rien, mademoiselle,*" he replied, bowing slightly and then walking away.

"*C'est madame!*" Marine called after him, waving her keys in the air. "Newlywed!"

She walked inside the building and picked up the bags as Antoine Verlaque came running down the stairs. "I have the living room windows open and could hear you. You should have called me when you were on the rue d'Italie," he said, panting.

"It's fine," she answered. "The bags never feel heavy in the beginning—"

"I know," Verlaque said, "until you get partway home." He lifted up the shopping bag and her briefcase and kissed her. "The wine is breathing. You'll love it."

"Oh, goody," she answered as they walked up to his fourth-floor apartment. "I shared a bottle of wine with Sylvie at lunch today. Well, she had more than I did as I had an afternoon class."

"Where did you eat?" Verlaque asked as they walked into his apartment together and he set the groceries down on his kitchen's white Carrara marble counters.

"La Fontaine. It was great."

"What did you have? In detail."

Marine recounted her cod curry. Verlaque laughed as he poured them each a glass of 2003 Mercurey.

"Mmm, this pinot is stronger than usual," said she, taking a sip.

Verlaque tried not to smile and pretended it was natural for his wife to leave off the "noir." "It's a 2003," he answered slowly.

Marine thought for a moment and then put her index finger in the air. "The heat wave."

"Yep," he answered. "I talked to another Burgundy wine-maker who said he didn't even like selling his 2003."

"I think it's delicious," she said, taking another sip.

"Me, too," Antoine agreed. "It has the perfume and velvetiness typical of Burgundy but the punch of a—"

"Côte du Rhône."

"Exactly." He picked up the bottle and looked at the label. "Alcohol content fourteen percent. That's unheard of in Burgundy. Which is why that one vintner didn't want to sell his . . . He said it was unrepresentative of their region."

"I get it," Marine said. "All that terroir stuff." She winked at her husband and put on an apron. "I'll make the salad, you prep the steaks to grill?"

They worked quietly side by side, listening to the public radio station's nightly jazz show. Marine swayed back and forth, slowly pouring olive oil into her salad vinaigrette as Gregory Porter sang. Verlaque got out a mortar and pestle and began to grind peppercorns.

"Why not use the pepper grinder?" she asked, looking over at him.

"Bear told me about this," he answered, bending into the task. "He said it's a classic prep job in any kitchen, and I thought the steak deserves this treatment."

"Can you flambé the steak in cognac for us?"

"Sure." Verlaque picked up a handful of crushed peppercorns and rubbed them into the steaks with the palm of his hand. He turned on the gas burner.

"Something odd happened at lunch," Marine said. "Thomas Roche stormed into La Fontaine with some crony and shoved a petition to stop the outside expansion in Bear's face."

"You're kidding?" Verlaque asked. "What did Bear do?"

"He didn't have to do anything," she replied. "His dishwasher came forward to protect him and Roche's friend fled. Literally fled. Roche wasn't far behind him."

"Excellent!" Verlaque said. "That guy is such a schmuck."

"Let me know when the steaks are almost finished," Marine said, taking off her apron. "I have a treat to put on them."

"Salted butter from Brittany?"

"Even better," she answered. "Truffle butter. I stopped in at André's cheese shop and bought you some. Plus three cheeses for dessert."

He smiled. "Thank you. You already had enough shopping to do. You know, I used to get Arnaud to buy me groceries. When we got married I stopped; I'm not sure why. Should we get him to continue? The kid can use the money and you've seen his muscles. Carrying groceries isn't a big deal for him. He's on the university volleyball team."

"Fine with me," Marine said. "And he knows what you—we—like."

"I'm—we're—lucky to have such nice neighbors."

"Mmm," she said, sneaking another sip of wine. "How did Arnaud's father die?"

"Cancer or heart attack," Verlaque answered. "I can't remember. Arnaud was about thirteen."

Marine thought about the cheeses and the steaks they were about to eat and her husband's paunch. Antoine Verlaque had played rugby while at law school, but that had been a long time ago. As if reading her thoughts, he lifted up the wine bottle. "Red wine," he said. "Good for your health."

Verlaque tapped his empty wineglass three times. "I have a piece of chèvre to finish, but no more wine."

"Classic problem," Marine said, pouring the last of the wine into his glass.

"Save some for yourself."

"No, I'll have a cognac instead."

He raised an eyebrow. "Would you like a cigar to go with that?"

"I'm not there yet," Marine said, laughing. She walked across to the Art Deco liquor cabinet and poured herself a cognac, sniffing it before she took a sip. "No classes tomorrow, thankfully."

"What did you teach this afternoon?" Verlaque asked, popping the last of his cheese into his mouth, then walking over to the living room to sit in his favorite leather club chair.

"History of law." She sat down on the sofa opposite him and kicked off her ballet flats. "I threw in some Rabelais and Montaigne."

"Ah, Montaigne is your man of the moment."

"It was easy to fit him in," she answered. "He was a lawyer after all, and he called for legal reform in the sixteenth century. There was widespread corruption among lawyers, and Montaigne saw that ordinary citizens avoided the law instead of seeking it out."

"I remember," Verlaque said, savoring the last few sips of his wine. "My grandfather told me a Montaigne story when I started first-year law. Montaigne once saw a man lying on the road, bleeding after having been stabbed. A group of peasants, who had water and bread, also came upon the dying man, and Montaigne begged them to give him some water, but they ran off."

"Terrified they would be held responsible if they helped," Marine suggested.

"Exactly. My grandfather used the story as a moral lesson— help thy neighbor—but Montaigne used it to tackle judicial problems. His complaining actually resulted in some real improvements, if I remember correctly."

"Absolutely," she agreed. "Although some of his opinions were too . . . original . . . for sixteenth-century lawmakers. For Montaigne believed that the greatest problem with the law was that it did not take into account our common human condition: our fallibility."

"Who's flawed?" Verlaque asked, smiling. "*Pas moi.*"

"Evidence, especially in those days, was often faulty or inaccurate," Marine went on, speaking louder and faster. "So how could a judge reach a decision that was one hundred percent accurate?"

"And yet he had to make a decision."

"Right. Montaigne joked that judges' verdicts often depended upon how well they digested their lunch."

Verlaque laughed. "Spoken like the true Périgourdin that Montaigne was. And Rabelais? What did he think?"

"Rabelais's character, Judge Bridlegoose—"

He laughed. "Which book did he appear in?"

"One of the Gargantua and Pantagruel books," she answered, getting impatient. "The judge had this mountain of paperwork on his desk, and he'd spend hours reading the documents and pondering, unable to make a decision, until he finally figured out a solution."

"What was that?" Verlaque asked, finishing his wine.

"Simple," Marine answered, getting up and running her fingers through his thick graying hair. "He tossed some dice."

Chapter Eight

❧

A Day in the Life

Verlaque was out the door the next morning at 8:30 a.m. He walked down the rue Adanson and would make his way along his usual route, turning left on Littéra and then immediately right down Aix's narrowest street, less than a meter wide, the rue Esquicho-Coude. The mornings were getting warm enough to leave the apartment with just a suit jacket, and as long as the sun stayed out, by noon the café terraces would be full. Since getting his new cell phone he had become obsessed with the weather and had programmed into it his favorite cities: Paris, Stockholm, Dublin, Rome, and Aix. It amused him how varying the weather in these cities—all of them in Europe— would be on any given day. It was his way of armchair traveling, for in that minute that he had the time to check their heat, or cold, or rain, or fog, he would picture himself there, standing on a bridge or sitting in a café. For fun he added Havana, which always seemed to hover around eighty-eight degrees. Someday he would go and see for himself.

As he approached Esquicho-Coude he felt his shoulders involuntarily narrowing, as they always did, as if they wouldn't fit down the tiny street that in Provençal meant "street of the squeezed elbows."

He heard voices—a man and a woman—discussing "rocks" and "stones" and as he got closer to them, the words changed to "lab" and "Palais de Justice," and then segued into what they were going to eat for lunch that day. "Good morning," Verlaque said, holding out his hand to Officers Jules Schoelcher and Sophie Goulin.

"Sir!" Jules, a transplant from Alsace, said, giving the judge a Herculean grip.

"Good morning, Judge Verlaque," Sophie Goulin echoed, shaking his hand.

"What's going on here?" Verlaque asked, pointing to her gloved hand.

Goulin gestured up to the oratory, a statue of Mary holding Jesus that sat in a niche on the corner of Esquicho-Coude. "Someone attacked the statue early this morning," she replied. "A neighbor who heard the rocks hitting the wall called us."

One of the dozens of oratories put up in Aix during the seventeenth century, the Esquicho-Coude statue had little protection: just three thin metal bars going across the niche and two down. "Is she hurt?" Verlaque asked, immediately regretting his choice of words.

"No, not badly," Schoelcher replied, nonplussed by his boss's sentimental language.

"There are some nicks on her face," Sophie Goulin said, pointing up. "But those might have been there before. We're going to call in the historical society; they have detailed photographs of the oratories."

"Some drunken fool," Verlaque murmured, looking up at the statue.

"Perhaps," Goulin agreed. "It's especially sad as there are so few black virgins left. There used to be more."

Verlaque looked at the young officer, impressed by her knowledge. He looked up again at Mary holding her infant. "I just always saw a mother and son," he said. "I never noticed the color of her skin."

"Someone did," Jules Schoelcher said. He did not have to remind his boss or his fellow officer of the recent rise of France's right-wing nationalist party Le Front National. "I would bet on it."

Verlaque left the officers to their work and carried on down through the narrow streets of old Aix toward the Palais de Justice. As he walked he kept an eye out for other oratories, trying to remember why so many were built in Aix in the seventeenth century. *Something to do with the plague,* he thought. Were they a request to a saint to intercede with God to prevent another deadly outbreak of the plague? Or were they a thank-you for sparing people during the epidemics? He thought the former. His cell phone rang; it was Rebecca Schultz, his father's girlfriend.

"Good morning, Rebecca," he said. She was bilingual, and

they sometimes spoke in French, sometimes in English. He chose the latter that morning.

"I see you have my number programmed into your phone," she replied. "Am I disturbing you?"

"I'm walking to work," Verlaque replied. "It's fine."

"Two things," she went on. "We want you to get us good seats for the summer opera festival."

"Done. At least I'll try my best."

"Great. The second: I have some questions about the French judicial system."

He laughed. "Go on."

"We—your father and I—have been following the Roland Perdigon case. Your dad has been trying to explain the role of the examining magistrate—your job—which I just don't get. If you don't mind me saying, I think it's outrageous that the judge who gathers evidence and launches a probe, in this case against an ex-president, is the same judge who orders a formal investigation. Will he also be the one to judge the case if it goes to trial? Wouldn't he be biased by that point?"

"Didn't you wonder all of that when I was questioning you here in Aix?"

"Of course," Rebecca replied. "But I was too terrified to ask."

"I'm sorry," Verlaque said, smiling. "The examining magistrate in the Roland Perdigon case, who's an old school friend of mine, *has* called for a formal investigation. I heard about it early this morning."

"So he thinks that the ex-president is guilty."

Verlaque paused. "Yes," he said slowly. "Suspicious enough to warrant an investigation. Let me explain. Your system in the United States is the adversarial system. Have you heard of that term?"

"I'm an art historian," she said, sipping some orange juice. "So, no."

"In your system, it's up to the plaintiffs and defendants and their lawyers—*many* lawyers—to gather evidence in their favor or evidence that incriminates the other party. The judge is there to make sure the law is respected, and the jury decides if the accused is guilty. The judge is more of an observer."

"So our system is like a competition where two sides try to prove their case."

"Exactly," he answered. "In fact, the parties are encouraged to win. That's the emphasis."

"Isn't that normal? You want to find out if the accused is guilty, right?"

"I like to think that my job, here in France, is more about uncovering the truth." Verlaque realized immediately that he sounded like a prig, and he thought about his conversation with Marine the previous evening, and Montaigne and Rabelais. He could picture Rabelais's judge's gnarly hands throwing a pair of dice across his desk. He smiled and went on. "The adversarial system can be like those puppets—Punch and Judy, right?— where it becomes a war between the defense and the prosecution."

"Now describe your system," Rebecca said. "If you have time."

Verlaque opened the front door to the Palais de Justice and sat down on a bench in the inner courtyard, thankful that he had decided to speak to Rebecca in English. "Ours is the inquisitorial system," he began. "The rest of continental Europe uses it, along with most of South America, Africa, and Asia. It's tied to common civil law."

"Okay."

"The truth is uncovered through questioning those most familiar with the dispute by a judicial authority. An independent prosecutor, or an investigating magistrate, will then distinguish between reliable and unreliable evidence. By interviewing complainants, witnesses, and suspects, we will steer the investigation in the interest of the State. We then decide whether there is enough evidence to go to trial."

"So in your system there's less trial time."

"Yes," Verlaque answered, watching people come and go across the courtyard. "But the system is slow and secretive, and many think inefficient. It can take two years to gather evidence. But in answer to your first question, yes, if a judge here orders you to court, there's a strong chance he or she presumes you are guilty, as is the case with Roland Perdigon. In his trial, and in other serious ones, which are held in courts of *assize*, there are nine jurors and three judges." Verlaque didn't tell her of the lack of resources; how there were only 562 examining magistrates in France who had to deal with 60,000 cases a year. Some judges, especially in Paris, had 100 cases to deal with simultaneously.

"That must be a crazy waste of a magistrate's talent," Rebecca mused, "if the judge spends all that time looking at evidence for all kinds of crimes, big or small. Surely the police should take on some of the ordinary crimes so that the magistrates could concentrate on bigger ones?"

He laughed. "That would be a great idea." Magistrates already worked with the French police in towns and cities, and with national gendarmes in the countryside, but it was a relationship often fraught with tension. He knew that the current system demotivated police, and that was something he had vowed to try to improve in Aix. Both old-fashioned and high-tech forms of police detection were downgraded by the system, as the emphasis was more on what judges knew best: interrogation and mindgames. But having a commissioner as sympathetic as Bruno Paulik helped enormously. He hoped that Paulik was available for lunch. "Are things clearer for you?"

"Yes, thank you," Rebecca answered. "I'll be able to argue intelligibly with your father now."

"By the way, have they decided about the painting?"

"*I* have," she said. "It's a real Cézanne. But the director of the Musée d'Orsay is calling in more experts. One of them won't be able to come to Paris until midsummer. So wait we must."

"Well, I'd better head upstairs." Verlaque got up, stretched, and hesitated a moment before adding, "Send Dad my love."

"Will do!" Rebecca cheerily replied, as if a Verlaque son telling his father that he loved him was the most natural thing in the world. She set her cell phone down and turned it to silent; she had research to do for a paper she was giving in Amsterdam on Cézanne, and she needed silence. Lying on top of her laptop was a padded manila envelope that Marine had sent; in it were five photographs of the wedding. Rebecca picked up the envelope to move it aside but then hesitated and reached in, taking out one of the photographs. It was the one she had already chosen to frame for their living room. The young photographer—she couldn't remember his name but he was dark-skinned like she was—had positioned himself inside the church, in the doorway, just behind Marine and Antoine, who were standing on the steps, looking down at the square. The morning light streamed into the church. Marine and Antoine waved to their friends and family down below. Someone had thrown handfuls of rice, and it floated around in the sky, caught by the camera. Rebecca smiled. She loved this photo: the blue-green sea, out beyond the village; the red rooftops of the ancient palazzos; and although the wedding party was small, there was so much joy seen in the guests' expressions. She brought the photograph up to her nose and looked at herself, her arms around Antoine's father, Gabriel, who was waving. Marine's mother had made it clear that she disapproved of their age difference, and that hadn't bothered Rebecca as much as it did Gabriel. Her own parents probably would have disapproved, had they still been alive. She knew that in ten years Gabriel would be over eighty and she only in her forties, but they had agreed not to think past a year, or even months. They were lucky to have found each other, which they said aloud every evening, just before falling asleep, holding hands.

Bruno Paulik was indeed available for lunch. Verlaque put in a good case for eating at La Fontaine, but Paulik complained that he was trying to lose weight and that he didn't have time to walk across town. So they ate salads in a café in the Place de Verdun, across from the Palais de Justice, and both regretted their decision.

"If you get a salad with potatoes and bacon in it, you might as well eat homemade pasta," Verlaque said once they were back in his office and, after a series of afternoon meetings, were finally ready for coffee.

Paulik rubbed his stomach. "I know," he replied. "And La Fontaine wouldn't have been much more expensive."

"But we would have ordered wine," Verlaque said, turning on the espresso machine in his office. "That would have doubled the bill."

"Hélène was impressed with La Fontaine's wine selection the last time we ate there," Paulik said. Paulik's wife was a winemaker who, thanks to Antoine Verlaque's financial contribution, now made her own wine at the foot of Montagne Sainte-Victoire. "Hélène says hello, by the way."

Verlaque handed Paulik an espresso and began preparing a second one. "Give her my best. How are the wines looking?"

"Fantastic," Paulik replied. "And I have big news. A journalist came last week from New York, from, I'm proud to brag, the world's most-important wine magazine."

Verlaque turned away from the espresso machine and stared at his colleague. "Are you joking?"

"Nope."

"And? So?"

"He loved the wines," Paulik said, grinning. "Hélène is going to be on the cover of the September issue."

Verlaque raised his hands in the air. "Hallelujah!" He walked over to Paulik and wrapped his arms around him. "Congratulations!"

"*Oh, excusez-moi,*" Mme Girard, Verlaque's secretary, said from the open door.

"Come join in the love," Paulik said, laughing.

Mme Girard, a well-off sixty-year-old who didn't have to work but did so because she loved the job, replied, "Another time, perhaps, Commissioner. Judge Verlaque, the report is in from the car accident." She handed Verlaque a manila envelope and, after giving the two men a quizzical look, turned around on her low-heeled Chanel pumps and left.

Verlaque took the envelope and sat down behind his desk. "She thinks you're gay," he whispered.

Paulik pointed a finger at the judge. "I've been resisting your advances for years, it's true." The two men broke out laughing. He sat down. "Is it the double car accident?" he asked.

"Yes," Verlaque said, putting on his reading glasses. He read while Paulik finished his coffee. He took off his glasses and rubbed his eyes. "Poor girl."

"Suicide?"

"It seems so, according to Dr. Cohen. There was no alcohol or drugs in her system, and she had just texted a friend a sort of farewell message."

"Very sad," Paulik said.

Verlaque looked at the photographs of the twenty-two-year-old's crumpled Renault Clio, which she had driven into a tree at four in the morning, the day after speeding through a pedestrian crossing and killing an elderly woman.

Paulik looked at his watch and got up. "I have to go to Le Tholonet before going home," he announced. "Caroline Rosa and her lawyer are countering."

"As we knew she would," Verlaque said. "I liked Aix better before there were famous actors moving here. Did she think that no one would notice an illegally built fifteen-hundred-square-foot guesthouse on her property?"

"It was done in good taste," Paulik said, heading toward the door. "That was her reply when handed the papers."

"In good taste but without a permit."

"She was shocked when handed the court order," Paulik said as he paused at the door. "Life has been good to people like Rosa . . . rich parents, private schooling, beauty . . . and so they're genuinely surprised when things don't go their way. Anyway, she's to be charged three hundred euros a day for every day she's late in demolishing the guesthouse. I get to go tell her that."

"See you later," Verlaque said. "And tell Hélène congratulations." He put on his reading glasses and picked up a file from his desk and began reading interview reports taken from witnesses to an armed robbery, thinking of his conversation with Rebecca. His commissioner was being sent off to slap a wealthy actress's hand, and he was working on what Rebecca had called "ordinary crimes" instead of taking corrupt officials, businessmen, and crime bosses to court.

Jules Schoelcher knocked on the door and Verlaque waved him in.

"Sorry to disturb," Schoelcher said, "but we've just had a call from a restaurant owner in the Mazarin neighborhood. He's really shaken up."

Verlaque took off his reading glasses and looked at Schoelcher. "Sigisbert Valets? Did something happen to him?"

"Yes, that's the guy, and he's fine," Schoelcher replied. "But his dishwasher is in hysterics. He was digging in the garden behind the restaurant over the afternoon break and came across a skeleton."

"I take it you're not talking about a cat."

"Correct, although he did find some of those," Schoelcher said. "But this one is human."

Chapter Nine

❧

Five Conversations

Verlaque stood beside Dr. Agnès Cohen as they looked at the shallow grave. The sun shone, and the sounds were a fusion of singing birds, hushed voices from inside the restaurant as police officers took statements from the shaken staff, and the hum of distant traffic. "Homicide, I assume," Verlaque said, "given the shallow grave."

"Yes, I'm surprised it took someone this long to uncover it."

"The chef told me he's been too busy working on the restaurant to work in the garden," Verlaque said. "And after the previous owner died the property sat vacant for four years—"

"Succession dispute?"

"Naturally," Verlaque replied. "Nieces and nephews in this case. I'm told that the restaurant renovations then took two years and the place has been up and running for two years, so that makes this skeleton at least eight years old. But don't bodies take longer than eight years to decompose?"

The pathologist knelt down with an elbow on her knee and looked at it. "It normally takes ten to twelve years to decompose a body in a temperate climate in average soil . . . but we don't have a temperate climate here. Especially in 2003 . . . the whole process gets sped up by extreme heat. There are bits of skin and internal organs still intact . . ." She pointed and Verlaque looked but stayed standing. "So seven to eight years might be about right."

Verlaque reflected that a downtown garden seemed an illogical place to bury a body. And had the victim been killed there, in the garden? Or brought there, already dead? "Sex?" he asked.

"Male," the doctor quickly answered. "Big bones, and look at the pelvis area." She pointed again. "Females have a larger subpubic area. Plus his chin is nice and square, and the forehead slants backward, whereas a female has a rounded forehead."

Verlaque tried not to stare at Agnès Cohen's own forehead and instead tried to picture Marine's. But all he could see were Marine's hazel eyes and freckles.

"His skull doesn't seem damaged, but I'll know more once I get him into the lab," Cohen said as she brushed more dirt off the skeleton.

"You always say that," Verlaque said, smiling.

The pathologist returned his smile. "I'll be able to check his teeth against dental records and look at the bones for cracks or fractures that can be traced back to previous injuries. I'm guessing that he once broke his left leg, but it's hard to tell right now.

There's a new test we can do by extracting mineral samples from the bones and cross-referencing them against various drinking waters found across the globe. My intern is obsessed with it."

"Perhaps your intern will be able to tell us whether he was an Aixois," Verlaque said, looking down at the skeleton. He recited the first phrase of Aix's slogan: *"Ville d'eau—"*

Dr. Cohen finished it for him, *"—Ville d'art, ville de musique.* We have too few Cézannes and in my opinion our opera is overpriced, but we do have excellent spring water." She looked over at the ancient fountain that stood less than a meter from the skeleton. "But this fountain isn't running, poor old thing."

Bear Valets stood in his restaurant, relieved that the investigation team had gone. He turned around and surveyed his dining room: the judge was insistent that La Fontaine would have to stay closed for the time being. "Believe me," Verlaque had said, smelling the meat stock gently boiling in the kitchen, "this hurts me as much as it hurts you."

Bear looked over at Mamadou, who was sitting on one of the dining room chairs and had finally managed to stop rocking back and forth. Florian had made Mamadou a cup of hot chocolate, and Bear could hear their conversation, or rather Florian's monologue, in bits and pieces: "My grandmother's recipe," Florian coaxed. "She always swore that any good cook only needs one or two sharp knives, but one day she ordered, out of the blue, a *saucier* from the La Redoute catalog. We still don't know why—"

Mamadou gave Florian a puzzled look and Bear bent his

head down to hide a grin. *Who cares about your grandmother, Florian?* But all the same, Bear was touched by his employee's sensitivity. Mamadou was in shock by the discovery of the skeleton, more than Bear himself. Florian went on, now sitting back in his chair and looking up at the ceiling with his hands behind his head. "She'd use eighty-five percent Lindt chocolate, add some milk, cream, a vanilla pod, and a small amount of sugar, and set the saucier to go. The chocolate would swirl around in there for what seemed like ages. When my family would visit her in her tiny apartment in Poitou, we could smell chocolate in the stairway. My brother and I would run up the last two flights. Do you know what she'd add to it at the end?"

Mamadou sipped the hot chocolate and shook his head back and forth.

"Butter," Bear whispered to himself, as Florian exclaimed, "Butter!"

Bear thought of Jane and Judith, who'd also make hot chocolate, usually laced with grappa, for the team on a rainy day. "They're really aren't many rainy days in London," Judith would try to argue, looking out the giant windows at the river and the sky. "It's just gray, that's all."

José, a sous chef from Seville, would loudly snort.

Bear now missed that London gray: the color of slate, or silver, or even sometimes mauve. Today he found the Provençal blue sky oppressive.

Gaëlle Dreyfus sat in the duke's well-appointed sitting room, surrounded by first-edition books and mediocre oil paintings of stiff, unsmiling ancestors. She held the porcelain saucer up in the air so that she could read underneath it.

"Do you approve?" the duke asked, walking in from the kitchen carrying a silver tray with a teapot on it. It was Manuel's afternoon off.

"Oh yes," Gaëlle answered, smiling, and in no way embarrassed to have been caught trying to determine the origin of his china. In fact, she thought the colors of the flowers too garish, but she was about to drink out of a Meissen porcelain cup, made in Germany, she was almost sure, in 1790, and it took her breath away.

"They were my late wife's favorites," the duke said, pouring out the tea. "I personally find the colors too loud, as you probably do."

"Yes . . . ," she slowly replied. "But to think that when this set was made, Louis XVI and Marie Antoinette were still alive."

"For another three years," the duke said, sitting down. "Our beloved fountain stopped the day they were killed. I read it in the historical records, which I have here on my bookshelves. It's well documented."

Gaëlle leaned forward. "You're kidding me."

"I wouldn't tease you, dear Gaëlle." The way he said "dear" made her body tingle in a way it hadn't done in more than a decade. But she couldn't decide what was more exciting: being charmed by a handsome and wealthy nobleman or drinking out of a cup that was more than two hundred years old. The duke asked, "Do you believe in the fountain's curse?"

"Oh yes."

"Funny, I wouldn't have thought the Jews were as superstitious as we Catholics."

"I was raised agnostic," Gaëlle replied. "My father was Jewish, but nonpracticing, and my mother was Catholic but stopped going to Mass when her parents disowned her after she announced her engagement. So there you go; I come by my superstitions, and dislike of organized religion, naturally." She picked up her cup and examined its delicate paintwork, not wanting to stare into his blue eyes, which she decided were beautiful.

"And so it won't surprise you if I tell you that the fountain has once again stopped," the duke said. He leaned forward. "Because of the murder, no doubt," he added.

"Murder?" she asked, looking up. "Who says?"

"Well . . . of course it was murder," the duke stammered. "My manservant, Manuel, says the whole rue d'Italie is talking about the skeleton. Buried in a shallow grave. Seven or eight years ago. You didn't hear anything?"

"I heard about the skeleton, of course."

"No, I mean seven or eight years ago. Someone digging?"

Gaëlle looked at the duke and noticed that his blue eyes had turned gray. "That's a long time ago. I hardly remember. And Mme Germain was always making noise back there, with her cats and her tin can collection." She added, quite unnecessarily, "Béatrice was a packrat."

"I had forgotten about all those cats," he said, leaning back.

"And you didn't see or hear anything?" Gaëlle asked. "An argument? Someone calling for help?" She felt more and more guilty since the discovery of the skeleton. Someone had been murdered and buried, and none of them had heard anything.

"Not from here, that would be quite unlikely."

"Upstairs?" She pushed on.

The duke nodded. "Perhaps from the third floor, where Manuel has his apartment. Yes . . ." He now seemed lost in thought.

"Well, no doubt the police will be coming around to ask us all these questions," Gaëlle said. She suddenly felt relieved. The professionals would take the investigation in hand, an answer would be found, and they could all get back to their dull lives.

And the antiques dealer was right: in the days that followed, the police—Bruno Paulik, Sophie Goulin, and Jules Schoelcher—interviewed the residents whose apartments and businesses gave onto the shared garden. No one had seen or heard anything unusual. Some could barely remember Béatrice Germain.

"She only died eight years ago," Sophie Goulin told her husband one evening after they had tucked their two small sons into bed. "Isn't that sad? People's memories vary, too. Some people remember very specific things about her: a blue apron or her battered white running shoes. Are they right? Or is their memory failing them? Or are they convincing themselves that that's what she wore? Others remember nothing at all."

"At any rate, the old lady was no longer around, right? When the murder took place?"

Sophie nodded. "The only thing the residents can agree on is that Mme Germain made a lot of noise in the garden."

"So if they heard noise that night, they didn't think anything of it."

"Exactly," Sophie said, sighing, "even though Mme Germain

was no longer alive. *That's* what's so sad. They had forgotten she was dead."

Her husband tilted his head. "You could look at it in a more positive light," he said. "Mme Germain had been such a presence in the neighborhood that if the neighbors had heard a commotion that awful night, they assumed it was her. She was still around, in their minds. I think that's touching."

"I ran into Bear today," Marine said. "He was sitting in a café, looking glum."

"Naturally," Verlaque said, twirling his pasta against the edge of his bowl. "The restaurant has been closed for a week. That's gotta sting. Did you put chili flakes in this? It's great."

She put her fork down and sighed.

"*Quoi?*" Verlaque asked.

"You're not being very sympathetic."

"What can I do, Marine? A skeleton was found on his property."

"I know, I know."

"I spoke to Arnaud, by the way, about buying us groceries. The food will get delivered to my place, as Arnaud has my keys."

"Ah," Marine said. "Which means we'll be eating dinners at your place."

"Do you mind?"

"No," she said. "We're married, so it's my place, too."

He smiled. "I'm glad you think so."

Marine looked around her dining room, which opened onto

an even bigger living room. Verlaque saw his wife looking around her apartment and said, "This has always been too much space for you."

"I knew that when I bought it," she answered. "But I loved the location, and I could afford it then. I couldn't now."

As he continued to eat his pasta—pancetta, pine nuts, olive oil, and arugula around fresh linguine—Marine twisted in her chair and looked behind her, toward the living room. "It's the perfect size," she mused.

Verlaque took a big gulp of Italian red wine and wiped his mouth with his napkin. "Don't even think of it."

"It's a brilliant idea and you know it."

He laughed, putting his napkin down. "It would be total chaos, not to mention it would get me into trouble. A skeleton of a murdered victim has been found on a chef's property, which makes him a suspect—"

"Bear was a kid in London eight years ago."

"Okay, but I'm involved in the investigation, and you're proposing to open your apartment to Bear to resume his restaurant business. Right?"

Marine beamed. "It's big enough here, and my kitchen is in okay shape, and we don't need two apartments. Why not help Bear out?"

"I've already told you why," Verlaque said. "And you're a law professor, so you know how tangled up this could become."

She smiled, not sure how much longer she even cared to be a professor. She briefly closed her eyes and imagined her apartment as a restaurant. She imagined they might squeeze in twelve, perhaps fifteen diners. Wine storage might be a problem, but maybe Bear could rent a wine fridge and set it up in the back corner of her office? Or he could bring over enough wine for a night by hand? Or in a wheelbarrow? She only had four burners and one oven, but she had seen industrial-grade single burners for sale in a restaurant-supply shop in Marseille she had once visited with a friend. They were heavy-duty gas burners, not at all like the rickety camping stoves her parents had used to make coffee on their roadside picnics. And, best of all, her downstairs neighbors were away for two months, visiting their daughter in Nantes who had just given birth to their first grandchild. Marine poured more wine and happily dug into her pasta.

Chapter Ten

❧

Snooping Around for Bones

"There is no more beautiful life than that of a carefree man; Lack of care is a truly painless evil,'" Frère Joël said as he set down his coffee cup. It was a cold morning, and the duke had suggested they have coffee inside, not in the garden. Manuel had baked a lemon loaf and the young friar hoped he would be offered a second piece.

"Euripides?" the duke asked.

"Sophocles."

"*Ah oui, Sophocles, bien sûr,*" the duke said. "In the Renaissance, when one retired one withdrew to discover what life was all about. To contemplate. It was considered part of a well-managed life."

"The great Stoic Seneca urged his fellow Romans to retire in order to—and I'll use one of our modern expressions here—to find themselves."

The duke laughed—he was hardly the kind of man who would go to India, or on a retreat, to "find himself." But he knew what Joël meant, and he was impressed with his classical knowledge. He was mad at himself for having mistaken a Sophocles quote for Euripides. "Yes, the Romans withdrew from their period of civic business, not only to find themselves"—here he smiled, then went on—"but also to prepare for their next stage. Death."

"With an emphasis on contemplating life," Frère Joël quickly added.

The duke got up and began pacing the room. "And now we, poor sods of the twenty-first century, live longer. We have even more time to prepare for dying."

The duke was in a particularly blue mood, and the pragmatic friar wanted to steer the conversation away from death. Why worry about death if it may be—in the duke's case—years away? The duke hadn't given him any more details of his illness or the doctor's prognosis. But before Frère Joël could change the conversation, the duke blurted out, "You've heard about the skeleton?"

"Ah, that explains all this talk about death," Frère Joël said, setting his coffee cup down. "Yes, we did."

"What do your colleagues think?"

"What do you mean?"

"Well, who is it?" the duke asked, still walking around the room.

The friar looked up, surprised. "I haven't thought about that."

"Yes, yes, you've only just arrived in Aix . . ."

In fact, Frère Joël had heard Père Jean-Luc speaking with

one of the other priests, Père Guillaume, in hushed tones, about this very subject, and a name had been whispered, but he didn't want to say anything to the duke. They could very well be wrong, or he may have misunderstood. He looked around at the oil paintings—relatives, he presumed—admiring them. The duke watched the friar and wanted to say how mediocre the paintings were—the artists had been incapable of revealing character or personality traits. Each female and male sitter resembled the next, a blur of chubby, rosy-cheeked, boring oafs. "You have so many memories in this room," Frère Joël said. "Family portraits, travel mementos—" He reached over and stroked a long wooden cane that was leaning against the bookshelf.

"African," the duke said. "It's a dancing cane used in ceremonies."

"I once visited Sigmund Freud's last home, in London. It was much like your home: stuffed with books, papers, paintings, and objects of every sort . . . anthropological curiosities. He, like Montaigne, thought that such busy surroundings stimulated the intellect."

"I remember that house," the duke said, sitting down and crossing his long legs. "It's in Hampstead. It was such a lovely day . . ." He stayed lost in thought, then after a few moments passed the cake plate to the young friar. "I know what you're trying to do," he said. "You want me to stimulate my intellect. To be occupied. Hence the Sophocles quote."

"Is that a bad thing? Look around and lose yourself in the variety and sublimity of everything around you."

"You think me a spoiled old man."

The friar laughed. "We all go through moments of boredom and self-doubt, whether rich or poor, old or young. Montaigne said that salvation lies in paying close attention to nature."

"That I do . . . my garden—"

"Yes, but the one natural phenomenon that lies closest at hand is not out in your garden but here"—Frère Joël tapped his chest with the flat of his palm—"yourself."

"What if I started writing? A journal? My memoirs?"

"There you are," Frère Joël said, smiling. He sat back to enjoy his well-deserved second piece of lemon cake.

Verlaque slept well and arrived at the Palais de Justice that morning before 8:00. Marine was already up and he drank some of the coffee she had made, forcing himself to eat a small bowl of muesli. He hated breakfast, but since getting married—and approaching forty-five—he decided to try to take better care of himself. His mother's death, too, he realized, had had an effect on his decision, but it had been Marine who had pointed that out. He rinsed the bowl and placed it in the dishwasher, then kissed Marine goodbye. She had a tape measure in her hands, and he remembered that she had said something a few days earlier about new drapes or a new shower curtain or something like that.

Once at his office he made himself another coffee; while drinking it he pictured the many gleaming stainless-steel espresso machines he could buy for Marine for Christmas. But was that necessary? Would they soon sell her apartment? The phone rang; he sat down and answered it. "Verlaque."

"Good morning," Dr. Cohen said, pausing to sip water out

of a recycled San Pellegrino bottle she always kept in her purse. "I have news."

Verlaque picked up a pen and grabbed his notepad. "Go ahead."

"The victim, a male as I suspected, died of a traumatic head injury, an epidural hematoma."

"A hemorrhage?"

"Exactly. After a trauma, in most cases a fall. Pressure builds on the brain, causing a herniation." She paused and Verlaque could hear her chewing. "The whole brain actually shifts, cutting off the blood supply to the brain—"

"Would it be a quick death?" he asked.

"It can take anywhere from minutes to hours," the doctor answered. "The signs aren't always clear, but the victim will develop a headache, then loss of consciousness, and if not quickly operated on, death."

"Was the skull fractured in any way?" Verlaque asked.

"Not at all," she answered. "But that can happen with an epidural hematoma. Sometimes there are no outward signs of damage to the head. Michel de Montaigne's brother died that way."

"I vaguely remember the story. Captain Saint-Martin?"

"Yes, he was twenty-three and had been playing tennis. The ball struck him on the side of the head. He felt fine at first, and there were no signs of injury. Hours later he complained of a headache and then fell down unconscious, later dying. All from a tennis ball."

"And our victim?" he asked. "Were you able to determine more about him?"

"Mid to late twenties," Dr. Cohen replied. "And judging by his bones, especially the femur, fibula, and tibia, we know he was short, less than five foot seven. And I was right about his broken left leg."

Verlaque wrote down the information. "Dental records?"

"My intern is looking at his teeth right now. We'll know more about that by the end of the day or tomorrow. Let's hope he's had some fancy dental work done."

"Thank you for this," Verlaque said.

Dr. Cohen held the phone between her ear and shoulder as she tore her *pain au chocolat* in half. "My intern wants to know if the water has come back on."

"*Quoi?*" he asked, not understanding what she meant. "Oh! The fountain . . . I have no idea. Why?"

"No reason," she answered. "He's superstitious, that's all."

As Verlaque hung up, Bruno Paulik walked in, turning on the espresso machine and then crossing the room to shake Verlaque's hand. They had been working together for more than six years, and Paulik wondered if the judge would ever be able to give him the *bise* as a greeting. He knew that it took guys from the north longer to get used to the idea of giving another man a peck on either cheek and to add to that Verlaque had that weird mixed-Anglo heritage. "Do you want another one?" he asked, pointing to the espresso maker.

"Why not," Verlaque answered. "I just got off the phone with Dr. Cohen," he continued. "Our victim, male, in his mid-twenties, died from a head injury. A fall. The outer skull appears untouched, but the damage was all done internally. The murderer, or whoever was there, must have watched him die."

Paulik handed Verlaque an espresso. "And then buried him?"

"Yes, and somehow the murderer got his body into that garden in downtown Aix. Wouldn't you take the body somewhere else? A forest? A lake?"

"There aren't any lakes around here."

"You know what I mean."

"What if the murder took place in one of the properties along that garden? Then it wouldn't be far to carry the body."

Verlaque sipped his coffee and said, "You're right. And the guy was short, too. Easier to carry." He looked at Paulik and tried to imagine anyone carrying the dead weight of the commissioner, who played rugby on the weekends and, at six foot two, was solid muscle. "Or, the death took place right there, beside the fountain."

"I like that scenario best."

"So do I."

Verlaque finished his coffee and leaned back. "Why a shallow grave?"

"The murderer ran out of time?" Paulik suggested. "They got freaked out and left in a hurry?"

"Or ran out of energy," Verlaque said. "It takes hours, and lots of muscle, to dig a deep grave. What does that suggest to you?"

"Someone out of shape. Or elderly."

"Or a woman," Verlaque added.

Paulik grimaced. "I just spoke to Schoelcher and he and another officer are starting to look at missing persons reports going back ten years. We'll begin in the Aix area, then if nothing pans out go larger. I'll tell him that we're looking for a young adult male."

"Dr. Cohen is forwarding you her report," Verlaque said. "She's probably already sent it, given how efficient she is."

"A shallow grave . . . ," Paulik mused as he finished his coffee. He leaned back and Verlaque guessed that he was in for another Paulik family story. The commissioner had been raised on a farm near Ansouis in the Luberon, a farm that his parents, now in their early seventies, still worked. "My grandparents used to talk about a guy a few farms over who disappeared before the war. Everyone thought his young wife did him in and that she buried him somewhere in the back forty. Anyway, I don't know if you read it in *La Provence* last week, but some hikers just found what looks like his skeleton on their old property, buried in a shallow grave. The widow is long dead, and the farm has switched hands twice since then—"

"Nice thing to tell a newly married man."

Paulik laughed and went on. "He had been cheating on her, and he was heavy-handed." He made a slapping gesture with his right hand, waving it back and forth in the air. "Twice the local doctor had to be called in to give her stitches, and once at a village fête my grandmother had to pull him off her."

"Your grandmother?"

"Yeah, you didn't fool around with her," Paulik said.

"Was the woman questioned when her husband disappeared?"

Paulik shrugged. "Yes, but she told the police that he had been threatening to leave her and emigrate to Quebec. The neighbors stayed quiet, or lied, as my mother thinks my grandmother did, confirming the woman's emigration story. In those days people handled that kind of thing on their own and helped one another. Everyone was glad to be rid of him. He was a terrible husband and neighbor. But when I was a kid, I had a hard time believing the gossip—that she could kill, and bury, her husband. My brothers were all into it, and they used to make halfhearted efforts to sneak back there and snoop around for bones. But I thought that he just went to Canada, end of story."

"Looks like your brothers were right."

"Yeah, for once."

"What happened to the widow?" Veralque asked.

"The priest in Ansious annulled the marriage after two years, and she went on to marry a really nice guy from Lourmarin and they had a bunch of kids, and each one did really well in school. You know, one of those kinds of families where there's a doctor, a lawyer, a professor, and I think one of the sons even became a cardinal. Not a bad one in the bunch."

Chapter Eleven

❧

The Wayward Son

Officer Sophie Goulin ran through the Palais de Justice carrying a yellowed folder. Jules Schoelcher had been called away on another case and she had continued going through the missing persons reports, eating her packed lunch at her desk, comparing the reports with the pathologist's findings. Many of the missing were female—runaways?—and she deleted those. Many, too, were over fifty, and some were elderly when they had gone missing—Alzheimer's? And then she found one: Grégory de Castelbajac. At first it was his name that caught her eye—posh—she even had to say it aloud a few times in order to figure out how it was pronounced. Her heart raced when she read that he was five foot six and had been twenty-six when he was first reported missing by his parents, the Comte and Comtesse de Castelbajac. The parents stated in the report that Grégory "had traveled the world" and returned home briefly, eight years ago, for his grandmother's funeral, and then disappeared again.

Sophie put her sandwich down and turned a page, reading through the paragraph listing "distinguishing physical characteristics": a pear-shaped birthmark on his right hand. There was no way they would be able to see that now. Left leg: broken in skiing accident when twelve years old. "Bingo," she said as she sprung out of her chair and jogged on the spot, then reached down and quickly touched her toes. "Where are you, Jules?" She sat down again and finished reading the document. The count and countess's address had been crossed out with a pencil. (Who was the dork who did that? Sophie sighed, embarrassed by the nonchalance of some of her colleagues.) A new address had been messily written in, the name of the house, La Belle Vue, with a street address in Sanary-sur-Mer. She knew that Sanary was a seaside town about forty-five minutes south of Aix, but she had never been there. They usually took the kids swimming in La Ciotat—there were lots of sandy beaches and, if you got there early enough, parking close to the beach. She lowered her head to try to read their old address and then let out a yell.

After a few phone calls, she made her way to the commissioner's office. "You missed all the excitement, Jules," she muttered. Paulik's office door was closed, and she could see through the frosted glass that the lights were off, so she kept running. She passed through a large communal office space, where police officers worked in relative silence due to the sobering presence of Mme Girard, Judge Verlaque's formidable secretary. She saw that the judge's door was open and that Mme Girard wasn't at her desk. It was then that Sophie remembered it was lunchtime and her stomach growled as she had eaten only a few bites of her ham sandwich. She saw the commissioner and the judge sitting around the judge's big glass desk and she slowed down, hesitating at the door. Antoine Veralque put his sandwich down and looked at her, recognizing her from the rue Esquicho-Coude and the defaced black Madonna. "Come in," he said, waving her in.

Paulik turned around and quickly wiped his mouth with a paper napkin. "Hello. Any news?"

"I'm sorry," she said, gesturing to their paper bags and sandwiches.

"That's okay," Verlaque said. "There's nothing more depressing than eating sandwiches at your desk. You can cheer us up." In fact, he and Paulik had been having a good time talking of Hélène Paulik's new wines and the interview that had taken place with the American journalist. A photographer had even been along and had taken dozens of photographs of Hélène, which included two costume changes, inside their ramshackle eighteenth-century farmhouse, in the wine storehouse, and in the vines.

Sophie held up her prize, the yellowed folder. It was then that she saw the two small wineglasses, the kinds used in wine tastings, on the judge's desk, both full of red wine. She quickly looked away, but Verlaque caught her eye and held up a wine bottle. "The commissioner's wife's new Syrah. Would you like to try it?"

"No, no," she stammered. How could they be sitting there

drinking wine when she had made such an important discovery? "But thank you."

"What's in the folder?" Paulik asked.

What do you think? she almost answered, but instead said, "Grégory de Castelbajac."

"Take a chair, please," Verlaque said, quickly moving aside the paper bag and wine bottle. "This sounds interesting."

"He's been missing for eight years," Sophie began, trying to keep her voice steady. "His parents, a count and countess, only reported him missing four years ago because he used to travel a lot, all around the world, apparently. They claimed in their statement that it was usual for Grégory to disappear for years at a time with no word. He would come back for money, which he spent on his travels and on drugs. He was the youngest of four boys. He was referred to by the parents as their, and I quote, 'wayward son.'"

Verlaque and Paulik exchanged looks, nodding to each other for a reason Sophie couldn't understand.

She continued, "He is—or was—five foot six and broke his left leg skiing when he was twelve."

"Sounds like we've found him," Paulik said.

"Yes, I'm sure of it," Sophie said, opening the folder and passing the last page to the men. "Because the count and countess now live in Sanary-sur-Mer, but when they filed this search they still lived here in Aix. On the rue Cardinale."

Paulik whistled.

"Which number?" Verlaque asked.

"Number 18," Paulik answered, reading the report.

"I've just checked with city records," Sophie added. "They owned the whole house and sold it three years ago. It was bought by a developer and has been split up into offices and apartments now, except for the top floor, where one of the brothers lives."

"I assume their old house gives onto the garden where the body was found?" Verlaque asked.

"Yes," Sophie answered. "It's next to the antiques store."

Paulik ate the last bit of his sandwich, washing it down with a large gulp of wine. "Here we go," he said.

"Interview everyone on that entire garden," Verlaque said.

"Thank you, Officer—"

"Goulin," Sophie replied.

Paulik said, looking at Sophie, "Great research. You can help with the interviews." He got up, brushing bread crumbs off his pants. "Sorry," he mumbled, looking down at the now-spotted blue carpet and then over at Verlaque.

"No problem," Verlaque said. "Mme Girard will magically appear in a few moments with her DustBuster. I'll call the pathologist right away to see if she has any dental findings we can use to verify, one hundred percent, that the skeleton is in fact Grégory de Castelbajac, before his parents are told."

"His dentist is here in Aix, and still in practice," Sophie offered. "Rue Mistral. His phone number is in the report."

Verlaque almost smiled, noting how his fellow Aixois tended to stay close to home when shopping or going about their business. Heaven forbid that the Castelbajacs had a dentist on the wrong side of the Cours Mirabeau.

Chapter Twelve

⚘

Sanary-sur-Mer

Verlaque parked his Porsche at Portissol, a small beach to the west of Sanary's downtown. He had once had drinks at Portissol's restaurant, long ago, with a former girlfriend. She had liked the bar's sleek pseudo-contemporary interior—lots of black and gray and too-loud house music pumped in—and he had winced. But the harbor had magnificent sunsets—that he remembered fondly—and he had returned with Marine a couple of times.

"We need to move to Sanary," he said into his cell phone as he looked at the sparkling sea.

"We already have two apartments," Marine answered. "I'm going into class. I'll phone you when I'm through."

"No, it's better if I call you before I head back to Aix," Verlaque said. "I'm just about to tell two people that a skeleton found in a garden is their son, and I don't know how long I'll be."

Marine held her phone against her chest and closed her eyes. "Are you sure?" she asked a few seconds later.

"Yes, just confirmed by his dentist, whose office is on the rue Mistral."

"Victim found; now find the murderer."

Verlaque sighed. "This is an amazing place, and only forty-five minutes from Aix. I'll take some photographs for you." He looked at the sea, framed by pine trees, and continued walking along the narrow sea-cliff road.

"All right," Marine answered, smiling. She knew that he'd come home with bundles of free real estate magazines. "See you tonight."

He had been given vague directions by the count, whose voice barely disguised his anguish when Verlaque introduced himself over the phone and asked if he could visit the couple that afternoon. "Across from the chapel," the count had twice mentioned, and Verlaque continued walking along the road, stopping to admire the houses on the right-hand side of the road, those directly on the sea. He was a happy, self-confessed real estate junkie and didn't bother to disguise his voyeurism, almost peeking through holes in fences to get a better glimpse at the homes and their gardens. The architectural styles varied from Mediterranean to sleek flat-roofed contemporary to ramshackle beach homes that probably weren't even winterized: those were clearly closed up for the season and their Parisian owners would reopen the homes sometime in July.

The road then narrowed to such a point that the seaside homes no longer had room for driveways and cars could no longer pass. The chapel appeared to the left, perfect in its proportions and framed by pots of palms and flowers, with benches for the weary. He stood in the doorway and turned around, looking at the sea, and saw the Castelbajacs' house, La Belle Vue, across the way. Verlaque nodded to himself, realizing now why they had chosen such an unimaginative name for the house. What else could you call it? Not only did they have a sweeping view of the sea, but they probably also had a view of the charming *vieille ville* of Sanary.

He was ten minutes early for his appointment, so he went inside the chapel, passing through honey-colored wooden doors that were covered with deep, dark grooves: names and dates carved into the doors dating back to the nineteenth century. He hated graffiti and didn't bother to stop to read the names, no matter how old they were. Once inside, he loved the simplicity of the chapel's interior. The barrel-vaulted ceiling and walls were painted white, showing off three or four small statues of saints, each one painted. Small marble plaques—ex-votos, offerings given to saints in fulfillment of a vow—lined the north and south walls. Each one was engraved with a name of the saved, the donors, and a date. Above the plaques were a dozen or so naïve paintings, and when Verlaque approached them to get a better look, he realized that they were not seascapes or landscapes but were also ex-votos. A woman, in long, flowing white robes, fell from a sea cliff. A man lay on the ground, injured in a railway explosion. The Virgin Mary hovered in the top corner of each painting, assuring their safety. He pulled out his phone and took a few photos to show Marine and Sylvie, both fans of the genre, and then left the chapel, taking in a large breath of sea air to prepare himself for the Castelbajacs.

It had been fifteen minutes since Verlaque had given the Count and Countess de Castelbajac the news. After he had gone over the details of the police report and Dr. Cohen's findings, he offered to leave and come back another time, but the couple had insisted he stay. They ordered coffee from a young maid who looked horrified by the sadness in the house. She almost ran out of the room, tripping on the rug.

"A year ago we came to accept, with the help of a therapist, that Grégory might be dead," the count said. Verlaque was surprised by the nobleman's candor. "But you've just told us that our son was murdered and we must know more, no matter how painful." Verlaque looked over at the countess and she nodded in agreement. "How did he die?"

"Grégory died of internal head injuries, due to a fall," Verlaque said. "The person who buried him probably pushed him, but we don't yet know where or when."

The countess let out a yelp, then covered her mouth. She grew ashen and silent, staring at her folded hands on her lap. Her husband paced the library, mumbling to himself. "Is it really Grégory?" he asked. "Might the pathologist be mistaken? Or the dentist? They could mix up files, couldn't they?" The count looked over at his wife, who mumbled a "Hail Mary" with her eyes closed. Verlaque saw that she had a rosary in her hands. Had it been there the whole time? Or had she just pulled it out of a pocket? The count continued his pacing, pulling books at random off the bookshelf and then replacing them. "Who would want to hurt Grégory?" He sat down and buried his head in his hands.

"Eight years ago," Verlaque said, "Grégory was back in Aix for your mother's funeral. Is that correct?"

"Yes," the count answered, rubbing his forehead.

"Were you and the countess at home, on the rue Cardinale?"

"Yes, as the funeral was at Saint-Jean de Malte, on August eighth. But three days after the funeral we came here, to rest."

"Grégory was alone—" the countess whispered.

"We were expecting him down in Sanary on Sunday, for a family lunch, but he never came. We assumed he had headed back south."

"Was it usual for him to turn up at family get-togethers?" Verlaque asked.

"Not for a few years, no," the count answered. "But Grégory had assured us he'd be here, so we were disappointed. His favorite cousin was here, too, so we thought he would come."

Verlaque asked, "What was Grégory like?"

"We spoiled him," the count said, looking from his wife to Verlaque. "Grégory came late, almost ten years after Emile, twelve years after Philippe, and fifteen after Ludovic." The countess continued praying, and so the count went on. "He was born premature and tiny. We were worried sick that he wouldn't make it out of the hospital. He did, but he was prone to illness, and a dreamer, and we catered to him. We had been strict with our first three sons, so by the time Grégory was born we were exhausted and not as disciplinarian as we should have been. Now I think . . . no, I know for certain . . . that we should have been even tougher on Grégory, as he needed it more than the other three boys."

Verlaque nodded, remembering the missing persons report, and the wayward son. He saw two framed photographs on the walls of two families of six, each with a smiling husband and wife and their four children. "Your sons?" he asked.

"Philippe and his family on the left," the count replied, "and Emile and his family on the right."

Verlaque nodded, wondering why there wasn't a photograph of Ludovic. Perhaps it was in a different room? Or only those sons with large families made it onto the library walls? On a bookshelf a small framed black-and-white photograph leaned against a vase of dusty dried flowers, and Verlaque got up to look at it.

"That's Grégory," the countess said, in such a clear voice that Verlaque swung around to face her, holding the photograph in his hands. "Machu Picchu."

"He *did* visit historical sites," the count said, "when he wasn't buying drugs."

"Did he buy drugs in Aix?" Verlaque asked, setting the photograph back and stealing a look at the young man: Thin. Thick tousled hair. Ripped jeans and Converse sneakers. Grinning.

"I would suppose so," the count replied. "But when he came back to Aix, he was on good behavior."

"*Il était toujours sage*," the countess interjected. The maid came back in and set a tray of coffee down on a side table, then left quickly. Verlaque didn't blame her. "Grégory was a good boy, Judge Verlaque," the countess continued. "He was weak, that's all."

The count nodded, looking at his wife. Verlaque saw the look of love they exchanged, and it made him ache for Marine. "You're right, dear," the count said. "Grégory *was* good natured, but he was too easily swayed by others. Deviant others."

"I'd like a list of his friends' names," Verlaque said.

The count paused and rubbed his chin. "Most of them live abroad," he answered. "Ibiza, Rome, London . . ."

The privileged set, thought Verlaque. He understood why the count referred to them as deviant. "What about friends in Aix?" he asked. "When he was a teen?"

"He had two good friends," the countess offered. "The Three Musketeers we used to call them." She looked toward Grégory's photograph and managed a smile. "They were always causing a ruckus—"

"We've forgotten the coffee," the count said, pouring out three cups. "Sugar?"

"One, please," Verlaque said. He looked at the countess, hoping for more information. "If you could give me their names . . ."

"Oh, it was so long ago," she answered. "But I'll go through our photo albums and let you know."

It wasn't so long ago, thought Verlaque. *Grégory was only in his mid-twenties.* But he knew that the countess was grieving and that shock can make one forget what he or she had just eaten for breakfast. "I'd appreciate that," he said. "We'll need to speak to you both again, in the next few days, and to your sons."

"Absolutely," the count answered. "Emile and Philippe live in Paris but will no doubt come down once they've heard the news. Ludovic lives in Aix, in the top-floor apartment of our former home on the rue Cardinale. Grégory was never very close to his brothers, but he was extremely attached to my brother's daughter, Juliette. She may be able to help you. I'll give you her number, but give me a day or so to break the news to her."

"Certainly," Verlaque said. "And thank you." He finished his coffee and set the cup down. Grégory de Castelbajac had probably been killed over drugs, most likely by a dealer who was owed money.

"I'll see you out," the count said. "I'm suddenly very tired."

"I understand," Verlaque said. He shook the countess's hand and thanked her, then followed the count out of the library. The count excused himself to look for Juliette de Castelbajac's phone number, and Verlaque looked around the spacious entryway. This room, as was the library, was on the north side of the house, without sea views. Small oil paintings—seascapes—lined the walls. A large Chinese vase held two umbrellas and a carved walking stick. In a gold gilt mirror he looked at himself, the newly married man. He was sure he had fewer wrinkles, but the happy state of matrimony could do nothing for his broken nose. It would always be crooked. Then he saw a reflection of a framed verse, executed in needlepoint, and he turned around to look at it. *Un roi, une foi, une loi*; the border outlined with fleurs-de-lis. Verlaque smirked; a needlepoint with the verse *One king, one faith, one law* was in keeping with the books he had seen in the Castelbajacs' library: biographies on French kings and queens and various conservative politicians and, just above Grégory's photograph, a multi-volume set of the *Livre d'Or*, a detailed Who's Who of French nobility published yearly.

Chapter Thirteen

❧

Philomène Off on Her Rounds

*B*runo Paulik and Sophie Goulin walked together along the Cours Mirabeau, crossing the street at Le Mazarin Café, and then walked down the rue Mistral. "I thought we'd start at the antiques place," Paulik said, looking at a list of addresses on his notepad. "Officers Schoelcher and Caromb are starting at the other end of the block, on the rue d'Italie, and the judge is interviewing the Duke de Pradet and the priests and brothers at Saint-Jean de Malte."

"And the family and friends of Grégory de Castelbajac?" Sophie asked.

"Judge Verlaque is working on obtaining a list from the parents. He visited them yesterday."

"How awful. I can't imagine losing a child."

"Do you have kids?" Paulik asked as they turned left at the Quatre Dauphins fountain.

"Two holy terrors," Sophie replied, smiling. "Ages three and six. Boys."

"Ah, we lucked out with one girl."

"Here we are," Sophie said, staring up at the wooden storefront painted an elegant matte black and the sign ANTIQUAIRE DREYFUS. She wondered why the commissioner and his wife had chosen to have just one child. Perhaps it hadn't been a choice? At the same time Paulik thought of his little Léa, at eleven already a star singer at Aix's prestigious music conservatory. What would he have done with two boys, two holy terrors? And besides, Léa even watched the last World Cup rugby tournament with him and had recently put up a poster of Morgan Parra in her bedroom. The French scrum-half now shared wall space with Kiri Te Kanawa and Jessye Norman.

Paulik opened the door, which jammed when it was half open. "Give it a shove!" came a voice from within the shop. "It's older than the hills."

Gaëlle Dreyfus moved out from behind her desk—Jacques Adnet, circa 1940, steel with brass corners, stitched leather drawers—and looked at the pair. She sized up Paulik, thankful that he hadn't broken the door when she had ordered him to "give it a shove." He was enormous. "Police?" she asked.

Neither Paulik nor Sophie were in uniform, and he introduced themselves. "How did you know we were police?" he then asked.

"I've been expecting your visit," Gaëlle answered, tapping her right cheek with the pencil she had been holding. "Although you might have been a recently married couple looking for the perfect Baccarat vase or Art Deco silver-plated tea service, both of which I have, at very reasonable prices."

Paulik laughed and said he'd pass, while Sophie stayed silent, eager to begin but knowing that this kind of chitchat was very important, sometimes even more revealing than routine questions.

"Please sit down," Gaëlle said, choosing a solid leather club chair for Paulik and a small, elegant Thonet bistro chair for his unsmiling cohort. "It's Grégory, isn't it? The body . . ."

"Yes," Paulik answered. Sophie pulled out a notepad and began writing, while Gaëlle watched her, one eyebrow raised. "How did you know?" he asked.

Gaëlle made a gesture with her fingers, opening and closing them. "Everyone in the neighborhood is talking."

"Does that surprise you?" he asked. "That it was Grégory de Castelbajac . . ."

Gaëlle thought for a moment before answering. "No. He was always getting into trouble, poor thing. I liked him. He used to come in here to chat after he had argued with his parents."

"Was that often?"

"Yes, I'd say so. More than I ever fought with mine, but every family's different. Then he'd go away for years at a time, sometimes coming back with very chic friends who were tanned and multilingual and knew a thing or two about antiques. I usually sold a lot then, small pieces that they could stuff into their Vuitton carry-ons."

"Do you remember the last time you saw him?" Sophie asked.

"Years and years ago," Gaëlle answered. "I think he came

back to Aix for his grandmother's funeral, Vicomtesse de Castelbajac. A real nutter."

"That was eight years ago," Paulik said. "How was he behaving?"

"If I remember correctly, he came into the shop complaining of being back in France. He reeked of pot and his eyes were red. Obviously not from tears for the old lady."

"Did he seem frightened?"

"No," Gaëlle said slowly. "Agitated, perhaps, but at the time I put that down to the drugs. Is that when he was killed?"

"Yes," Paulik answered. He didn't offer any more information.

"Did he mention seeing any friends while here?" Sophie asked.

"Not by name," Gaëlle answered. "He didn't stay in my shop long, which was unusual. Sometimes he'd sit in the chair you're sitting in"—she pointed to Paulik's weathered club chair—"for hours. He'd read or do the *Le Monde* crossword with me. But that day he was restless."

"Thank you," Paulik said. "Will you please call us if you think of anything else?" He gave her a business card and he and Sophie got up, shaking hands with Gaëlle.

The antiques dealer set the card in a small silver envelope holder, engraved with palm trees.

"That's a beauty," Paulik said, pointing to it. "Much nicer than IKEA."

"It's a rare one," Gaëlle answered, flattered. "Late nineteenth century, Brazil. It came from a wealthy sugarcane baron's estate."

Sophie Goulin opened the door, giving it a strong pull at the halfway mark. They walked out into the sunny morning and stopped at the next door, number 16, a law office. "Did you intentionally comment on that envelope holder?" Sophie asked.

"Yes, in a way. It looked very South American, or Caribbean, to me."

"Grégory de Castelbajac spent a lot of time in South America," Sophie said.

Paulik shrugged. "You never know. Just trying to make connections."

"And by the way," Sophie added, "I love IKEA."

Paulik laughed. "So do I. So do I."

Verlaque walked down the rue d'Italie, looking for a brightly painted red door that he knew led to the offices of Saint-Jean de Malte. The medieval building that housed the offices of the eleventh-century church had recently gone through two years of renovations, the details of which Florence Bonnet had recounted during a family dinner. It had been an entertaining narrative, full of the same trials and tribulations that every home owner experiences while renovating in Provence: Workers who don't show up for days or weeks. Materials not ordered on time or in the right size. Internal squabbles between the priests themselves over interior spaces and furnishings. He began daydreaming, imagining a scenario of two priests arguing over paint swatches, and stopped suddenly at the red door, tripping up the person who was walking too closely behind him. "*Je suis vraiment désolé*," Verlaque said, turning around to apologize.

"*Ça va*," the man grunted, pulling a scarf up around his face despite the warm day. Verlaque grinned; two or three of the employees at the Palais de Justice swore by the benefits of keeping one's neck warm, even in clement April weather. Antoine and Sébastien Verlaque had been partly raised by their English grandmother, who thought the opposite: Bedroom windows were left open in winter, and if it was lightly raining, the boys were still sent outside to play. "Come back in if you see lightning," Emmeline would joke, and the boys would do as they were told, as they knew in an hour she'd have a warm tarte tatin ready for them to eat, served with dollops of whipped Normandy cream. He looked at the man, thinking that they knew each other, but he couldn't place him. Aix was that kind of small town: He was continually embarrassed by running into people who seemed to know him, often by name, but he couldn't even remember if they were colleagues or assistant butchers at the Boucherie du Palais.

When he walked into the church's offices a bell sounded. An elderly woman (*Why do elderly women always take care of priests?* he wondered) turned around from a filing cabinet and waved her hands in the air. "You're here!" she bellowed, walking across the office in long steps, giving the judge a handshake that might have even hurt Bruno Paulik's hand. He knew immediately that she was Philomène Joubert. "A few minutes late, but no bother," she added. She picked up a telephone and dialed one of the offices, bellowing into the receiver, "The judge is here!," hanging it up with a thud. "Did you get held up or what?"

"Yes," Verlaque answered, enjoying the interrogation of the infamous Mme Joubert, director of the church's choir, friend of Florence Bonnet's, and neighbor, across the courtyard, of Marine's. "At Michaud's, as a matter of fact."

"What's your fancy there?" she demanded, her hands on her hips.

"*Facile. Brioche glacée à chaque fois.*"

"Umph. I would have taken you for a croissant man."

"Too many crumbs," Verlaque said, patting his jacket, "on the Ralph Lauren jacket."

Philomène laughed, slapping his upper right arm. "I must say, it looked like you had a lovely wedding, even if it wasn't here in Aix."

"I agree," said a voice behind them. "I, too, saw the photos." The priest extended his hand and said, "I'm Père Jean-Luc. I'm very pleased to meet you. Please come into my office."

Père Jean-Luc's office was just as Verlaque imagined a priest's office to be: a heavy wooden desk, a bit too big for the room, dark wood floor-to-ceiling bookcases with mostly hardbacks, thick red curtains. Verlaque sat down opposite the priest and asked, "Did my secretary explain why I'm here?"

"Yes, sadly," Père Jean-Luc answered. "The skeleton found in the garden. It's the Castelbajacs' youngest son, isn't it?"

Veralque nodded. "Yes, it's Grégory. Did you know him well?"

"I baptized him." The priest's eyes watered and Verlaque stayed silent, waiting for him to continue. He went on. "And I saw him through his communion and confirmation. And then Grégory's rebel years hit, and he stopped coming to Mass. It was a sore point between him and his parents, but I didn't take it personally." The priest stopped to blow his nose. "Grégory came to me here, in this office, and apologized. You see, it seems he had been introduced to the atheist texts of Jacques Derrida by his philosophy teacher."

"There is nothing outside the text," Verlaque said, smiling. "That's all I ever got out of Derrida."

"That's more than me, I'm afraid."

"Did you see Grégory the last time he was here, eight years ago?" Verlaque asked.

"Yes, but only briefly. I was much occupied with the funeral of the vicomtesse, Grégory's paternal grandmother. But I saw that he had changed . . ."

Verlaque leaned forward. "How so?"

"Thinner, more wiry. But more than the physical change, I saw that the joy had gone from his face. He had always been a rascal, that's true, but he was a sweet boy and an optimist. I spoke to him after his grandmother's funeral and he seemed depressed and agitated. He said he was going to leave France and go back down south as soon as possible. But he never got there—"

"Did you know any of Grégory's friends?"

"Oh no," the priest answered. "I don't get involved in their private lives. There was a retreat just before the kids' confirmations, but I don't know if Grégory went or not. The younger priests always accompany them. Frère Joël, my current assistant, only arrived three years ago. I'll look up in our records who was here at the time and give him a call. Would that help?"

"Yes, thank you very much," Verlaque said. "I asked the countess, but she had forgotten their names."

"Shock," Père Jean-Luc suggested. "I've heard she isn't doing well since they heard the news."

"I'm sorry about that," Verlaque said. He got up and shook

the priest's hand, said goodbye, and left his office, walking into the waiting room, where Philomène was watering a giant potted palm. The front door opened and an elegantly dressed older man walked in, taking off his hat. "*Chère madame*," he said, exchanging the *bise* with her.

Philomène took Verlaque by the arm. "Judge Verlaque, please meet the Duke of Pradet."

The duke stared at Verlaque, then forced a smile. "I'm sorry, Judge Verlaque. We're all upset over the skeleton. Grégory." He held out his hand. "I'm pleased to meet you."

"I was going to call on you today," Verlaque said, shaking the duke's hand. "Perhaps we can talk here?"

"You can use my office," Père Jean-Luc, who had just walked in, said. "I'm on my way into the church."

"Thank you," Verlaque said.

The duke followed Verlaque down the hall and into the priest's office. "I didn't know the young Castelbajac," the duke began before he closed the door. "Although I knew his parents."

"Not at all?"

"No, I don't think we ever met."

"Did you hear anything unusual in the garden eight years ago, a few days after the vicomtesse's funeral? It was on August eighth."

The duke shook his head. "In August I'm usually in Burgundy; it's too hot for me here. I'll check my diaries. But my house is at the opposite end of what is a very long garden, so it's unlikely that we would have seen or heard anything."

Verlaque said, "I can see your house from my wife's terrace. But if someone is making noise in the garden, we hear it."

"A lovely woman, Marine Bonnet," the duke said, ignoring his comment. "I've met her once or twice at dinner parties. You're going to think that's all I do . . . go to dinner parties."

Verlaque pursed his lips. "And your wife? Did she know Grégory?"

"Highly unlikely," the duke quickly answered. "Anyway, it's impossible to ask her now. She died of cancer six years ago."

"I'm sorry," Verlaque said. "Are you friends with the Castelbajacs?"

"Yes, I guess you could say that," the duke answered. "But we don't see as much of each other now that they've moved permanently to the seaside."

"How was their relationship with Grégory?"

The duke glared at Verlaque. "I don't know what you're insinuating, but they loved that boy unconditionally."

"I'm only trying to work out Grégory's state of mind eight years ago," Verlaque explained. "I'm not blaming anyone."

"They adored the boy. Well, if that's all, I promised Père Jean-Luc I'd help prepare the church for a fund-raising event. We're buying a badly needed new organ."

"Good luck to you, then," Verlaque said, shaking his hand. "I'll leave a donation with Mme Joubert."

"That's very kind."

They left the priest's office together; the duke then passed through a small wooden door that Verlaque assumed led into the church. It was the same one Père Jean-Luc had used. Verlaque got out his checkbook and wrote a check for fifty euros, giving it to Philomène. "For the organ," he said.

She opened a file and slipped the check in, thanking him. "I'll leave with you," she said, looking at her watch.

She locked the red door behind her as they stepped out into the street. A battered three-speed bicycle was locked to a lamppost and Philomène quickly undid the lock, hanging the thick, plastic-covered chain around her neck like a giant oversize necklace. Verlaque found it hard to keep a straight face. "You bicycle here from your apartment around the corner?"

Philomène laughed, walking beside her bike. "I have errands to run," she explained, pointing to her rear pannier in which she had set a basket covered with a tea towel. "I visit elderly and sick parishioners and take them treats."

"How kind," Verlaque said earnestly.

"What else am I going to do all day? Twiddle my thumbs?"

"That I can't imagine," he said. "What did you make?"

Philomène patted the tea towel but didn't lift it. "Little cookies and cakes; whatever strikes me. They like anything."

"I imagine they do."

She pushed her bicycle along, then looked behind her and leaned into Verlaque. "I wanted to talk to you in private."

"Yes?"

"The Duke de Pradet has always been kind enough to me," she said. "But I couldn't stand his stuck-up wife. She always thought she could fart the highest."

Verlaque stopped walking and bent over, laughing.

"I thought maybe you had never heard that expression," Philomène said, glancing over at the judge and allowing a sly smile to form at the corners of her mouth. "Marseille. Menpenti, to be exact. My husband grew up there. Anyway, the duchess was as thick as thieves with the Castelbajacs. They all belonged to this ridiculous group; you may have seen their stickers around on lampposts and signs: *Le Roi Pourquoi Pas?*"

Verlaque laughed again. "They're for real? I thought those slogans were some drunken university students' hoax. But I do know that monarchy groups exist."

"Of course they exist."

"Very interesting . . . ," said Verlaque, trying to amuse her. "So you knew the Castelbajacs?"

Philomène shrugged. "Just to see them. We'd nod in each other's direction. My husband and I ran a print shop. Not exactly the same walk of life."

"And Grégory?"

"Same," she replied. She looked pensive, as if she was about to add something interesting, but instead she said, "Well, I've got to shove off." She stopped walking and straddled the bike, putting on what looked like a pair of WWII aviation goggles. "I need these! Car exhaust!" she called out, waving goodbye.

Verlaque returned her wave, wishing she would have offered him one of her little cakes. He was famished.

Chapter Fourteen

❧

Verlaque Eats a Disappointing Lunch

I'm on the rue Mistral and starving," Verlaque said into his cell phone. "I could have been eating at Bear's."

"I'm at school," Marine replied. "I'd come and meet you, but we have a faculty meeting in a half hour."

"*Merde.* I'll just swing by your place then."

"No!" she quickly said.

Verlaque was about to reply when Mamadou walked by, whistling, pushing a wheelbarrow full of kitchen supplies. He asked, "Why no—"

"Empty fridge," Marine said. "Sorry."

"I ate a sandwich at my desk yesterday," Verlaque said, walking along the narrow street toward the Cours Mirabeau.

"Poor boy," Marine replied, laughing. "Just get the *plat du jour* at the office."

He hesitated before replying. The "office," or their regular meeting place, Le Mazarin Café, was a great place to meet for morning coffee or early-evening drinks, but not to eat. But if the *plat du jour* wasn't to his liking, he could at least get two fried lamb chops—surely the cook couldn't mess that up—and a glass of Hélène Paulik's wine. "Okay, the office it is. See you tonight at my place, I presume."

"Sounds great. I'll pick up stuff for dinner on my way home. I may be a little late—"

"Your civil-servant endless meetings, I know."

Marine bit her lip—her husband was also a civil servant, but he had both the power and the nerve to skip meetings whenever he saw fit. "It's for a good cause," she said.

"What?"

"Gotta run!"

Upstairs from where Verlaque stood, Bear sat on his weathered sofa, smoking a rare cigarette. He kept a pack of Marlboros in a drawer for times like this, smoking one or two a few times a month. Bill time. He had the living room window open and had heard Verlaque's low voice, but not the conversation, and could tell from the judge's tone that it had been a light one. A pile of mail sat in front of him on the coffee table and he flipped through the envelopes: electricity bill, a bill from one of his organic farmers, a wine supplier bill, and, finally, what looked like a personal letter, with his name typed and posted in Avignon. He ripped it open and read. His hand began to shake and he quickly set the single sheet of paper down, getting up to make himself an espresso. He downed the coffee in one go, then walked over and read the letter again. It contained two sentences and was fashioned with letters of various sizes and colors cut from newspapers and magazines, like in a 1940s American movie. It read: *I know who you are and what you did. Leave Aix now.*

An hour and a half later Verlaque was walking back down the rue Mistral. He had eaten the lamb chops—slightly over done—at the Café Mazarin with Jean-Marc Sauvat, a childhood friend of Marine's and now one of his best friends. Jean-Marc was a lawyer, a quiet and reserved man with a dry sense of humor. He was also a member of Verlaque's cigar club, so they passed the time talking of all the other members behind their backs.

Verlaque stopped in front of La Fontaine, whose door had two notices, an official one from the city of Aix's department of police declaring the restaurant a crime scene, and a second one, handwritten: "Closed until further notice. Sorry, Bear." Verlaque cupped his hands at the window and saw the interior of the small restaurant, chairs stacked on tables, and then through to the back garden via a rear window. Two police officers were on their knees, slowly digging with what looked like tiny forks.

To the right of La Fontaine he stopped and rang the bottom of three bells, marked TIVOLLE. The door quickly opened as if the Tivolles had been expecting him, and Bénédicte Tivolle ushered the judge into a spacious hallway. He looked up and saw that the grand stone staircase went up at least three floors, leading the eye to the ceiling with a painted fresco of some flying mythological gods and goddesses. Those kinds of paintings always bored him.

"My husband, Serge, has his interior design office on the second floor, and we have to rent out the third," Bénédicte said, following the judge's eyes up and down the stairs. "A Canadian family is here for two years. He works for Shell."

"It's a grand house," Verlaque said. "And it's beautifully preserved. I've always admired it from the street." He noted that she had said "have to rent out" instead of, simply, "rent out."

"Thank you," Bénédicte replied. "That's Serge's profession, so it had better be well taken care of. For more than a year he labored over these paint colors for the walls of the stairwell. I won't tell you how long he took fussing over the rest of the house." She waved her hand in the air. "The pink going up the stairway walls is actually called Pale Trout. Have you ever heard of such a thing? Serge thinks it's the bee's knees." She rolled her eyes and sighed, and Verlaque felt a twinge of sympathy for poor old Serge. She said, "Follow me into the living room."

They passed through a small music room—a white piano faced one wall and a cello leaned against a bookcase full of books and sheet music—into a larger room that was sparsely furnished. A large black marble fireplace graced the far wall and opposite it two French doors gave onto the back garden. Verlaque walked up to one of them and looked out. A stone wall surrounded the garden, low enough so that it could be easily climbed over, but high enough so that he couldn't see the police officers digging next door. An olive tree sat in the middle of the Tivolles' garden, the trunk surrounded by a circular wooden bench. "I have a terrace," Verlaque offered, "but have always dreamed of a garden." He was lying, of course. He much preferred a terrace, high up, with a view. But he wanted to hear Bénédicte Tivolle speak of the garden.

"I won't beat around the bush," she said. "It is our haven,

despite the fact that nothing except for olive trees survive in it. But if the restaurant next door is permitted to install outdoor seating, we won't be able to use it except in the early morning."

"I'm sorry to hear that. Are you friends with your neighbors?"

"Do you know the Castelbajacs?" she asked. "Is that what you mean? We know them, yes. We were neighbors for decades. And Serge renovated their kitchen before they sold the house. They underpaid him, naturally. And he didn't complain, naturally."

Verlaque asked, "So you've heard about Grégory—"

"Yes. Very sad news."

"Did you know him?"

"Not well," she answered. "I teach at Lycée Vauvenargues, but Grégory went to La Nativité."

"Do you have children?"

She nodded toward the music room. "Two, a boy and a girl. She plays the piano and he the cello. They're twins, and both go to Vauvenargues."

Verlaque looked at Mme Tivolle, trying to guess her age.

"They are fifteen and were born when I was forty-two. A miracle."

He smiled. "Congratulations. So they were too young to be friends with Grégory—"

"Yes, and I didn't trust him to babysit. Besides, my husband has two nieces who live nearby who dote on the twins."

"You didn't trust Grégory?"

She winced. "He was a nice boy—"

"That's what everyone says."

"But he was restless and fidgety. I couldn't trust him with my babies."

Verlaque had the feeling that she was leaving something out. She had just said that she didn't know him well, but she somehow knew him enough not to want him to babysit. Perhaps she thought that boys couldn't babysit as well as girls and didn't want to say it. He asked her if she had heard anything unusual eight years ago, but she answered, logically, that it was too long ago to remember. "And besides," Bénédicte added, "Béatrice was always making noise out there." She realized what she said and quickly added, "But not as much as the restaurant!"

"You teach philosophy," he said, changing the subject.

"Yes. I'll retire soon, thank God. Classroom etiquette has gone way downhill in the past five years. There's no respect for the teacher. And the poor pay is no secret. I make ends meet by tutoring."

Verlaque nodded. "And this house?" he asked, gesturing at the living room that was at least sixty-square-meters big, larger than many Parisian apartments. There was no way a high school teacher and her self-employed husband could afford it.

"*My* family," Bénédicte explained. "*Je suis née Bénédicte de Vitrolles.*"

Verlaque almost let out a whistle, à la Bruno Paulik. Vitrolles was a large town south of Aix, and he had driven around it a number of times, to go to the airport, but had never ventured in. The old town was surrounded by a sea of giant commercial spaces—car dealers, *hyper-marchés*—and an IKEA that he had never set foot in. He imagined that the Vitrolles family must have owned a château there at one time, but it was probably long gone. *What irony,* he thought, *if the bright blue and yellow Swedish megastore now sits on the château's grounds.*

He said, "The Castelbajacs belong to a royalty group. Trying to bring the monarchy back. Do you?"

Bénédicte Tivolle laughed. "Are you crazy? I'm a member of my teachers' union; nothing could be further away from royalists than a bunch of underpaid, striking teachers. No, I do not belong to their group. My husband, on the other hand, would be a member before I ever would be; he's much more impressed with the various counts and dukes who have lived in this house and on our street. But of course he can't . . ." She saw Verlaque's puzzled look and continued. "I've broken the chain by marrying a nontitled man, so my husband and children aren't noble."

Verlaque thought he detected sarcasm. Or was it regret?

She said, "I do belong to a historical society here in Aix. You're welcome to come anytime."

Verlaque quickly pictured a meeting with the historical society: everyone talking at once and arguing for hours over minute details of some building's paint color. "Thank you," he said. "I'll think about it. Has your historical society dug up a lot about this neighborhood?" He immediately regretted his word choice of "dug up," but Mme Tivolle didn't seem to have noticed.

Bénédicte nodded. "Why don't I make us some coffee?" she offered. "I can tell you as much as you have time for." She disappeared behind a swinging door and a few minutes later came into the living room with a tray laden with coffee and LU chocolate cookies—he imagined they were bought for the twins' after-school snack. She told Verlaque of Louis XIV and his entourage arriving in town and the brave peasant who refused to pledge allegiance, then the hanging of that peasant in the garden just behind her house. She included in her narrative, which he found fascinating, Béatrice Germain's stories of the fountain's curse and the murder of Béatrice's brothers.

Verlaque finished his third cookie, got up, and looked out the window. He asked, "Is the fountain still dry?"

"Yes, but hopefully not for long."

"When will it start up again?"

"When you solve Grégory's murder."

Verlaque walked slowly back to the Palais de Justice, smoking a wide Churchill. It had recently been given four stars in *L'Amateur de Cigare*, and he agreed with the magazine's generous grade—it smelled both like warm brioche and black pepper and tasted of dried fruit and caramel and . . . leather, he thought. But he had a problem with paying thirteen euros for a short cigar, even if it was wide. He never used to care about prices, but now, even if Marine made no comment about the amount of money he spent on wine and cigars, he had begun to pay attention.

He wondered if Serge Tivolle had married Bénédicte for her house and title. She didn't seem to care about either. Bénédicte Tivolle was neighbors for decades with the Castelbajacs but hadn't been friends with them. In fact, all the neighbors seemed to know the Castelbajacs, but no one claimed a friendship with the couple. He had found them quite pleasant, despite their mourning, and despite Philomène's scoop about their royalist group affiliation. And Grégory de Castelbajac? Everyone, from the parish priest to the antiques dealer, found Grégory to be a "good boy," but restless. And Bénédicte Tivolle, "*je suis née Bénédicte de Vitrolles,*" admitted that she hadn't trusted him but wouldn't elaborate further.

Bruno Paulik was sitting at his desk when Verlaque walked through the open office, and Verlaque tapped him on the shoulder and whispered, "Espresso." Verlaque went into his office and turned the machine on when Paulik walked in. "Could you please close the door?" Verlaque asked.

Paulik closed the door and saw why the judge had made such a request: It wasn't about privacy but about cigar odor, as he took out his lighter and relit the inch or so that was left of his cigar. The sound his lighter made—the initial click; then the whoosh of the torchlike flame that Verlaque ran back and forth against the tip of the cigar in a circular motion would, for years to come, remind Bruno Paulik of the judge. His friend. He walked over and opened one of the windows, as he always did when Verlaque lit up, and then sat down, putting his notebook on the desk. Paulik had grown to love the smell of Cuban cigars—but Mme Girard had not.

"Is she around?" Verlaque asked, taking a puff while he made Paulik a coffee. He'd had enough espresso at Bénédicte Tivolle's.

"Mme Girard's on a training session," Paulik replied. "But she'll be back any minute. How were your interviews? Mine weren't at all fruitful."

"Ditto. Although I did find out that Grégory de Castelbajac's parents belong to a bring-back-the-monarchy group."

"Don't all nobles belong to those kinds of organizations?"

Verlaque thought of Bénédicte Tivolle, a public-school teacher. "No, they don't."

Paulik shrugged his shoulders and flipped through his notebook. "None of the lawyers or real estate agents whose offices give onto the garden could offer any help, understandably, as they're there only during the day. The hotel manager at La Fleurie vaguely remembered a guest about eight years ago complaining of someone screaming in the garden, but the hotel staff took it for a couple having sex in one of the apartments." He looked at Verlaque and winked as a thank-you when the coffee was handed to him.

"Guests at La Fleurie must complain all the time." He sat down. "The Quartier Mazarin is quietier than this side of Aix, but there's a surprising amount of noise, especially for people used to the country or suburban living."

"That's what I suggested, but the manager said she remembered it so clearly because the guest was so insistent; he was Parisian and insisted he was used to city noises at night, so his comments stayed in her head. The only other interesting bit of info was from the antiques dealer, Mme Dreyfus, who confirmed that Grégory smoked pot and probably experimented with other drugs as well."

Verlaque watched as Paulik got up and paced across the room. "Any other news?"

"Yes—"

"You're hesitating, and pacing."

"Do you remember Kévin Malongo?"

"Yes, of course," Verlaque replied. "I sent him to prison for twenty years."

"He hanged himself last week. In jail. He ripped his pajamas into pieces and tied them together—left a note saying he was innocent."

"He was seen at the scene of the crime, by the sister of one of his fellow thieves."

"Her evidence was shaky, and she hated him," Paulik said.

"Of course she did. Her kid brother died during the robbery, but so did a security guard. Father of three kids."

Paulik finished his coffee and set his cup down. "Her brother was seventeen—"

"I remember, Bruno." Verlaque finished his cigar and got up, setting the stub on the windowsill to let it burn out on its own. They smelled less that way. He turned around and said, "You're telling me I was too hasty in my judgment."

"I just hope we didn't make a mistake."

How like Paulik, thought Verlaque, *to take the blame with me. But I'm the examining magistrate here.* He remembered Marine's story of Rabelais's judge who, unable to decide, threw dice across his desk. *If there was a Judge Bridlegoose who decided the fate of Kévin Malongo, it was me, not you,* cher commissaire.

Chapter Fifteen

❧

Trois Frères et Une Cousine

*T*he Castelbajac brothers are on their way up," Mme Girard told Verlaque twenty minutes after his conversation with Paulik. Her nostrils wriggled and she raised an eyebrow in his direction. He pretended to move papers around on his desk. "I'll leave your office door open," she added, quickly pushing and pulling the door back and forth a dozen times to let in fresh air.

A few minutes later Emile, Philippe, and Ludovic de Castelbajac were sitting across from Verlaque at his glass-topped desk. He offered them coffee but all declined. They were tall men—notably taller than Grégory—but he saw a family resemblance in their fair skin, strong jawlines, and wide mouths. The two younger brothers had the same thick curly hair as Grégory, but Ludovic wore his in a brush cut. They looked tired, and Ludovic and Philippe had dark circles under their eyes. Emile's hair needed washing. "Thank you for coming," Verlaque said. "I could have driven back down to Sanary—"

Philippe waved his hand in the air. "We needed a break from there."

Emile nodded and looked down at his lap.

Philippe went on. "Papa keeps talking of Grégory and Mama hasn't left her room."

"Understandably," Verlaque answered. "When is the memorial service?"

"The day after tomorrow, at Saint-Jean de Malte," Philippe said. He seemed to be the spokesperson of the trio. "At 11:00 a.m."

Verlaque nodded and said, "I'm going to have to ask your help in trying to figure out what happened to your brother. I know it was eight years ago—"

"Exactly," Philippe cut in. "I've lived in Paris for more than twenty years. I had long given up on keeping tabs on Grégory's movements. He was in contact with us only when he needed more of Papa's money. We both went to school" —he looked at Emile— "and we worked hard at our exams, got jobs, and made our own money."

Verlaque looked at Ludovic, the eldest, who had been obviously omitted from his brother's list. "No school for me," Ludovic said.

"But you were employed!" Philippe protested. "I didn't mean to—"

"No offense taken, dear brother," Ludovic said, not hiding his sarcasm.

"Don't fight," Emile pleaded. "Not now."

Ludovic looked at Verlaque and said, "I was at sea . . ."

"Oh?" Verlaque asked, leaning forward.

"I was a captain on a freighter," Ludovic explained. "I just retired. Twenty-five years at sea is a long time. I started when I was just out of high school."

Verlaque looked at Ludovic de Castelbajac, who, as the eldest son, would carry the title. But there he was a retired sea captain and, to Verlaque's knowledge, not married, as there had not been a family photo displayed at his parents' house.

Verlaque also looked at Emile, who was still engrossed with the subtle stripes in his linen pants. He wondered if the sons were any help to their parents during this difficult time. He imagined that Emile was the doctor and Philippe the lawyer. Philippe then surprised him by saying, as if they were still speaking of his education, "Nine years it took me to finally get a medical degree and then become a specialist in cosmetic surgery."

"Grégory wasn't always asking for money," Emile said in almost a whisper. He was apparently the world's most softspoken lawyer.

"*Bof,*" Philippe grunted. "No, when he was selling drugs he didn't need money."

"Did he sell here in Aix?" Verlaque asked.

"Yes, we think he did," Ludovic answered. Emile looked across at his brother, visibly annoyed, but stayed silent. Ludovic went on. "I came across him once, coming out of Saint-Jean de Malte, all happy because he had a pocketful of cash. How else does an unemployed youth get a wad of cash like that?"

"He said he was doing odd jobs," Emile offered.

"Ludovic just said Grégory had come out of the church!" Philippe said. "What kind of odd jobs could he have been doing at Saint-Jean de Malte?"

Verlaque raised an eyebrow and remembered his conversation with Père Jean-Luc, who had said he liked the boy but couldn't remember much about him or his friends' names. He made a mental note to harass the priest for more information.

Emile blew his nose on a linen handkerchief, then carefully folded it and put it back in his front pants pocket. "Who would want to hurt Grégo?" he asked.

"Quite right," Philippe added, for the first time his face revealing some kind of sadness or grieving.

"What can we do?" Emile asked.

"Tell me everything you knew about your brother," Verlaque said. "Who were his friends?"

Ludovic offered, "Our cousin, Juliette—"

"I've left two messages on her answering machine," Verlaque said.

Philippe rolled his eyes. "Typical of Juliette."

"But she's rarely at home," Emile explained. "She works in a school for handicapped children. Keep trying. You'll get her, perhaps on the weekend."

Verlaque tried another avenue. "Did Grégory contact you from South America?"

"Postcards," Philippe said. "Of historical sites. He was big into Indians and their rights. I once got a postcard of Machu Picchu; Grégo had written on the back 'to think, the Indians of Peru made this.' A day later I got a postcard of an aerial view of Lima, in smog, with the *favelas* stretching as far as the eye can see, and he had written 'and the Spaniards killed the Indians, and destroyed their cities, to create this.'"

Verlaque nodded, noting that even Philippe was now referring to Grégory as Grégo. "Where did he stay when he was in South America?"

"With friends, we think," Ludovic said. "Or in youth hostels."

"Sometimes I think he slept on beaches or in parks," Philippe added. "He was like that—he didn't need any refinements. I *can* say that for him: He didn't need luxuries or possessions. But still, it takes money to travel, and not work."

"What kind of drugs was he into?" Verlaque asked.

"We don't know for sure," Emile said.

"He did send me long rambling letters at times, on that thin blue paper meant for cheap air post. I'm sure he was high when he wrote them," Philippe said.

Emile nodded. "I got those, too. I still have them."

Ludovic said, "Me, too."

"Could I see all of Grégory's correspondence?" Verlaque asked.

The brothers exchanged looks. "Mine are all in Paris," Philippe answered.

"Mine, too," added Emile. "I didn't even think to bring them. Stupid of me—"

"How were you to know?" Philippe asked.

"I'll dig around in the attic for mine," Ludovic said.

"You could box them up and mail them to me," Verlaque said. "Mme Girard, my secretary, can give you our details. We'll pay for it."

"I need to get some fresh air," Emile suddenly said, standing up. He had turned pale, and beads of sweat appeared on his face and neck.

"Please," Verlaque said, gesturing toward the door and quickly standing up. "Do you need anything? Are you all right?"

"I feel like I'm suffocating," Emile said. "I just need to walk around a bit."

"I can speak to you another time," Verlaque said.

"I'll come with you," Ludovic said. "Is that all right?"

"Fine," Verlaque said. "I'll visit you on the rue Cardinale if I have any more questions."

"Go along," Philippe said, looking visibly concerned. "I'll finish up here and meet you both at the car."

Emile de Castelbajac opened the door and walked out, his shoulders hunched, followed by his eldest brother.

"Will he be all right?" Verlaque asked, sitting back down.

"Yes, I think so. His wife is leaving him."

"I'm sorry."

"Yes, it's bad timing. But Emile's more shaken up by Grégory's death . . . murder . . . than us. He was closer to Grégo than we were. Grégo frustrated me to no end. I'm sorry if I sounded uncaring."

"What did Grégory do when he was in Aix?" Verlaque asked. "I take it he wasn't a good student."

Philippe laughed. "No, poor guy. Emile and I were the good students, and Ludovic was above average but needed to be outside, on the sea. My father loves the sea, so that was okay. Grégo . . . it was exasperating for our parents, to have what the teachers called 'a slow learner.' Grégory had zero concentration and he couldn't keep still. The Americans called it ADHD, but we're still trying to understand it here. But Grégo was smart and good with his hands. He should have been channeled into a manual discipline, an electrician, for instance. But of course that wasn't good enough for the Castelbajacs."

"Do you belong to that monarchy group that your parents belong to?" Verlaque wasn't sure why, but he couldn't get the needlepoint in the Castelbajacs' front entryway out of his head. Perhaps Philomène was on to something?

"Yes," Philippe answered frankly. "That's one of the many points where Grégory and I disagreed. The Indians would have been better off with some guidance from a strong monarch."

But the conquistadores were sent to the New World by monarchs, thought Verlaque. He wanted Philippe to continue speaking and so merely nodded, as if he was in agreement.

"All those migrants coming in droves across the Mediterranean, for example," Philippe went on. "Fifty years ago they didn't want the colonists leading them anymore—us, the English, the Dutch; we who gave them roads, hospitals, and schools. And so we gave them their independence, and they throw themselves into chaos—civil wars, dictators, genocides—and now they are all coming here. To us, their colonists. What irony. But they'll be in for a surprise, as our politicos are just as crooked and stupid as theirs." He sighed and looked up at the ceiling.

"Do you belong to the same group as your parents?"

"No, I go to meetings in Paris. They go to meetings in Aix."

"Can you—?"

"Give you names?" Philippe asked. "Sure. It's not like it's a secret society or anything. They're the local chapter of the L'ANF."

"Association de la noblesse française?"

"The Association for the Mutual Assistance of the French Nobility, to be exact," Philippe answered. "The Aix president is Casimir de Tressan. My father is vice-president."

"The Duke de Pradet is a member, isn't he?" Verlaque asked, trying to sound casual, like a friendly neighbor chatting between hands at a bridge game. He added, for extra insurance, "My wife owns an apartment on the same garden and quite likes the duke. Fascinating man—"

Philippe de Castelbajac made a snorting sound. "Not nearly as clever as he makes himself out to be. Quit the monarchists in a huff. But Marguerite stayed on, bless her. She was good friends with Maman."

Verlaque was already scheming about who he could send to the association in the guise of a new member when Philippe got up and stretched. "Is that everything?" he asked. "I should be getting back to the car to check on Emile."

"Yes," Verlaque said, shaking the doctor's hand. "Thank you for driving up to Aix. Just one last question. Grégory's friends—"

"He had two best friends," Philippe said. "In junior high, I think."

"The Three Musketeers," Verlaque offered.

"Exactly. One guy had a common name. Jean something or other. Jean-Yves? Jean-Louis?"

"And the other one?"

"Easy name to remember," Philippe said. "Sigisbert. Can't remember his last name, though."

Verlaque tried to hide his surprise at hearing the name. He said, "It's no matter. Thank you." *He isn't a noble*, he thought. *So you had no need to remember his last name.*

Philippe de Castelbajac left, looking much more tired—deflated, even—than when he had first shaken hands with the judge. He looked to Verlaque like he had officially entered the stage of mourning. Verlaque thought about his own brother, Sébastien. They had nothing in common and rarely saw each other; much like Philippe and Grégory de Castelbajac. But the last time they met, in Italy, at his wedding, Verlaque had felt closer to Sébastien than he had in years. Perhaps it was the fact that Sébastien had made the effort to come, or was it because he was so elated that day that he would have welcomed an enemy to his wedding table? Or it may have been Sébastien's funny crack about the age difference between their father and Rebecca Schultz or the smile it brought to his face watching Sébastien and Sylvie laugh together.

He watched Philippe de Castelbajac disappear around a corner, his shoulders getting smaller and smaller. A young policeman walked by, pushing a cart full of documents. The image of Mamadou walking down the street, pushing a wheelbarrow, suddenly came into his head. He moaned out loud. He had been so fixated on finding a decent lunch that he had ignored La Fontaine's dishwasher. He now knew where he'd be able to find Bear that evening. But first he had to drive to Avignon.

There was a long-standing competition between Aix and Avignon. Both were ancient cities, built of the same golden stone. Avignon had water—the Rhône—and Aix didn't, unless you considered its fountains, which Antoine Verlaque didn't think counted as a body of water. Aix had the opera festival and

Cézanne, Avignon the pope's palace and a well-respected summer theater festival. They both had elegant shops, although one dined better in Avignon. *That, along with the river, makes two points for Avignon,* thought Verlaque as he slowed his car down at a toll gate. The toll detected the transponder that his ancient Porsche had permanently displayed in its windshield; the bar lifted and he drove on. He grimaced as he thought of wine: Avignon had Châteauneuf-du-Pape within reach; Aix had the younger Côteaux d'Aix. Hardly the same ballpark. Another point for Avignon.

One hour later Verlaque had exited the highway at Avignon sud and was directed by his phone's GPS through the city's suburbs toward Juliette de Castelbajac's school, the name and address of which Mme Girard had easily located. He looked around at the barren streets and shoddy buildings and gave Aix another point. Aix's outskirts, even the Jas de Bouffan, were not as desolate or poor. As he approached the old town it did not get better. His grandparents' neighborhood in Paris's 17th arrondissement was much like this, with the regular smattering of services that catered to the needs of immigrants: shops that offered phone booths for making long-distance calls, usually back to Africa; ethnic restaurants lit up with neon lights; wig shops; and the usual corner pharmacy and bar. In Paris there was a municipal swimming pool, a theater, and a community arts center where his grandmother Emmeline had volunteered as a drawing instructor. In the 17th the ambience was a happy one and the streets were busy. Not so here.

It was with some relief when, five minutes later, he pulled

up in front of Juliette de Castelbajac's school. It was new, built with much glass and steel, probably by a young architect getting his or her first big commission. The building's tidiness gave Verlaque hope; he saw it as a sign that he would find Mlle Castelbajac and that she would be able to shed some light on her cousin Grégory. Since she had not returned his phone calls, he had decided to come to Avignon without warning. It was a Tuesday, so in all likelihood she would be at work. At least that was what he was betting on.

He could hear laughter and shouting as he walked toward the front door. To the right of the door was a window and he could see the concierge sitting inside, reading a magazine. She looked up and saw him, then pointed to the speaker to the right of the window. "Oh, all right," he said, doing his best to look helpless.

He pressed a white button beside the speaker and she spoke into a microphone on her desk. "Parent? School doesn't get out for another two hours."

"Um, no, I'm not a parent," he replied, smiling. He showed her his badge. "Judge Antoine Verlaque. I'm from the Palais de Justice in Aix and I need to speak to one of your faculty members."

The concierge shot out of her chair and stuck her nose to the glass to read his badge. He imagined that he had made her day. "Whom would you like to speak with?" she asked.

"Juliette de Castelbajac."

Without a word the front door opened with a click, and he walked into the large, bright foyer filled with colorful drawings.

"Follow me," the concierge said, walking out of her office. "Mlle Castelbajac is outside, in the back, with the children."

He followed the short, wide woman through a long hallway lined with backpacks and jackets that hung from pegs about a meter off the floor. It looked like any school except he knew that this one was for children with special needs. They walked out through a set of double doors into the courtyard, where children ran in every direction. A group of three teachers were standing in a huddle, talking. The concierge held up a finger, motioning for Verlaque to stay where he was, and walked over to the group and spoke to them. The tallest—a thin woman with dyed pink hair and harem pants—looked over and then slowly walked toward him.

"Mlle Castelbajac?" he asked as they stood face-to-face.

"Yes, I'm Juliette de Castelbajac." She had big brown eyes in a round, childlike face that was slightly at odds with her tall, angular body. He had to stop himself from staring at the small hoop earring pierced through her left eyebrow.

"You are hard to get a hold of."

"My cell phone is broken," she answered flatly.

Verlaque didn't ask how she knew that he had tried her cell phone. Perhaps he had called the school or her landline? Instead he said, "I need to ask you some questions about Grégory, your cousin."

"Go ahead."

The children's screams were deafening, but it somehow helped the situation, as the noise forced them to move closer together. "Your aunt and uncle tell me that you were very close to Grégory."

"Yes," she said. She swallowed, and Verlaque saw that her nerve was slowly weakening. "We spent holidays together when we were kids, in Sanary."

"And as adults?"

She closed her eyes slightly, then said, "Still close." She tilted her head as she looked at him, then asked, "What do *you* know of Grégory? What kind of a person do you think he was?"

Verlaque didn't mind her cross-examination. He just wanted her to talk. He said, "I know that he loved traveling, South America especially, and that he loved history and the rights of man." A smile formed at the sides of her mouth, and her eyes filled up with tears. Verlaque continued. "And that he was the black sheep of the family."

Juliette held out her harem pants on either side and then gestured to her piercing. "We were two. Two black sheep. I abandoned law to take a degree in education."

"What else did you have in common?" he asked.

"Not drugs, if that's what you mean," she answered. "I'm into clean living. I could never keep up with these kids if I had a drug or alcohol habit." As if on cue, two boys, ages seven or eight, ran around them in circles, laughing. Verlaque saw that they both had Down syndrome. The taller of the two tugged at the back of Verlaque's jacket and then they ran away.

"Did Grégory sell drugs?"

Juliette de Castelbajac flinched but replied in the negative. "He *took* drugs, though. I don't think anything strong. Hell, they will soon be legal here, anyway. Grégory was harmless." She closed her eyes and when she opened them Verlaque saw her anger. "Who would want to hurt him?"

"I don't know," he answered as he watched the children run

and play. He turned to her and asked, "Was he frightened when you last saw him?"

She shook her head. "I saw him at our grandmother's funeral. He seemed angry about something, or agitated. I assumed he had had another argument with his parents or with Philippe. Philippe was hard on him."

"But Grégory didn't tell you what was bothering him? Didn't that strike you as odd, given how close you were?"

"It was a funeral, with all the social muck that goes with our family gatherings. We didn't have time to sit down and talk."

"Your uncle, the count, belongs to a royalist group. So does Philippe. How did Grégory feel about that, given his socialist leanings?"

Juliette shrugged. "I wouldn't know." It was an entirely unsatisfactory answer, but before Verlaque could challenge her on it, the boys came back, running more circles around the pair of them. Juliette called out their names and told them to go back and play with the other children.

"Boyfriend!" the taller child called out, pointing at Verlaque. The boys exploded into laughter.

"Husband!" his comrade cried, jumping up and down. They fell into each other's arms, laughing.

"I'm married to someone else," Verlaque said, smiling. "Marine. Her name's Marine."

"I don't like you anymore," the smaller one said to Verlaque. "And I don't like Marine."

They hugged Juliette's legs, one on either side. "Juliette," the taller one said, staring up at her, "don't be frightened.

We heard you telling Agnès that you were afraid. We'll take care of you."

Emile de Castelbajac sat in the passenger seat, staring straight ahead. Ludovic and Philippe stood beside the car that Philippe had rented, arguing. They had been lucky to have found a spot in the small public parking lot across from the Palais de Justice. A large Range Rover slowed and stopped behind their car, the driver rolling down his window to ask, "Are you about to leave?"

"Get lost," Ludovic called over.

"No, sorry," Philippe said, waving the driver on. He looked at his brother and said, "Still the chip on your shoulder."

Ludovic shrugged.

"You really should be coming with us to Sanary," Philippe went on. "I can drive you back up here when Emile and I catch the TGV back to Paris."

"I was already in Sanary—"

"For a few hours," Philippe protested.

"You've always enjoyed telling me what to do. That's one of the reasons I went to sea. To get away from all of you."

"Forget about our squabbles for a moment and think of Maman and Papa. And Grégory."

"Grégory was a loafer," Ludovic said. "You were the one always saying that."

"Perhaps I was too hard on him."

Ludovic snickered.

"Well, at least now we know what happened to him—"

"He won't be causing any more trouble," Ludovic said, turning to go.

"I can't believe you just—"

Emile opened the car door. "We should be going," he said. "Maman and Papa are all alone."

"Are you just going to walk away?" Philippe asked.

"That's what I'm doing," Ludovic said, walking away through the parking lot toward the Cours Mirabeau.

Philippe got into the driver's seat and started up the car. "Can brothers ever really know one another?" he asked Emile.

Chapter Sixteen

La Fontaine Up and Running

"O kay, we have seating for sixteen and it's a full house to-night," Bear said, looking at each member of his team. His voice was shaky, and he seemed unusually pale. Marine assumed that it was due to the stress of moving locations. He continued. "It doesn't sound like a lot of people, but we have limited resources and equipment here. No offense, madame."

"Please call me Marine," Marine said. "And no offense taken."

"I assume you all have the table numbers memorized," Bear went on. "There are no odd-numbered parties tonight, thank God."

Marine looked surprised, and Florian explained, "Tables of five, for example. The biggest table we have right now fits four comfortably. Five would be tight, although we have an extra chair if need be."

"Florian is my sous chef," Bear said.

"More like your wife," Florian replied, laughing.

"What he means by that," Bear said, "is that he watches my back and knows my every move. If you aren't sure where to find something, ask Florian. I don't know why we're telling you all this; it's not as if you are going to work with us tonight."

"It's fascinating," Marine said. "I'd just like to watch you all in action for a bit, then I'll leave and let you serve your customers."

Bear's cell phone rang and he excused himself, taking the call in Marine's former living and dining room, which was now set up with six tables for two diners and one for a party of four. Marine had left Sylvie's large color photographs of people swimming in the sea but taken down personal or family photos. She and Mamadou had set the tables with small candles and she was impressed by how good her apartment looked in its new guise as a restaurant. The sofa and armchairs were now stacked on top of one another in the guest bedroom.

"Something smells wonderful," Marine said as she lifted the lid off a giant stainless-steel pot.

"Tuscan bread soup," Florian said. "Bear and I made it this morning, along with ravioli, which will be the other starter. The mains are grilled calamari, linguine with roasted vegetables, or osso buco in bianco."

"White osso buco?" Marine asked. "No tomatoes?"

Florian lifted the lid off another pot. "White wine and anchovies instead of tomatoes."

Bear walked back into the kitchen, sliding his cell phone into his back pocket. "Bad news. Jacques is sick. His doctor says it's pneumonia."

Mamadou set down the stack of plates that he was about to

take out into the dining room and Florian set his head in his hands.

"I'm guessing Jacques is your waiter," Marine said.

Bear nodded, looking at the vintage clock that hung on Marine's kitchen wall. "One hour until the first clients arrive."

"This is my apartment, and I know a thing or two about wine and food," Marine said. What she didn't tell them was that her knowledge was newly acquired. She had rarely eaten in restaurants as a child, and as a law student in Paris had been either in the library or meeting friends for drinks in cheap bars. But the more that she ate in restaurants with Verlaque, the more interested she became in how the place was run, who did what, the orchestration of it all. She had a friend in law school who had dropped out in order to study theater, not because she had wanted to be an actress but because she had wanted to work behind the scenes. "Whenever I go to a play I lose track of the text," she had complained to Marine while they drank beer with grenadine (something she never admitted to Verlaque) in one of the many student bars near the rue Moufftard. "I keep looking at the lights and trying to work out where they bought the furniture for the set." Last time Marine had heard, her friend was married with three children and still worked in the theater—La Comédie Française, no less.

"What are you suggesting?" Bear asked.

"I'll stay and serve tables," she said. "Florian told me about tonight's dishes, so I'll just need to look at your wine list. Is it Tuscan or Piedmont based?"

Bear smiled. "Piedmont, of course. And some Friuli."

"Friuli whites, I hope," Marine said. "What's tonight's ravioli?"

"Spring peas from the market," Florian said, "with ricotta and Parmesan and a sage butter sauce."

Marine grinned. "Did you get the sage from my terrace?"

Bear laughed and pointed to Mamadou. "He did."

Two hours later the La Fontaine dinner hour was in full swing. All but two of the tables were occupied, but in another half hour the dining room would be full. Marine's dishwasher had already been run twice, and Mamadou, having done much of the prep work earlier that day, had stepped in to bus tables. A large pot of water was kept on a permanent boil for the ravioli, and the kitchen felt like a steam bath. Marine opened the door to the terrace to cool off the kitchen, and she was happy that they had decided not to set up a few tables outside. She was already concerned about the noise level and what her neighbors must think, although these were noises that she loved and she could tell that Bear and the others loved it, too: the sound of forks hitting plates, wineglasses clinking, and diners laughing and chatting.

"Table one has just finished their first courses," Marine said to Bear as she set a stack of dirty plates in a corner.

"Righto," Bear said without looking up from his frying pan.

"Excuse me," Florian said as he squeezed by with a knife in his hand. Marine had a galley kitchen, and while it was practical for her, with everything within reach, it now seemed minuscule. She remembered that table three had just asked for a

Barbera wine, so she hurried into her bedroom where the wine was being kept. She grabbed the right bottle and on her way back into the dining room table four asked for more water. "Of course," she said, showing the Barbera to their neighbors at the next table and slowly opening it for them, thankful that Bear had brought a proper corkscrew from the restaurant. As the husband? lover? cousin? tasted the wine, Marine studied their faces, trying to remember them, but she was so busy that each diner's face that night was a blur. She had no time for her usual restaurant game of making up stories about the clients.

She walked quickly back into the kitchen and out onto the terrace, where the bottled water was being kept.

"*Merde*," Florian said when she came back into the kitchen. "We're out of chili flakes."

"I have some," Marine said, "bought in Liguria this year. Second drawer on your left."

He nodded and Marine realized that restaurant kitchens were too busy for the niceties of "Thank you" and "Please, Marine." Simple nods sufficed.

Mamadou walked in and set more dirty dishes on top of the pile. "Table seven has finished their aperitif and just told me that a friend would like to join them."

A communal "*Merde*" sounded, including Marine.

"Mamadou, slice me some garlic," Bear said.

"I will in a second, Chef. Table two just finished their soups and told me they are in a hurry. I'll go clear their bowls."

"The dishwasher has just finished its cycle," Florian said to no one in particular as he slid ravioli into the boiling water.

Marine left with the water for table four, grabbing a small

bowl of olives for table three to snack on as they studied the menu. Water and olives delivered, she was walking back toward the kitchen when she saw two new clients standing in the front hall (they had given the clients the door code and left Marine's apartment door slightly ajar). It was Gaëlle Dreyfus with a distinguished-looking elderly man dressed in tweeds. Marine shook their hands, embarrassed that she hadn't immediately recognized the Duke de Pradet, who reminded her about a university dinner party they had both attended years earlier. She showed them to table six, beside the unlit fireplace, and they both ordered champagne.

She hurried back to the kitchen to ask Bear if they had champagne (normally they did, but had they remembered to bring it?) and as she crossed the front hall she ran into her husband. "Table for one, please," Verlaque said.

She quickly kissed him. "Sorry, we are full this evening. You could eat in my office, if we have enough food."

"You were going to tell me about this, weren't you?"

"I did," Marine answered. "I left a message on your phone."

"Ah, I saw that you had called but haven't listened to your message yet. I was in Avignon—" He looked toward the kitchen and saw Bear, who quickly glanced at the judge and then looked away. "I need to speak to Bear—"

"After the dinner rush," she said.

Their laughter was interrupted by Mamadou, who stood beside them, beads of sweat glistening on his forehead. "The next courses are up," he said, looking at Marine. "I need to empty the dishwasher and reload it, and also cut more garlic and parsley—"

Marine looked at Verlaque. "Which job do you prefer?"

"Cutting, definitely," he replied. "Really thin, right?"

Mamadou said, "Paper-thin, the chef always says."

Verlaque hung up his jacket and rolled up his shirtsleeves as they followed Mamadou into the kitchen. "Good thing I bought you those good knives for your birthday," he said to Marine.

"And what a romantic gift it was, darling," she answered as Florian handed her two plates of grilled calamari.

"When you go out there eavesdrop on the duke and the antiques monger," Verlaque whispered.

Marine nodded and smiled as her husband began to peel cloves of garlic at lightning speed.

At twenty minutes after eleven the last clients had gone. Bear, Marine, and Verlaque sat in the dining room, having pushed two tables together. Florian stood outside on the terrace, a cigarette in one hand and a can of beer in the other, and he waved at them through the window. Mamadou was in the kitchen, whistling, doing the dishes.

"That was tremendous fun," Marine said. "But I couldn't do it every night. *Chapeau!*"

"And every day at lunch," Bear said as he stretched his back muscles.

"I always wondered why in Italy the pasta isn't a watery mess when delivered to the table," Verlaque said. "Now I know."

Bear nodded. "You blanch dried pasta in small undercooked batches, then lay it out on an oiled sheet."

"And you finished cooking it in the sauce," Verlaque said. "The pasta stood up on the plate instead of swimming around."

"That last couple who came late," Bear said. "Who were they?"

Verlaque sighed. "A police officer and her husband. I'll have to deal with that tomorrow."

"*Merde,*" Bear said.

Sophie Goulin had heard about the pop-up restaurant through her sister-in-law and made a reservation to celebrate her wedding anniversary. She hadn't realized that it was La Fontaine just changing addresses, as her sister-in-law hadn't mentioned the name, only saying that it was "*hyper branché.*" When Sophie had called to reserve a table, the young man on the other end of the phone had answered with a quick "*Oui?*" and hadn't said the restaurant's name. After the babysitter showed up a half hour late and her younger son threw a temper tantrum, they had arrived at the restaurant almost forty minutes late. When she and her husband had been greeted in the front hall of that large *quartier* Mazarin apartment she wasn't sure who was more surprised—she or Judge Verlaque.

Verlaque thought of Officer Goulin and the possible uproar she could cause at the Palais de Justice. He folded his arms and stared at Bear. "I hate to break this evening's reverie, but we need to talk about—"

"I wanted to talk with you about Grégory," Bear cut in, taking a sip of the Lagavulin that Verlaque had offered to him.

"So why didn't you?" Verlaque asked.

"Shock," Bear replied. "I knew that he had sort of disappeared, but I never imagined him dead." Bear's voice shook again, and Marine now realized why. He had known Grégory.

"Murdered," Verlaque said.

Bear groaned and leaned forward.

Verlaque asked, "When did you meet?"

"Junior high, here in Aix. Collège Mignet, just around the corner. Grégory was rotten at school; his parents were always forking out for tutors. But he was funny and smart in other ways—like in history and politics. We hung around with this other guy, Jean-Baptiste Dellaney, who now lives in Australia and is making a mint in advertising."

"And did you have a falling-out?"

"No, no," Bear quickly answered. "Nothing like that. We just grew apart. Grégory went to La Nativité for high school, and Jean-Baptiste and I went to Zola. Then I moved to the UK for university. When I started working at Cavolo Nero in London, I got really focused on cooking. And I suppose I just ran out of time; you saw how it was tonight, and we only had seventeen diners."

Verlaque leaned back and folded his arms across his chest. "Do you have any idea who would want to hurt Grégory?"

"No, but—" Bear reached into the right-hand pocket of his chef's jacket and pulled out a folded envelope. He slid it across the table. "This is the second one I've received. I got it today, on my way here."

Verlaque picked up the letter and Marine leaned over to look at it. "It was posted in Avignon," he said. "Do you know anyone there?"

"No," Bear said.

"Ever met Juliette de Castelbajac?"

"Oh, yeah," Bear answered. "Once or twice, at Grégory's. She was weird." He drew out the word *weird*.

Verlaque read the letter. "Are they all the same?"

"Yes."

"Do you have any idea what it means?" Verlaque asked.

"No," Bear answered, shifting slightly in his chair.

Marine looked at him and saw that he slowly swallowed before answering and rubbed his sweating palms on his jeans.

Verlaque asked, "Nothing at all? What are they alluding to, do you think?"

Bear shrugged. "I have a lot of enemies since opening up the restaurant. 'What I did' could mean anything. I could have taken someone's preferred parking spot one night."

Marine thought he was lying. But if he was, why show them the letter? Unless he was truly frightened.

Chapter Seventeen

✦

L'ANF

Marine sat across from her student. Emilie Givron was in her third year of law; she'd made it past the grueling first two years, but just. Marine knew from past conversations that Emilie was a tennis player—a very good one—and on this warm spring day Emilie had come to school wearing her tennis clothes. Although her student was thick around the middle—this surprised Marine, as she normally thought of athletes as being quite thin—she could see that Emilie had powerful arms and legs, twice the size of her own, of solid muscle. But it was the girl's wide shoulders that awed her.

The two of them leaned together, looking at Emilie's essay, and Marine could smell the soft sweet smell of baby powder. "Look at this phrase," Marine said. "This is a great example of where you went amiss, trying to sound like an old fart of a lawyer—"

Emilie laughed, and Marine went on. "I'd like you to use your own voice. Please don't try to sound like a lawyer, or an academic, or how you think I want you to sound."

Emilie looked confused. Marine guessed that the girl had never heard anyone say that to her. She imagined that Emilie had studied hard for her French Bac but had simply memorized and regurgitated her lessons. Marine believed that any good writing began with clarity and a natural voice, but there was no time for that in law school. It was a constant battle that Marine had with her fellow faculty members. They accused her of not teaching law but creative writing. She also took the time to sit down with students, off hours, which had released a series of insults from her colleagues, ranging from her teaching "*à l'américaine*" to obliterating the good work the teachers' union had done by giving office hours on her own time. Part of the problem, she knew, came with her recent marriage to Antoine Verlaque, who hardly hid his family wealth. Marine looked at the text, pointed at it with her pencil, and then at Emilie. "Tell me, in your own words, exactly what you wanted to say here."

Emilie sucked on the end of her pen and then gave Marine a sentence that, while a little dull, made absolute sense and was nothing like the jargon she had written in her essay.

"That's it," Marine said. "Just get rid of all the 'so it would seem' and 'however' expressions and write in simple clear prose. If you confuse your reader, especially the person grading your paper, what will he or she do?"

"Give me a poor grade?"

"Yes," Marine said, smiling, "after I get up and change the

radio station, and make myself another tea, and check my phone messages. Do you see what I am saying?"

"Yes, don't confuse the reader or he or she will be bored."

"Exactly. Have you heard of Luc de Clapiers?"

Emilie shrugged her shoulders.

"The Hameau de Claps? On the north side of Saint-Victoire, just after Vauvenargues?"

"Oh yes! I've hiked up there, with my family."

Marine went on. "Luc de Clapiers was the Marquis of Vauvenargues. He was sickly and died when he was only thirty-one in 1747, but he was helped financially and morally by Voltaire, which enabled him to write. His strength was in aphorisms. Do you know what that means?"

"Sayings?" Emilie asked.

"Yes, sort of miniphilosophies. One of my favorites is: 'When a thought is too weak to be expressed simply, it should be rejected.' So, before you write, say it out loud and try to express your idea in the simplest way possible. If you can't, it means you are too muddled—"

"Like I'm not sure of my idea."

"Exactly."

Emilie gathered up her papers, stuffing them into her backpack. "Thank you so much, madame."

"You're welcome." Once Emilie left the room, Marine sat back and thought of Luc de Clapiers, whose own father, Joseph, had stayed behind in plague-stricken Aix in the early eighteenth century, risking his life to tackle the crisis. There were certainly good people in the world: nobles and nonnobles, chefs and dishwashers, teachers and police officers. She thought of another of Luc de Clapier's aphorisms: "Everyone is born sincere and dies a liar."

Marine drove her bright green subcompact Renault through the château's gates and pulled up beside the other dozen or so cars that were parked beside an outbuilding. She smiled at the collection of nondescript, older model cars, most of them made in France. No Mercedes or BMW, and certainly nothing as bling as Antoine's 1963 Porsche. The French nobility may still live in châteaux—although some were crumbling—but outward displays of wealth, especially fancy cars, were frowned upon. That much Marine knew. The rest of this evening's meeting was an unknown, and she was prepared for it to be dull. But Antoine was convinced that the ANF had something to do with Grégory de Castelbajac's death—perhaps directly, perhaps indirectly—and Marine was being sent to infiltrate the nobles.

It was not quite 7:00 p.m. and the sky was still light. The château was big and blocky, built in a U-shape, and she could see a man standing in the imposing front door, waiting for her, or the other ANF members, to arrive. She smiled as she approached and extended her hand. *"Bonsoir,"* she said,

"Dr. Bonnet," the man said, shaking her hand. "Welcome. Please come in. I am Casimir de Tressan."

"Thank you," Marine said. So the count had been waiting for her, and he had assumed that the woman who had parked her beat-up Renault was the law professor, their special guest. "Lovely château," Marine said, smiling at the count.

"Please, Dr. Bonnet," the count said, "you must admit

that it looks like a big boxy train station. But my great-great-grandfather built it." He threw his hands up in the air. "And I inherited it, including its taxes and upkeep. Please—" He ushered her through a set of double doors, where twenty-odd people, not all of them with white hair, were mingling around an unlit, oversize fireplace, two sagging nineteenth-century sofas, and a collection of caned armchairs mixed with folding chairs with cracked leather seats. He led her to a small cocktail table. "I'll introduce you in a bit," he said. "But first, would you like something to drink? Juice? Wine?"

Marine looked at the wine, a supermarket brand, and replied, "Juice, please."

The count poured her some juice with a shaky hand and passed it to her. He smiled a genuine, warm smile and she felt guilty that her husband had sent her to this meeting, to eavesdrop, or whatever it was she was supposed to be doing. She felt like a fraud, which made her uncomfortable.

"Let's begin the meeting, if everyone would take a seat," the count said. "We should have enough chairs." He smiled as his fellow nobles sat down in a semicircle, and Marine thought that he looked like a grandparent or a preacher, proud of his flock. "Welcome, everyone, to the April meeting of the ANF, Aix-en-Provence chapter. We have a few things on this evening's agenda and then we'll adjourn for some light snacks, but first I'd like to introduce our guest, Dr. Marine Bonnet, from the law faculty of our university here in Aix."

Marine stood up and did a small wave, then sat down. The count once again smiled and said, "Dr. Bonnet is researching European nobility and how current European laws can help—

or hinder—us. She has proposed to deliver one of the lectures at our annual meeting in Paris this September—"

"Provided I finish it in time," Marine cut in, smiling. The crowd laughed; Marine knew how to charm a room. She had, in fact, quickly looked at the lectures offered at the previous year's Paris meeting and threw together a synopsis, which she had emailed to the count the previous afternoon. There had been four lectures offered, all with almost exactly the same titles and themes: "The Role of the Nobility in the Evolution of Europe," "Nobility in a Europe on the Move," "The Role of the Nobility in European Civilization," and "The Place of Europe in the World and the Nobility in Europe." The count had replied to her email almost immediately, obviously thrilled to receive an offer of a lecture given by a professor who had been widely published. Marine had been confident that she could bluff her way through the meeting and that her lecture topic, "New European Laws and the French Nobility," would be greeted with enthusiasm.

As the count began—citing two new families to have joined the association and questions regarding an upcoming rummage sale—Marine looked around the room. Judging from Antoine's description, the Castelbajacs were not present. But that did not surprise her. She had been wrong; not all those present were over seventy. There were three couples in their forties, perhaps fifties. Their clothes—at least the women's—were the same as their cars. Practical, inexpensive, and in dull colors. When one of the husbands smiled at her, raising his eyebrow then winking, she looked down, pretending to read an ANF pamphlet. She recognized him as a lawyer whose firm shared the same building at the top of the Cours Mirabeau as the firm of her friend Jean-Marc's.

The tone of Count de Tressan's voice then lowered, becoming somber. "Of course, the Count and Countess de Castelbajac couldn't be with us this evening," he began. "I would encourage you all to attend their son Grégory's funeral tomorrow morning at eleven at Saint-Jean de Malte. They will need their noble friends now more than ever. Let us recite our Lady's prayer." Marine had spent enough time at Saint-Jean de Malte to know how important the Catholic Church was to France's nobility, and when the group lowered their heads and began the Hail Mary, not mumbling but in loud, clear voices, she was moved.

The meeting ended fifteen minutes later, after a member—the man who had winked at her—recited a surprisingly long list of families who had recently been stripped of their falsely claimed nobility. Count de Tressan leaned over to her and whispered, "It can be quite traumatic, to find that your ancestors gave themselves noble-sounding names in the nineteenth century and then have the title taken away."

Marine nodded, and as they got up and headed toward the food table, he continued. "Of course, to join us, one needs to offer historical proof that a French king or emperor bestowed a noble title on their family and that they are directly linked to that noble via male heirs."

Marine was surprised that the ANF accepted nobles titled by Napoleon as nobility. In some circles, only those titled before the revolution were considered "true" nobles. "So a letter from the king would suffice as proof?" she asked, smiling.

The count laughed. "Absolutely," he answered, leading her to a table laid out with sandwiches.

"When did the ANF begin?" she asked, taking a small ham-and-butter sandwich.

"In 1932," he answered, pausing to swallow. "A group of nobles waiting for a train in Paris noticed that the porter carrying their baggage was a fellow aristocrat. They were shocked. That's why it's so important that we help families in need—"

Marine nodded, realizing that these "families" were nobles, not single-parent families who lived on the edge of Aix. "Hence the rummage sale you're planning," she said.

"Yes, that, with donations from members who are more financially comfortable. We also help low-income families with the school fees for promising children." He paused and looked across the room, and Marine pretended not to notice. Two men had started to argue, their voices raised. The count coughed and wiped the corners of his mouth with a paper napkin. He continued. "Every year we offer around two hundred thousand euros to help those feeling the pinch."

Marine wondered which branch he fit into—the helper or the helped—or the Castelbajacs, for that matter. "So sad about Grégory de Castelbajac," she said, lowering her voice. "I live across the garden from their old house on the rue Cardinale. Did you know him?"

The count shook his head. "No, I never did meet him. His older brother Philippe is quite active in the ANF, Paris branch."

Marine took another tiny piece of sandwich; this one was filled with a bland pâté. "The Duke de Pradet is also my neighbor," she said. "Is he a member?"

"Um, unfortunately, no," the count answered. "But his late wife, Marguerite, was." He gave a nervous laugh. "You might say she was a staunch royalist."

Marine was about to question his comment when the men who were arguing—one of them was her winker—left the salon, still bickering. She excused herself to use the ladies' room.

"Third door on the right," the count instructed. He gave another nervous laugh and said, "You have to pull the chain twice to flush!"

Marine walked down a long, wide corridor that was lined with old coats and rain boots, following the sound of their voices. A musty odor filled the hallway; she wasn't sure if it was the coats or the ancient wainscoting, but it was a smell that always reminded her of her maternal grandparents' vacation home in the Dordogne. She stopped when she saw light coming from under a door that was slightly ajar, and leaning against a black wool coat, she listened.

"You've gone too far this time," said one of the men. "I told you and Marguerite the same thing eight years ago."

The other, in an excited, rushed voice, replied, "If it were up to you, Louis, we nobles would just slowly erode, along with our properties and traditions. I'm not going to fade away. Nor will I let my family."

Chapter Eighteen

❧

The Story of Judge Joisson

Antoine Verlaque was usually one of the last members to arrive at the cigar club, but this evening he got to the rue Papassaudi thirty minutes early. The meetings were usually held at Jean-Marc's apartment at number 6; he lived alone and didn't mind a dozen cigar smokers in his home. But a plan was under way to find a clubhouse, where the members could meet once a month and use it as a place to relax and smoke when they were in downtown Aix. Both Jean-Marc and Antoine lived in the *vieille ville,* but most of the other members lived in the countryside around Aix or in villages close by. José and Georges drove up from Marseille for the monthly meetings. The potential clubhouse was to be one of the topics on tonight's agenda, along with a proposed trip to Cuba.

Verlaque rang the buzzer on the street and Jean-Marc buzzed him up. He walked up one flight of stairs then stopped on the landing before going up to the next floor, pulling out his cell phone and dialing Bruno Paulik's number. "Bruno, it's Antoine. I hope I'm not disturbing you."

"No, we haven't sat down to eat yet. But shouldn't you be getting ready for your first clients? What's today's special?"

Verlaque groaned. "So you've heard about Marine's pop-up restaurant. That's all I need, with the local press all over Kévin Malongo's prison suicide."

Paulik said, "The restaurant news has made its way around Aix fairly quickly. But I shouldn't have teased you about it . . . Roussel told me that people in Marseille and Paris weren't very happy about your wife offering her apartment to a chef whose restaurant has been closed by us. That, added to the suicide, has him beaming."

Verlaque closed his eyes and nodded. Yves Roussel was Aix's chief prosecutor and a thorn in his side. Ever since Verlaque had arrived in Aix, Roussel had made it clear that he regarded the judge as too cultured, too educated, and too rich for their little lot at the Palais de Justice. Verlaque brought with him rules, Parisian rules according to Roussel, whereas they had always gotten by in Aix by bending the rules. And now the examining magistrate was doing just that, by letting Bear run his business in an apartment owned by his wife. "I'll deal with Roussel," he said. "But right now I need you to arrange a visit to Juliette de Castelbajac's home in Avignon, tonight if possible. Sigisbert Valets has been receiving anonymous letters telling him to leave town. They may be harmless, but—"

"They were mailed from Avignon?" Paulik asked.

"Exactly. And I'm worried. Something's frightening her. Even her students noticed it."

"I'll call the Avignon precinct right away," Paulik said. "Have a good evening."

"You, too, and thank you." Verlaque put his cell phone back in his pocket and walked up the next flight of wide stone steps to Jean-Marc's apartment. The door was open, as Jean-Marc had heard Verlaque on the phone and gone back into the kitchen to check on his coq au vin.

"Smells good!" Verlaque called as he stepped into Jean-Marc's apartment.

"You're early," Jean-Marc replied, coming out of the kitchen and wiping his hands on a tea towel that was tucked into the waist of his pants. "What's up? You're usually the last to arrive."

Marine had texted Verlaque about the argument she overheard at the ANF meeting, and Verlaque had arrived early in the hopes of asking Jean-Marc a few innocent questions. He wished he could talk to Jean-Marc about the Castelbajac case, but he knew that he couldn't because of confidentiality laws. His friend was even more of a stickler for the rules of the court than he was. "Sorry, I lost track of the time," Verlaque said. "I hope that's okay."

"Of course it is," Jean-Marc said. "You can help me set up a bit, if you don't mind." Verlaque took off his jacket and helped Jean-Marc set out ashtrays and wineglasses. "Here," Jean-Marc said, handing Verlaque three slim objects. "I'm putting out three cigar cutters. Put these on the coffee table. And they'd better be there by the end of the evening."

"I think you can count on losing one," Verlaque said. He set them down on the table and then thought of a way to ask Jean-Marc a few questions. "Marine called me earlier, in a rage over some guy who snagged her table at the Mazarin this morning, even though she had left her coat there while she went to use the toilettes. He was really rude about it. She thinks he works in your building, in the law firm downstairs. He's in his forties, blond."

"Charles de Saint-Félix."

Verlaque said, "That was fast."

"He makes it clear that he's better than everyone else, which irks everyone else."

"I can imagine."

"He gives nobles a bad name. My mother was a noble, from Perpignan, and her family was very sweet. The opposite of him. They were very old-fashioned, and always doing good work in the community. Poor as church mice, but rich in real estate."

"A castle and land doesn't necessarily feed you," Verlaque said. "I knew you were well bred, but I had no idea you had such a posh background. No offense."

Jean-Marc smiled. "I'm very posh. My mother's name was Anne d'Estève de Bosch. Of course she lost the title when she married my father, a dentist from Aix."

"How are your parents these days?"

"Very well, thanks," Jean-Marc said. "They fill their time gardening, in the house I grew up in, on a little dead-end street off the avenue Philippe Solari."

"So your mother has no contact with the local ANF—"

"No, not really," Jean-Marc answered. "But although my

mother may have left the nobility, she's still an incorrigible gossip when it comes to that set."

"Do you know Charles de Saint-Félix well?" Marine's text messages had been short: the men were arguing about something that happened eight years ago. In the next text she typed, in caps, WITH MARGUERITE.

"Hardly," Jean-Marc said. "He has nothing in common with a gay, cigar-smoking lawyer."

"Except you're both lawyers," Verlaque replied, laughing.

"You know, one of my colleagues is quite impressed with all the noble trappings, and he's been over to the Saint-Félix château a few times."

"Where is it?"

"On the way to Jouques, just past Vauvenargues."

"I know exactly the one," Verlaque said. "I've driven past it a couple of times. It's marvelous . . . that round medieval tower—"

The buzzer rang for the front door, and Jean-Marc walked into the front hall and lifted up the receiver. "*Oui*," he said. There was silence at the other end. He repeated, "*Oui, allo?*"

Ten seconds later came the reply, three deep voices growling, in English, from down in the street, "*Wassup?*"

"Come on up," Jean-Marc replied, rolling his eyes and buzzing them in. "Fabrice, Julien, and José. So immature." He saw that Verlaque was laughing and he said, "I can't believe you think they are funny. Fabrice is almost sixty!"

Verlaque rubbed his eyes, still laughing. "It's good to be silly sometimes."

"Well, I never . . . ," Jean-Marc mumbled as he went back into the kitchen to start water boiling for the potatoes.

Just around the corner, on the terrace of Les Deux Garçons, the duke and Gaëlle Dreyfus sat, sipping champagne. "I could get used to this," she said.

"Don't you come here very often?" the duke asked as his eyes followed two female twenty-somethings who were walking up the Cours, wearing short skirts and high heels, their arms linked and their heads thrown back in laughter. The taller one looked vaguely like Marguerite had at that age. Marguerite had also been carefree; in fact, she had been happy well into her fifties. But at some point she had become cynical, obsessed with how people should and shouldn't behave.

"No, I mean the champagne," Gaëlle replied, lifting her glass.

The duke raised his glass and touched hers. "We should make a habit of this," he said. "It's a cliché, but—"

"Life's too short?"

"Voilà." He looked at Gaëlle, admiring her dark blue—almost violet—eyes and her perfectly coiffed thick white hair. Marguerite had dyed her hair up until the week before her death. Why was it that men his age didn't bother to dye their hair but the majority of his female acquaintances did? Well, he supposed it didn't matter, as long as their hair was clean. Why in this day and age did some people still walk around with greasy hair?

He realized that he must have been frowning, because Gaëlle was looking at him, her head tilted. "Is everything all right?" she asked. "You sometimes look worried."

"It seems that the older I get, the more questions I ask. From the profound to the silly. My head is swimming with questions."

"Oh, so it's nothing serious," she said, taking a sip of her champagne. "I'm glad."

There were some serious questions that he had, but he didn't want to bother her with those. Besides, they were, for the moment, just questions. His doctor promised that he would have some answers at the end of the week. But since the discovery of Grégory de Castelbajac's skeleton, more questions had come into the duke's head. "Did you receive a visit from the police?" he asked.

Gaëlle nodded. "I think the whole neighborhood did. I was quite hoping to get the handsome judge—"

"You think he's handsome?"

"Oh yes, in a rough kind of way. Or maybe it's just his charisma. But my interview was carried out by a very serious young female officer and the commissioner. She was in the restaurant last night, at the table next to us."

"They came in late," the duke offered. "Trouble with the babysitter."

"Eavesdropper."

The duke laughed, grateful for her company.

She asked, "Did you happen to read *La Provence* this morning?"

"Yes, I did. That crook who hanged himself in jail didn't sound like the holiest of men, but I somehow believed his story. The family and their lawyer sound quite determined to have a retrial and clear his name. Your handsome judge sounds like he's in a bit of trouble. And did that article remind you of a similar incident that happened here in the sixteenth century?"

She shook her head. "Sorry, no."

"It did me, straightaway, especially given that they share the same name, Antoine," the duke explained. "The fountain stopped then, too. The judge in this case was Antoine Joisson. The condemned farmer's family insisted he was innocent, as did all his acquaintances. Joisson had rushed it through the courts. Judges have always had to be careful who they condemned to prison, even in the sixteenth century. He was hacked to death by an angry grieving brother on a quiet street in Aix, in the middle of the night—"

Gaëlle shuddered.

"I'd like to think we've progressed since then," he said, finishing his champagne. "But sadly not much has changed in five hundred years."

"It has; we have. I just read a review of an American book whose author states just that," Gaëlle said. "He claims, backed by statistics, that compared to past eras the twentieth and twenty-first centuries have been relatively nonviolent."

"Well, that's something to celebrate," the duke said. He turned around until he caught the attention of Les Deux G's black-uniformed waiters and, pointing to their empty *coupes*, ordered more champagne.

Verlaque was the first to arrive and the last to leave. He enjoyed helping Jean-Marc clean up. They washed the wineglasses by hand, as they were too big to put in the dishwasher. After smoking two large cigars in the same evening he was rarely tired, even if it was after midnight. Marine called it his "cigar buzz."

Jean-Marc poured his friend a small whiskey, setting it on

the kitchen counter. "That apartment on rue Célony sounds promising," he said, pouring himself a whiskey as well.

"I agree," Verlaque answered as he dried a wineglass. "I've always liked that side of town."

"The wrong side of the tracks," Jean-Marc said, smiling. "The fact that it has a terrace sells it for me, even if I haven't seen it yet."

"But," Verlaque said, pausing as he dried, "financially the rent for a clubhouse will be a stretch for some of our members. That bothers me. We can't let this move be the reason that some members feel they have to quit."

"We could help fund them, as the nobles do with one another."

Verlaque laughed. "Yeah, I can really see Fabrice agreeing to that." Fabrice Gaussen was the club's president and a self-made millionaire who hadn't passed his Bac. At sixteen he had apprenticed with an uncle who was a plumber, and now Fabrice owned a chain of plumbing stores that spanned the entire South of France. He was even considering opening a shop in Paris. "I'll have to speak to my people up there first," Fabrice had said that evening, sitting back and resting his arms on his ample stomach. Verlaque and Jean-Marc had burst out laughing. "Hey, you two, you're not the only ones with connections in the capital!"

"One thing you can say about Fabrice is that he earned his money," Jean-Marc said. "My mother, although she loved her family, always complained that some nobles took their wealth for granted and hadn't done enough hard work to earn it." He finished his whiskey and set his glass in the dishwasher, and Verlaque did the same.

"Thank you for hosting another great evening," Verlaque said, giving Jean-Marc the *bise*. "I'll see myself out."

Once out on the street, lit by golden lights, Verlaque wished that he had saved part of a cigar. There was something about smoking as he walked along Aix's narrow medieval streets at night that he loved. As he walked he looked in shop windows, wondering who exactly bought all those purses, and expensive sunglasses, and shoes. He remembered a section of Hemingway's *A Moveable Feast* when Gertrude Stein instructed the young writer to buy art, not clothes. Hemingway had argued that he indeed did not buy clothes, and the formidable Stein had answered, "But your wife does." Marine thought the line sexist when he read it aloud to her, and she cited a few friends whose husbands spent more on clothes than they did, but he thought she was exaggerating in order to prove a point. At any rate, Marine didn't overspend, although lately she had been coming up with some kooky ideas, the pop-up restaurant being the winner. It was the thorn in his side that he had imagined it would be.

Despite himself, he slowed down in front of a men's shop and looked at the linen jackets in the window. He needed a new one—they were perfect to wear on summer evenings and always reminded him of Italy, with Marine. A man had stopped behind him, looking at the window display next door. Verlaque noted the price of a pale blue jacket and, for the first time in his life, decided he would wait for the summer sales to buy it. He walked on, as did the man behind him.

As he turned left on the rue Esquicho-Coude he received a text from Marine saying that she was at his place and hoped he would be home soon. He replied that he was about thirty seconds away and put his phone back in his pocket. Before walking on he turned around to look at the man behind him, who had also stopped. It was unusual that people walked up the tiny street, especially at night, and Verlaque was now sure that he was being followed. "Do I know you?" he asked as the man walked quickly toward him.

The man was about two feet away and Verlaque braced himself, his fists clenched at his sides. His follower slowly reached into his pocket, and Verlaque thought he recognized his face. But a sudden noise behind the man caused him to turn around. A group of three university students, laughing and singing a Daft Punk song, had pushed one another into the narrow alleyway. The man turned back around and pulled a pack of cigarettes out of his pocket. Turning his body sideways so that he could walk around Verlaque, he said, "*Pardon, monsieur.*"

Jean-Marc opened the living room windows to air out the room. All three of the cigar cutters remained on the coffee table, probably due to the fact that Verlaque had grabbed a white Magic Marker from Jean-Marc's desk and put the initials JMS on each one. Jean-Marc laughed, turned off the lights, walked down the hall, glad he had remembered to keep his bedroom door closed, and was relieved when the room didn't smell of cigars. He saw Marine's padded envelope on his dresser and picked it up, then sat on the edge of his bed, pulling out the photographs. It had been a wonderful weekend in Paradiso, and he fluffed up the pillows and leaned back, carefully looking at each photograph, enjoying reliving the moment. He looked closely at one of them and then began to laugh. Much to his surprise, there was Salvatore, leaning against a stone wall, smoking, watching the wedding group congregate on the square in front of the church. Jean-Marc hadn't noticed Salvatore when these pictures were being taken; it had only been at the lunch, in an elegant restaurant on the edge of the old town, that Jean-Marc first set eyes on the handsome young waiter. The lunch had lasted all afternoon, finally breaking up just before 6:00 p.m. The guests slowly ambled back to their hotel, laughing and chatting, and in the lobby wished one another a good evening, even though it was early. The Pauliks and Sylvie and Sébastien were taking the girls down to the sea for a walk, and Marine's parents were going to read in their room. Gabriel Verlaque and Rebecca were going to walk behind the village, through the olive groves. Verlaque invited Jean-Marc back to their suite for a pot of tea, but Jean-Marc could see the fatigue in his friend's eyes. "That's very kind," he said, playing with the folded piece of paper in his pocket, "but I think I'll read a bit and turn in early." They gave each other the *bise*, and Jean-Marc wished the couple a long and happy marriage. He turned around and walked out of the hotel, back to the church square. And there was Salvatore, his young De Niro, leaning against the same wall, with the same grin plastered on his face. Jean-Marc was relieved he hadn't needed to call the phone number written down on the piece of paper in his pocket, as his Italian was rough. But he somehow thought that that evening they wouldn't be exchanging many words.

Chapter Nineteen

ꝶ

Paulik Thinks,
"Welcome to the Real World"

I know it's difficult to solve a crime that happened eight years ago, but this case feels like it has stalled," Verlaque said.

"I agree," Paulik said, taking a seat at Verlaque's desk. "Not only has it stalled, it's never even taken off."

"No need to rub it in," Verlaque said. He got up and opened the window, looking out. "And it's a beautiful morning. Soon we'll be swimming in our pools."

Paulik laughed; neither of them had a swimming pool. He opened his notebook and took a pencil from his shirt pocket.

"I do have one new piece of info," Verlaque said, sitting back down. "Marine went to an ANF meeting last night, just outside of Aix. It was at that crumbling old excuse of a château owned by Casimir de Tressan. About twenty of the members showed up, and toward the end of the evening she overheard an argument between two of the men. One of them, someone named Louis, warned the other, a lawyer here in Aix, Charles de Saint-Félix, not to repeat his mistakes of eight years ago, something he had done with Marguerite."

"Marguerite de Pradet?"

"Yes, I'd assume so."

"Do we question Saint-Félix?" Paulik asked. "It's tempting, but that's not quite enough information."

"I agree. I'd rather bug the duke about it. But for now let's go over what we know. Or at least what we can deduce. Grégory was killed just after Grandma Castelbajac's funeral—"

"Grandma?"

"Can't be bothered to look up her name. Her funeral was eight years ago, on a Tuesday, the eighth of August. The count and his wife told me that they stayed in Aix for a few days afterward, then left for the weekend to their house in Sanary. I'm betting the murder took place that weekend. They told me that Grégory was alone in Aix. They had expected him in Sanary."

"No drug leads panned out," Paulik said, flipping through his notebook. "None of the regular small-time dealers say they knew him. He could have been bringing drugs in from South America and selling them here, but to whom?"

"Did you speak to his jet-set friends?"

"Yes; they all spoke excellent French, thank God. They were saddened by the news of his death, but none of them sounded surprised, except for the last friend to have seen Grégory before he came back to Aix, a photographer named Federico Renzi. He's from Milan. He and Grégory had spent a few days together in Rio before Grégory came back to Aix. Renzi told me that he thought that Grégory had 'calmed down' and was on better terms with his parents. That's at odds with what the antiques dealer, Mme Dreyfus, said about Grégory that week in Aix. She said that he was unhappy and restless. I had assumed he was fighting with his parents, as did she, until I got ahold of the photographer yesterday. It's possible that he was arguing with someone else, not his parents."

"With his murderer," Verlaque said. "And the chef—Sigisbert Valets?"

"One of our English-speaking officers phoned that restaurant in London and Sigisbert was working during the entire week of August eighth, and the weekend. They have kept all of their journals since they opened."

"Impressive. But I still think Bear is holding back information. He seemed frightened by the letters he was receiving, even if he wanted to appear casual about it."

"And you say Grégory's cousin Juliette is frightened, too?" Paulik asked. "So maybe she didn't send them."

"What happened last night in Avignon?" Verlaque asked.

"I was just thinking the same thing," Paulik said. "I haven't heard anything. I'll call them when we're through here."

"And Gaëlle Dreyfus? The antiques dealer?"

"She can't remember what she was doing that week. Says she's never kept a diary."

"The Duke de Pradet told me the same thing," Verlaque said. "He said that in the summer he's in Burgundy; he was going to check his journals for that year and get back to me. I had the funny feeling that he didn't want to talk about his late wife. She was still alive when Grégory was killed." He paused, looking at Paulik. "When I asked him if Marguerite knew Grégory, he answered very quickly and emphatically 'no.'"

"Like he's protecting her—"

Verlaque said, "Marguerite de Pradet was in that royalist group. I'm going to go call on the duke. Come to think of it, he was nervous when he met me. Men of his social standing are rarely nervous when introduced to someone new, even people like us who work in the law."

Paulik nodded and looked at his notes. "What about the Jouberts at number 10? You know Mme Joubert, right?"

Verlaque laughed. "Sort of. Philomène Joubert is a friend of Marine's mother. They sing in the choir together, and Philomène is one of those busy church ladies, always trying to help the priests. She knows of the family, but not Grégory. Very different social circles."

"And the Tivolle family?" Paulik asked. "They live next to the restaurant."

"Bénédicte Tivolle is a high school teacher," Verlaque said. "She was nobility until she married a commoner." Verlaque thought of Jean-Marc's mother, marrying a dentist.

"Sounds like a costume drama."

"I agree. She did offer that her henpecked husband, an interior designer, is quite taken with the noble set."

"Did it seem odd to you that she would offer that information?" Paulik asked.

"No, not really. It was in context with a conversation we were having about their house. Correction. Mansion. She knew the Castelbajacs, but not Grégory. And the other neighbors?"

Paulik flipped through his notebook. "We interviewed what seemed like dozens of lawyers and real estate agents—"

"Welcome to Aix."

"But none of them could shed any light on that week or on Grégory. We spoke with a family called Roche, too. They stick out in my mind. Neither Officer Goulin nor I liked them."

Verlaque pretended he had never met *la famille Roche*. He wanted to hear what Paulik had to say. "Go on."

"They complained more about the restaurant than the discovery of a skeleton in their backyard," Paulik said, speaking slowly as if trying to explain clearly what it was that had bothered him about Thomas and Stéphanie Roche. "They kept saying how France is going down the tubes and that Aix is changing . . . that too many people are moving in." He mimicked quotation marks when he said "people."

"Do you think they're racist?"

"Yes, that was what bothered us, although at first we couldn't pinpoint it. Of course that doesn't make them murderers, and Grégory de Castelbajac would certainly be their right kind of person."

"They make me think of the National Front . . . and people who do things like defacing that black Madonna. I've met the Roches, you see."

Paulik's cell phone rang and he looked at the caller ID. "It's an Avignon number."

"Go ahead and answer," Verlaque said.

Paulik picked up his phone and left the office, while Verlaque looked up the Duke de Pradet's phone number. He was about to call the duke when Paulik came back into the office. "She's gone," he said.

"Juliette de Castelbajac?"

"Yes. The concierge had to open her apartment. The radio was still on and clothes were scattered about. She left in a hurry."

Paulik got back on the phone with Avignon to try to sort out how to find Juliette de Castelbajac, and Verlaque left the Palais de Justice. He had decided not to telephone the Duke de Pradet but to pay him a surprise visit. It was just before lunch; a good time to catch the duke at home. He went down some of the same streets he had the previous evening, but in the opposite direction. It was a beautiful spring morning with a clear blue sky, and Verlaque tried to forget his paranoia, his fear that the dead Kévin Malongo's brother was following him. But all the same his body was stiff, on alert, paying close attention to the people around him. His fellow Aixois were out and about: mothers walking with small children, taking them home for lunch; retired friends, or groups of students, sitting in cafés; and people window-shopping, as he had been doing the night before. Nobody seemed rushed; it was as if no one here worked. But few people worked downtown—he knew that he, Marine, and Jean-Marc were fortunate, as those who worked in business or light industry had to drive each morning south of Aix, to its *zone d'activité*, or to Marseille.

The Castelbajac brothers had been sent out to Sanary's harbor to buy freshly caught fish for the evening's dinner. They were all surprised by Ludovic's unannounced appearance that morning. Their presence was heavy in the house, and both parents were relieved when the three brothers left together. Emile felt his parents' fatigue and suggested to Philippe and Ludovic that they lunch together on the port, after buying the fish. They agreed, and Emile prepared a foil-lined bag with ice cubes to keep the fish cold. He embraced his parents before they set off. He felt useless, unable to help them in their grieving. They both seemed more overly dependent on the maid than on their sons.

The brothers walked three astride down the hillside path that was lined with potted plants on one side and stations of the cross, leading to the chapel, on the other. From the path they had a view of downtown Sanary and the harbor, with its red-and-white-striped lighthouse. As they walked Philippe slowed down before each station, quietly praying and making the sign of the cross. Emile looked at the flowers, trying to name them. He knew that the tiny multipetaled orange-and-yellow flower was lantana. The tall, spiky mauve flowers, with their long, slim petals, were agapanthus. He stopped at a large terra-cotta pot that held a bell-shaped flower that fell gracefully upside down. He had no idea what it was. "I remember this flower," he said, "from a trip to Sicily that Julie and I did before the kids were born. There's something beautiful about a plant like this, with its naked stem topped by a crown of flowers. The green of the stem glows."

"The fish will be all sold if we don't get down to the port in the next few minutes," Ludovic said.

"You're right," Philippe said, picking up his pace, and soon they were at the bottom of the hill, which ended in a boules court and, across the street, the sea. *Les pointus* bobbed up and down in the water, like toy boats. "Look at their colors . . . ,"

Emile said, stopping to take a picture with his cell phone of one of the small wooden double-bowed sailboats. "Yellow and blue and orange. Look at that red and blue one, the same colors as ours. I always regretted Papa selling it. But today they just seem too bright and happy. Their joyfulness is completely incongruous to how I feel, to how we all feel . . . Grégory loved *les pointus*."

"You're a poet today," Ludovic said, sighing. "First the flowers, now the boats—"

"Let him be," Philippe countered, defending his younger brother. "I thought of Grégory, too, when I saw the boats. He always fancied buying one; he told me that the last time I saw him. You know Papa has a friend here in Sanary who rescues old *pointus* and stores them in a big hangar. He sells them for one euro, on the condition that the new owner makes the boat seaworthy within a year."

"It would take more than a year to fix one of those," Ludovic said. "Some of them are more than ninety years old."

"Mr. Negative at your service," Philippe said, bowing slightly before Ludovic.

"They can't be all that bad if they've been sailing on the Med for more than four thousand years," Emile said, ignoring his brothers' bickering. He stared at one of the boats, painted bright green with orange trim. It was called *Julie*, oddly enough the name of his soon-to-be-ex-wife.

"They're getting more and more scarce," Philippe said. He turned to his brothers. "What if we bought one? We could teach our kids how to sail, and Papa would have a grand time. Maman, too. She loved sailing. It would get their minds off—"

"I've always loved their lateen sails," Ludovic said, as if he hadn't heard Philippe's idea. He stopped and looked out to sea, shading his eyes from the sun. "The triangular rig rises better toward the wind. Do you guys remember how easy it was to maneuver? Tracking and beating the wind. Tracking and beating the wind. Tracking and beating the wind. When we were out in ours, it felt like we were the only people on the sea."

Manuel Arruda did not hide his surprise, or hostility, when he opened the front door for Verlaque. Manuel didn't know who Verlaque was, but that didn't matter. The duke was not to be disturbed. The servant was about to tell Verlaque that the duke was away when the duke walked into the town house's front hall and asked, "Frère Joël, is that you?" He saw the judge standing on the doorstep and mumbled, "Oh . . ."

Even from the front door Verlaque could smell the smoke. He smiled and asked, "May I come in, Duke? I have a few questions—"

Manuel quickly said, "The duke was about to have lunch—"

"I won't be a minute," Verlaque replied, walking across the tiled floor to shake the duke's hand. He looked to his right and could see the last tiny flames in the living room's marble fireplace. "Odd day for a fire," he said.

"Please, come into the salon," the duke said. "We won't be long, Manuel." He closed the door behind him and gestured for the judge to take a seat.

Verlaque sat down and leaned forward, picking up off the floor a piece of paper that had blown out of the fireplace, its edges still burning.

"You'll burn yourself!" the duke said, trying to stop the judge.

Verlaque put on his reading glasses to examine the paper. "A fleur-de-lys," he said, holding it up.

"I have a lifetime's accumulation of paperwork," the duke said. "I'm trying to tidy up."

"Funny time for it, on a warm spring day."

"You said you had some questions," the duke said, ignoring Verlaque's comment.

Verlaque continued holding the paper, but, raising his eyes over his reading glasses, he looked at the duke. "You left the royalist society here in Aix over a dispute."

"Not a dispute. I just no longer had the time."

Verlaque found it odd that someone who didn't work used lack of time as an excuse. "When did you stop going to their meetings?"

"Oh, long ago. Maybe ten or twelve years ago. You can check their records if you want an exact date." The duke knew that he sounded snarky, but he was tired and expecting his friend Frère Joël. He normally hid his impatience—it was one of the things he was proud of—but today he did not.

"But your late wife stayed in the association."

"That's right."

Verlaque thought that the duke looked uncomfortable. "What kind of a relationship did Marguerite have with Charles de Saint-Félix? He's a local lawyer—"

"I know very well who Charles is."

Ah, we're getting something here, thought Verlaque. "Did they work in the ANF together? Eight years ago?"

The duke shrugged. "Yes, they were both members, but as I

said, I was no longer a member." He knew very well what Marguerite and Charles were scheming, but he could not tell the judge about it.

"Did they have things in common? Did they want to bring back the monarchy, at whatever the cost? Did Charles and Marguerite see eye-to-eye on things?"

"You'd better stop there."

Verlaque persisted, "Did they have more in common than you and your own wife did?"

The duke finally lost his patience. "Yes, they probably did. If you must know, as we aged our interests changed. We loved each other but didn't always see eye-to-eye as we did when we were young. You're a newlywed. You'll see. It's entirely possible that someday you and your wife will grow apart."

By the time he got back to the front steps of the Palais de Justice, Verlaque felt like he had been punched in the stomach. The duke's words had saddened him, and he knew he had pushed the old man too far. He walked into his office and closed the door. He sat down, relit his Upmann, and pulled out the tiny piece of paper he had taken from the duke's fireplace. The fleur-de-lys was very clear, but it looked like there was a date written underneath it. He couldn't read it, even with his reading glasses. He got up and pulled the Oxford dictionary off his bookshelf. He had two: The OED in his apartment had been his grandparents', one of the few items he had taken from their Paris house, and this copy had been his in university. He put his big hands around the tiny brass knob and opened the drawer that was a part of the two-volume boxed set, pulling out the magnifying glass. Holding it up to the paper, he could now read what was written under the symbol of France, the symbol of the French monarchy. It was a date: August 15, eight years ago.

Verlaque was about to phone Marine when Paulik knocked on the door, opening it to stick his head in. "Sorry, but it's important. I think," he said.

Verlaque looked up, setting his phone down on the desk.

"You should come downstairs," Paulik continued. "They've brought in the dishwasher from La Fontaine restaurant."

"What?"

"He was picked up for loitering; at least that's what they're saying downstairs. Two of the officers have been following him the past week."

"Why on earth?"

Paulik said, "I think he was followed partly because of the scar on his face, his size, and—"

"The color of his skin," Verlaque cut in, standing up and walking to the window. He opened it and, reaching to the edge of the window, wedged his cigar in a space about half-an-inch-thick between the wooden shutter and its iron latch.

"Genius," Paulik said, watching.

"That way, the cigars don't roll off the windowsill," Verlaque answered, closing the window. "There's still five euros' worth of Cuban cigar there." They walked out of the office together and turned down a hallway, heading for the stairs. "Something's going on with me," Verlaque began. He stopped speaking when someone came up behind them, and after the colleague said

"*Bonjour*" and walked into the restroom, he continued, "I'm eating out less, waiting for the summer clothing sales, saving my cigar stubs—"

Paulik laughed nervously. He wanted to say "Welcome to the real world, " but instead said, "I don't think you're going to get canned over the restaurant or Kévin Malongo's suicide."

"Oh, you don't think so?" Verlaque asked.

When they got downstairs, Yves Roussel was pacing back and forth in front of room 104. "He's in there," he said, tilting his head toward the room's closed door.

Verlaque looked down, always curious about Roussel's footwear and how big a heel he'd be wearing.

"New boots?" Paulik asked, as he had been doing the same thing.

Roussel tapped his heels together. "Bought 'em in Dallas. At that law conference last month." They were cowboy boots—Roussel's preferred shoe—and the leather was turquoise, with yellow stitching.

"Nice," Paulik said flatly.

"So what is the dishwasher in there for?" Verlaque asked, pointing to the door.

"His name's Mamadou Zouma," Roussel said. "We'd had complaints that he was wandering the streets—"

"Walking around?" Paulik said drily. "Nobody ever does that in Aix."

"*Aaaand*," Roussel continued, "he's been sleeping in the Parc Jourdan. But what's more important is this." He held out an envelope folded in half, then handed it to Verlaque.

Verlaque opened it and then passed it to Paulik. "'Ludovic de Castelbajac, 18 rue Cardinale,'" he said, reading who it had been addressed to.

Roussel said, "Zouma had slipped into the building when the front door wasn't latched properly and the concierge caught him red-handed, going through the count's mail. That's Ludovic de Castelbajac I'm talking about. His father's actually the real count, but he gets the title, too, because . . ." Roussel paused, looking up at the ceiling.

"Because Ludovic is the eldest son," Verlaque said.

"Voilà," Roussel said. "We called Ludovic de Castelbajac after the police brought in M. Zouma, and he went berserk. He said to keep Zouma here, that he was dangerous, and that he'd like to press charges."

"*Dangerous?*" Verlaque asked.

"The count went berserk because someone went through his mail?" Paulik asked.

"No, no," Roussel replied impatiently. "The count insists that Zouma killed his brother."

Chapter Twenty

✢

L'Esmérelda

"We couldn't close our eyes because then we'd become seasick, so we squinted, with the rain pounding down on us," Mamadou said, holding his large hands around a white mug decorated with red hearts. Paulik had found the mug in the staff room and filled it with tea. "The storm lasted eight hours. Twenty-foot waves crashed over the dingy; we were lying on our backs, terrified that we'd fall out. Neither of us could swim. We stayed like that all night, and the next morning the sun came out. The sky was blue and the sea was calm, as if we had changed worlds. We were parched with thirst but managed to talk. We wanted to talk. We talked about our parents, about soccer. About Mandela. Obama."

There wasn't a sound in the room; Verlaque, Paulik, and Roussel, even Roussel, were mesmerized. Mamadou, hands trembling, lifted the mug to his mouth and took a sip of tea.

Verlaque imagined that it was almost as if they had just rescued Mamadou from that dingy and he was sipping his first drink in days. Perhaps they *had* rescued him by just listening to his story, by letting him speak.

Mamadou set the mug down and continued speaking. "And then we couldn't chat anymore. We were too thirsty, and when the sun went down it got unbearably cold. But at least the sea was calm. I don't know how we slept, but we did. I guess we were so exhausted that we slept. And then the next morning when we got up Vianney began vomiting, and there was blood in his vomit. He had been sick on the ship, too, and I knew that wasn't good. I prayed for someone to rescue us. And a few hours later, like a miracle, we heard someone calling. 'Hello!' they called. 'Hello!' We turned around and behind us was a fishing boat."

"Is Vianney your brother?" Verlaque asked.

"Yes. He was my younger brother. He's dead."

"When did this happen?" Verlaque asked.

"Ten years ago."

"What happened next?" Paulik asked.

"The fishermen were from Liberia, and they took us to the port authorities in their town. We were taken to a cell; it was a kind of temporary prison, until they figured out what to do, and we didn't mind . . . we were so relieved not to be out on the open sea anymore. But Vianney kept coughing. He had been too dehydrated from the seasickness, too hungry, too thirsty. Six days later he was dead. I stayed in that cell for five more months, thinking of Vianney, thinking of how I had let him down, let our dead parents down. I was supposed to protect him. The big brother. And then they flew me back to Togo. I soon left there for Cape Town, hoping to find work, but there was nothing. I lived under a bridge with dangerous people. But at least in Cape Town there were docks. And so I did it again."

"Stowed away on a ship?" Verlaque asked, not believing his ears. But how else had Mamadou gotten there?

"I knew I would. Living under that bridge was worse than the dinghy. That whole area was full of thieves and thugs."

"Is that how you got the scar?" Verlaque asked, gesturing to his own cheek.

"I got that before, when Vianney and I were kids, just after our parents had died. I took Vianney to Cape Town to find work, and we were attacked. Under that same bridge. So after Vianney died and I found myself back there, I knew I had to leave that place. And the next time I'd be smarter on the ship and not get caught. I'd be more prepared. And I'd be luckier."

"What happened next?" Roussel asked, like a child wanting to hear the rest of a fable before bed.

"A boat coming to Marseille had docked," Mamadou said. "France is a country that takes care of you. Free hospitals, good food, beaches." He managed to smile as he added, "So-so soccer players. But it sounded like a dream. And just like the boat that I took with Vianney, there was no night watchman. It was easy to slip on board."

"That seems unbelievable," Verlaque said.

"I was lucky," Mamadou said. Verlaque noticed that Mamadou used the work *luck* a lot. "Some ships are harder to get onto, but there's always a way. Some guys use a stowaway pole." Seeing the perplexed faces of his interviewers, Mamadou made a vertical gesture with his hand. "They are long bamboo poles with toeholds and a hook. Other guys get on when the love boat pulls up at night."

"Love boat?" Roussel asked.

"They bring prostitutes and drugs and liquor," Mamadou explained. "There are lots of them in the Cape. But this time I didn't hide in the engine room, like Vianney and I had on the *Esmérelda*. That was horrible—"

"The fumes?" Verlaque asked. He made a mental note of the ship's name; it was the first time Mamadou had mentioned it.

Mamadou nodded. "The fumes got to Vianney and made him lightheaded. But for me the worse part was the noise—"

"The turbines," Paulik offered.

"Yes, my ears kept ringing. And the heat was unbearable, with no fresh air. I thought: Next time, I'd rather be cold. Next hiding spot has to be cold and quiet. So in the ship heading to Marseille I hid in a big tool trunk next to the shipping containers. It looked like it hadn't been used for a long time. At night I could walk around the containers and stretch. I had taken some food with me and a bag filled with orange juice, and one night I found a bottle of water and some crackers that someone had left lying in a corner. I had no idea how long we were at sea, so when we docked and I slipped off the boat and got to a busy street, it was the first thing I asked. What the date was. I had been in that trunk for nine days." Mamadou finished his tea and set the mug down, his hands no longer shaking.

Verlaque leaned forward and said, "I'm sorry, but let's go back to that first boat, when you and your brother were forced off."

Mamadou hung his head.

"What exactly happened?"

"One of the sailors found us," Mamadou replied, his voice cracking. "Vianney was making too much noise; he kept coughing and retching. The sailor took us up on deck and called for the captain. They spoke Spanish, but I could tell that it wasn't the captain's first language. He terrified me. I thought to myself, This is it. You're done for."

"Mamadou, this is where things get tricky. I want you to tell me who the captain of the *Esmérelda* was."

Mamadou looked up. "Ludovic de Castelbajac."

"Did he force you and Vianney into the dinghy?"

"It was his order. One of the sailors had a knife, and he and another one—they were Filipino—forced us onto the dinghy. The captain looked at us with hatred, and he said to them, 'Just deal with it.'"

An officer brought Mamadou a sandwich and an apple—it was almost 6:00 p.m.—and Paulik, Verlaque, and Roussel met in Verlaque's office, where he could make them decent coffees.

"I don't trust him," Roussel said, pacing back and forth.

"You were riveted," Verlaque said.

"I always am when someone tells a good story," Roussel said. "But it's fiction. He chose that boat to Marseille not for the beaches and good food but because it was coming to France. He was going to come back and deal with Castelbajac. Vengeance is such a good motive for murder."

"But Ludovic wasn't killed," Paulik said. "His kid brother was."

"A mix-up," Roussel said. "Maybe it was dark and Zouma couldn't see well. Or the kid brother got in the way, trying to protect Ludovic."

"Grégory de Castelbajac was killed in a passionate attack," Verlaque said. "You make it sound like it was premeditated. Our African dishwasher has no motive. Besides, Mamadou's been working around the corner from Ludovic's apartment and yet he has never laid a finger on him."

"Until now," Roussel said. "We don't know what he had in mind this morning. Ludovic is responsible for the death of Zouma's kid brother. Maybe that's why Zouma killed Grégory . . . to hurt Ludovic, as Zouma himself had been hurt."

That theory made the most sense to Verlaque, but he said nothing.

Paulik finished his espresso and looked at his watch. Verlaque said, "You can go if you want. I can finish talking to Mamadou."

"Léa has a recital in half an hour," Paulik said. "Do you mind?"

"No, not at all," Verlaque replied. "I'll fill you in tomorrow."

"Okay," Paulik said. He began to walk toward the door but then turned around and asked, "Why *is* Ludovic de Castelbajac pressing charges? After what Mamadou just told us, Ludovic is in plenty of hot water himself. Wouldn't he want to keep what happened out there on the seas a secret? Mamadou's story makes the captain look like a monster."

"If it's true," Roussel said.

"Ludovic is afraid," Verlaque began.

"Voilà!" Roussel cut in. "He's terrified of Mamadou Zouma."

"What I was going to say," Verlaque said, trying to stay calm, "was that if Mamadou gets charged for murder, who would believe his story about the ship? Ludovic's cruelty out at sea would get swept under the rug." He paused and then thought of a way to irritate Roussel even more. "Or is Ludovic the murderer? Accuse a poor African dishwasher and hope that the magistrate is impressed by your career and nobility."

"He has no motive for wanting his own brother dead!" Roussel shouted.

"Well, I'll leave you two to it," Paulik said, opening the door and leaving after adding a quick "Good luck."

Verlaque smiled, knowing the good luck was more for dealing with Roussel than dealing with Mamadou Zouma.

Verlaque and Roussel walked back to room 104. Mamadou had finished eating and had his head on the table, resting on his forearms. Verlaque and Roussel sat back down and Verlaque resumed the interview. "Did you come to Aix then, after you landed in Marseille?"

Mamadou looked up. "I stayed in Marseille for a couple of months. It was summer and I got an easy gig selling knockoff watches on the beach. At night I'd sleep in a lean-to near the railway tracks. It wasn't dangerous like in the Cape. You have to hide your stuff from the gypsies, but that's all."

"But you knew that Ludovic de Castelbajac lived in Aix?"

"No, not straightaway," Mamadou answered slowly. "After I had been in Marseille for a couple of months, it was easy to find out where he lived. I was shocked. I knew he was French, but I had no idea he lived so close to Marseille."

"So you came to Aix?" Roussel asked.

"Yes, I came nine years ago in the fall," Mamadou answered. "I got a job in a restaurant right away, the Flunch at the Rotonde. Washing dishes. I became obsessed by Castelbajac. I used to watch his street, and I'd see him come and go. Follow way behind him while he did his shopping on the rue d'Italie. But then he went away—must have been at sea—and the following September a bunch of us at the Flunch lost our jobs because there was a crackdown on employees without papers, so I hitchhiked to Paris. I have a distant cousin there, in Barbès. And slowly, over time, I managed to forget about that sea captain. I stayed in Paris for eight years."

"Do you know that the skeleton you found in the garden was his brother?"

"No, no," Mamadou said, shaking his head. "I heard that his name was the same, but at first I didn't know it was his brother."

"Good motive," Roussel said, leaning forward. "You lost your brother, so he has to lose his."

Mamadou looked horrified. "What?"

"Ludovic de Castelbajac is accusing you of murdering his brother," Verlaque said quietly.

"That's crazy! When did he die?"

"Just before you went up to Paris. In August. What brought you back down to Aix?"

"I hated Barbès," Mamadou said. "It was almost worse than the Cape. And it was so cold. People here in the south had been nice to me, and it was warm and life was cheaper. I got the job at Bear's just after I arrived back in Aix."

"Coincidentally around the corner from Ludovic de Castelbajac's home," Roussel said. Verlaque couldn't help but agree with him.

Mamadou squirmed in his chair and went on. "No. It wasn't like that. It was a Tuesday when I got here, so I went straight to the big market, hoping a farmer might give me fruit or I could pick through the stuff they throw out. I heard Bear talking with one of the farmers—I buy from her now, for the restaurant, her name is Mme Martin—and he was telling her about his restaurant. I liked Bear straightaway. He was . . ." Mamadou paused, staring at the table, and then found his words. "Confident. And friendly. He had tattoos and yet I could see that Mme Martin really liked him. I followed him back to the restaurant, curious to see it, and after walking around for about an hour to build up my courage I marched in, asking if he had work. I was lucky—his dishwasher had just quit. But it was a coincidence that the restaurant was in the Mazarin. I swear."

"Have you been sleeping in the Parc Jourdan this whole time?" Verlaque asked.

"No. I was sharing an apartment in the Jas de Bouffan with a mechanic and he got engaged, so he left. I couldn't find another roommate, so I gave it up, thinking I could find a smaller place, but the prices have gone up so much here, even in the Jas—"

Verlaque nodded. "And what were you doing in the front hall of Ludovic de Castelbajac's building?"

"He came into the restaurant last week with another man. They came in at lunch and were threatening Bear, saying they were trying to close his restaurant. I had managed to forget about the sea captain and then there he was, trying to ruin the life of another person who had been so kind to me. I knew where he lived, and one day a woman left his building and I could see that the front door hadn't latched properly, so I slipped in—"

"You do a lot of slipping in," Roussel said. "Slipping onto boats, slipping into apartment buildings."

Mamadou continued as if he hadn't heard Roussel. "I was just going to talk to him. Okay, maybe I even had the idea that I'd threaten him, tell him to stop bugging Bear or I'd tell everyone—you the police, the newspapers—about what he did out at sea, to us, but also to the Earth."

"What do you mean?" Verlaque asked.

"When I was hiding in that tool trunk I overheard two of the sailors complaining. One of them was Filipino, but the other wasn't, so they spoke in broken English, which I can understand from my days in South Africa. They talked about how the captain ordered them almost every day to dump engine oil and sludge into the sea. The one guy said, 'I'm no tree hugger, but even I have a hard time doing that.' But I didn't know what floor of the building the captain lived on, so I went through the mail, hoping one of the envelopes addressed to him would say which floor, as the buzzers outside did not, and the apartment doors didn't have name plaques."

"The mail was out, easy to get at?" Roussel asked.

"Yes, on a fancy table in the hallway," Mamadou replied.

"It's like that at my place, too," Verlaque added. "We don't have mailboxes." He remembered that he had meant to speak to the other tenants in his building to get their okay to have someone fix their front door. Like Castelbajac's, it only latched properly every other time.

"And you weren't going to hurt him?" Roussel asked.

"I didn't have a knife on me, did I?" Mamadou said, holding out his arms.

Verlaque noted that for Mamadou a weapon of choice would be a knife, and Grégory de Castelbajac had been pushed.

"I'm missing the dinner rush," Mamadou said quietly, looking down at the table.

"You can go," Verlaque said. "Tell Bear where you were and that I'll be calling him. And you need to stay in Aix. I'm going to arrange for a Catholic hostel for you to stay in until you find an apartment. I want to talk to you more, especially about the *Esmérelda*."

Mamadou nodded and got up. "Thank you," he said.

"I'm very sorry about your brother," Verlaque said.

Roussel sighed.

Chapter Twenty-one

※

Blowup

I know I often say that I need a drink," Verlaque said as he hugged Marine, "but tonight I really do need one. A double."

"Coming right up," Marine said. "And I'll have one, too. I got into a huge argument with the dean today. She basically said that the other professors don't like me spending so much time with the students, that I was babying them." She threw her hands into the air and walked toward the kitchen. "Two rums coming up. Oh, by the way, I invited Sylvie over this evening. I hope that's okay. I should have checked with you first."

"That's fine," Verlaque said, taking off his tie and laying it on the back of a chair. "She can cheer us both up."

He sat down in his favorite club chair and rested his head on its back, closing his eyes. He couldn't get the image of Mamadou and Vianney lying in the dinghy, their faces pointing out to the storm and crashing waves, out of his head. He looked up when Marine came in, carrying two glasses of golden rum. She was wearing long white cotton pants that flared at the bottom, with high-heeled espadrilles, and a sleeveless dark green silk shirt. "You're lovely," he said, sitting up and taking a glass. "Maybe your students come to you for help because you're so beautiful."

"Thanks," Marine said, laughing and taking a sip of her rum. "As if they don't come to me for my wisdom!"

"That's not what I meant," Verlaque said. "Your beauty is a bonus—"

The buzzer rang and Marine got up to buzz Sylvie in. They could hear the front door bang shut, and they started laughing when Sylvie began swearing at the third floor. "Have you guys ever thought of putting in an elevator?" she asked as she walked through the front door, which Marine had left ajar.

"Not enough room in the stairwell," Verlaque called out, turning so that he could see her. Marine gave Sylvie the *bise* and Verlaque got up and did the same.

Sylvie handed him a wine bottle, wrapped in tissue paper. "A killer Burgundy," she said. "At least that's what the wine guys on the rue des Cordeliers said. It's from Santenay."

"That will be perfect with the roast pork," Marine said, taking the bottle.

Sylvie laughed. "Antoine, you've been usurped as the wine expert in the house. I hope you don't mind."

"I don't mind at all," Verlaque said. "Would you like a glass of rum? White wine?"

"Wine, thanks," Sylvie said. "I had a few run-ins with rum when I was in art school."

He laughed, and Marine came in and set a bowl of olives and a plate of sliced chorizo down on the coffee table. Sylvie leaned over and put one of the thin slices of chorizo in her mouth. "Have you guys noticed that chorizo can either be amazingly good—like this one—or really, really bad?"

"Absolutely," Verlaque said. "The grocery-store stuff is too fatty. We buy ours at the butcher's, who slices it wafer-thin."

"It was the butcher who gave me the recipe for tonight's roast," Marine announced. "He said to wrap it in cabbage leaves to keep it moist. But it won't be ready for another hour or so."

"We're so lucky," Verlaque said suddenly. "To have all of this." He motioned around the room with his head.

Marine and Sylvie looked at him.

"Today I heard the most horrific story," he went on, "of two brothers from Togo. They were stowaways on a merchant ship and were found out. The captain and crew forced them at knife-point into a dinghy during a storm . . ."

"Oh my God," Marine said.

"Marine, the captain was Ludovic de Castelbajac, the eldest son," Verlaque said. "And the castaway was Mamadou."

"Mamadou?" Marine asked in disbelief.

He said, "Yes. And his brother died after the ordeal."

"That's awful," Sylvie said.

"Wait a minute—" Marine said. She looked at Sylvie and said, "Remember our lunch when Thomas Roche came into La Fontaine with that military-looking guy?"

"Who was terrified of Mamadou!" Sylvie said.

"That's him," Verlaque confirmed. "And Mamadou was

caught today in Castelbajac's front hall. He claims he was just going to talk to Castelbajac."

"I'll bet," Sylvie said, snorting.

"Castelbajac has accused Mamadou of killing his brother Grégory," he said. "But he has zero proof, so I let Mamadou go."

"There's a motive, though," Marine said.

Sylvie said, "This whole story reminds me of Eric's photos—"

Verlaque and Marine looked at Sylvie. "Go on," he said.

"Eric Cassely and I went to the Beaux Arts together," Sylvie said. "He's a photographer in Marseille, and he just won an award for a series of photos he took of the merchant-ship life. The photos were amazingly beautiful, and the sailors' stories so heartbreakingly sad. Eric did a lecture on the opening night. I remember him saying that more than two thousand stowaways are caught each year. Those are the lucky ones; many die because they've chosen a dangerous hiding spot, like inside shipping containers that look cozy but are fumigated, or they're crushed by anchors. And many are forced onto rafts out to sea, like the dishwasher."

"Why not just hand the stowaways in at the next port?" Marine asked.

Sylvie took a big sip of wine and continued. "That's what used to happen, but European immigration laws have tightened and now port authorities give hefty fines to ships arriving with people whose names are not on the ship's manifest. The fines can be as high as fifty thousand euros and even more if the cargo is delayed."

"And so it costs nothing to force them overboard," Marine said.

Sylvie said, "Well, Eric explained it as kind of a catch-22. Captains are prohibited from keeping stowaways on board but are fined if they bring them to shore."

"There must be a solution," Marine said.

"No country wants to take responsibility," Verlaque said. "I've read that the seas are like the Wild West."

Sylvie continued. "My favorite photos was a series of portraits of guys who had spent all their savings to get to this one ship only to find it had been abandoned, with no captain or owners about. They didn't have enough money to get home, so they stayed on board, waiting for news, then slowly starved and fell into depression. That boat ended up in Marseille, after changing owners a couple of times, and while at sea it managed to avoid the port authorities."

"Should we look at the wedding photos before dinner?" Marine asked. As Sylvie had said, the sailors' stories were heartbreaking, and she felt guilty for changing the subject. But she doubted that Mamadou's story of the ship was related to Grégory de Castelbajac's murder; Grégory could hardly have been mistaken for his much-older sea captain brother. And she knew that if they didn't sit down together that evening to choose photos, it would be months before they could do it again.

"*Volontiers*," Verlaque said, reaching over and putting the album in the middle of the coffee table where they could all see it. Marine took in a relieved breath of air, seeing that he felt the same.

"I must say," Sylvie said, opening the album, "Régis did a bang-up job on the photos." She turned to the first page, a portrait in black-and-white of Marine and Antoine, slightly smiling—more bemused than anything—with the Baroque church in the background. "Okay-looking couple, I guess," Sylvie said, turning the page. "I love this shot." She said pointed to the photograph of Marine adjusting her lipstick.

Verlaque looked at it, then said *"Pardon,"* and picked up the album so that he could see it better.

"Can you get it any closer?" Sylvie teased.

After a few seconds he smiled and set the album down so that Sylvie could turn the next page. "There will be more choices once we get to the reception photos," she said. "But I love this one of your mom scowling, Marine."

They laughed and again Verlaque picked up the album and brought it up to his nose. "You need a new prescription," Marine said.

"He looks so much like . . . ," he mumbled.

"Who?" Marine asked. "Who looks like whom?"

Verlaque looked up at the ceiling and then closed his eyes. Sylvie and Marine exchanged glances. He opened his eyes and snapped his fingers. *"Mais oui . . ."*

"Antoine, what the—?" Marine asked. She picked up the album and looked at the photograph. "Who am I looking at?"

"The man watching my father and Rebecca get their photo taken," Verlaque said, pointing. "He's standing at the left edge of the photo, smoking, beside the bougainvillea that climbs up the church wall. He was in your lipstick photo, too."

"He's just some village local," Sylvie suggested.

"Yes, and I just finally figured out who he is," Verlaque said. "He's the waiter from the restaurant, Marine. The one we always joke looks like a young Robert De Niro."

Marine looked at the photograph. "Are you sure?" She looked again, then made a clicking sound with her tongue. "Yes, you're right. He's grown a beard now. I didn't recognize him."

"It's one of those scruffy beards," Verlaque said. "Patchy." He rubbed his eyes and Marine stared at him.

"What's wrong, Antoine?" she asked.

"Yannis Malongo," Verlaque said. "He's the brother of Kévin—"

"The guy who claimed he was innocent, then killed himself in jail," Sylvie cut in. "Sorry, I read about it in *La Provence* in a café this morning."

Marine shook then straightened her back. "Does the waiter remind you of Yannis Malongo? What's the connection?"

"The beard," Verlaque said. "Yannis has grown the same kind of half-assed beard, and I didn't recognize him. I've bumped into him at least twice in town in the past few days." He put the album down and walked across the room, standing with his body against the wall so that he could look out the window without being seen.

"Why are you looking out the window?" Marine asked. "Is Yannis there?"

Sylvie began biting her nails while she stared at Verlaque.

"No, of course not. But he followed me up the street the other night," he replied. "I knew I recognized him, but it was dark and he walked by me too quickly."

Marine picked up the album and looked again. "That De Niro look, with the beard . . . ," she said. "Now it's giving me déjà vu as well."

"You two are giving me the creeps," Sylvie said.

"Now I know who the waiter reminds me of," Marine said.

"That guy who helped me open the front door downstairs the other night, when I had my arms full of groceries." She looked over at her husband, who had now moved away from the window and sat back down on the sofa, putting his arm around her.

"Don't worry," Verlaque said. "He's probably lost interest in following me around." But he was lying. Yannis Malongo was on their street, looking up at their apartment, smoking. Verlaque suddenly thought that Mamadou Zouma, despite his tragic story, might be guilty. And, like Zouma, Malongo was obsessed with the man—be he sea captain or judge—who had hurt his brother. Verlaque tried not to shiver when he thought of the worst-case scenario: Yannis Malongo might take his vengeance out on the person dearest to him.

Chapter Twenty-two

The Duke Confesses

*T*hat evening after dinner Verlaque and Marine walked Sylvie home. The streets were eerily empty—Yannis Malongo had gone—and Sylvie lived just two streets away, where there were no restaurants or bars open late. Sylvie nervously chatted and smoked, as if to warn potential followers that they were three, not one. It reminded Verlaque of noises hikers in certain mountains of North America had to make to ward off bears.

Once upstairs in her apartment, Sylvie paid the babysitter and tiptoed into Charlotte's room and kissed her warm cheek. She stroked her curly hair, thinking of the wedding photograph Charlotte had chosen to frame. After school they had gone to the framer's together and chosen a simple silver frame. Sylvie could see why her eleven-year-old daughter liked the photograph: She was actually in it, along with her friend Léa, daughter of the Pauliks'. In fact, almost all the wedding guests were in this photograph, as it was taken inside the restaurant where the reception had taken place. Charlotte had said that it reminded her a little of *The Last Supper*, with Marine sitting in the middle of the table like Jesus. "Who is Antoine, then?" Sylvie asked her daughter. She answered, "He's one of the wise men." "But they weren't at the Last Supper," Sylvie corrected Charlotte. "I'm making it up, Maman!" One long table had been set up in an annex of the restaurant, and in this photograph only the faces of those sitting on the same side of the table as Marine and Verlaque could be seen; those on the opposite side had their backs to the camera, but even so their attitudes could sometimes be read in a turn of the head or the body posture. Three magnums of red wine, Barolo, set the scene of a good party. Antoine Verlaque had insisted on there being wild boar on the menu, despite the village's location on the sea, and he had fought and lost when Marine added a fish option. The table was dressed in white linen and there were no flowers on it: only dozens of wine and water glasses, baskets of bread, bottles of olive oil, and about ten Italian sparkling water bottles, the empties being taken away by the staff almost as soon as they were set down on the table. Régis had rightly chosen black-and-white for this photo, which gave it a timelessness. Charlotte and Léa were at the far right, huddled together, laughing about something. Their new friendship pleased Sylvie, as the girls were very different: Léa was a choral singer in Aix's prestigious music conservatory, and a serious and outgoing girl; whereas Charlotte was shy and a dreamer. "It's a perfect picture," Sylvie had said as they left the framing shop. "What were you girls laughing about, anyway?"

"Antoine," Charlotte answered matter-of-factly. "Marine's maman was speaking to him, and we were watching. He wasn't listening to her, but he was trying to make it look like he was. But she caught him not listening and grabbed his shoulder. That's when we got the giggles, and then Antoine heard us and winked."

On the way back to their apartment Verlaque held Marine close to him, and they, too, spoke a little too loudly, reliving their wedding day and fantasizing about buying an apartment in Paradiso. When they got back home, they quickly loaded the dishwasher and put the leftover food away. "I'll wash the Riedels tomorrow morning," Verlaque said of the three fragile wineglasses.

"All right," Marine said. "Thank you."

They turned off the kitchen lights, brushed their teeth, and changed for bed. "What's on for you tomorrow?" Verlaque asked as he buttoned up his cotton pajamas and got into bed.

"I'm going to stay here and work on the bibliography for my book," Marine said. "Antoine . . . are we in danger?"

He looked over at his giant black Pierre Soulages painting and then at Marine. "I don't want you leaving the apartment tomorrow," he answered. "Or if you do, take Sylvie with you or buzz Arnaud."

"Groceries?"

"Arnaud. Give him a list. Tell him you have too much work."

"And you?"

Verlaque answered, "The Palais de Justice is just around the corner, and it will be broad daylight, with lots of people about."

"You could say the same thing about me going out tomorrow—" Marine argued.

"Okay, I'll get Bruno to come and pick me up. He can bring some brioches from Michaud's."

Marine smiled, relieved that Verlaque would call Bruno Paulik, relieved that her husband was back to his cheery self, already thinking of his next meal. She reached over and turned off the bedside lamp.

Paulik arrived on the rue Adanson just before 9:00 a.m. Marine was already upstairs in the loft, in the office that Verlaque had set up for her, working. She called a good morning down to the commissioner, leaning over the balcony's contemporary black-iron railing. "I brought you a brioche," Paulik said, holding up the bag.

"No thank you," Marine said. "I ate muesli this morning."

"Muesli?" Paulik asked, looking bewildered.

Verlaque shrugged, putting on his jacket. "I know; it's a mystery that someone would choose to eat what tastes like wood shavings over Michaud's brioches." His cell phone rang and he looked at the number and then excused himself, taking his phone into the bedroom at the back of the apartment. Paulik sat in the club chair and checked his own messages. After ten minutes Verlaque came out and apologized. "It was Jean-Baptiste Dellaney."

"The third musketeer with Sigisbert and Grégory?" Paulik asked.

"Yes," Verlaque answered. "We've been playing phone tag because of the time difference."

"Was it interesting what he had to say?"

"Very. Listen, I have one more quick phone call to make. To London. Do you mind?"

"Go ahead," Paulik said.

Marine came down the stairs and said, "Bruno, would you like a coffee?"

"No, no—" he protested.

"I'm making one for myself," Marine said.

"In that case, yes, thanks."

A few minutes later Verlaque came back into the living room. He appeared agitated and eager to leave.

"Should we go?" Paulik said. "We can eat as we walk."

"Yes, let's." They said goodbye to Marine and left the apartment, opening the bag on the landing and pulling out a brioche each. "We'll split the third one later," Verlaque said. "I'm keeping track."

When they were down on the street Paulik said, "There's still no news from Juliette de Castelbajac."

"Mmm," Verlaque grunted. He looked behind him toward the Place des Martyrs de la Résistance but only saw a group of tourists taking pictures of the Théâtre de l'Archevêche, where the summer opera festival was held.

They turned right and walked down Adanson, which almost emptied into the tiny Esquicho-Coude. "Every time I look up at that defaced statue," Verlaque said, looking at the oratory behind its wrought-iron grille, "I think of people like Mamadou Zouma—migrants, or refugees, looking for a better life. And then they come here and there are people like Thomas and Stéphanie Roche."

"And Ludovic de Castelbajac," Paulik added. They turned left on rue Paul Bert then immediately right on Granet, which would take them directly to work. "Do you want to tell me what's going on?" he asked, finishing his brioche and getting the third one out of the bag. "Or did you just feel like a Michaud's delivery?"

"Let's get a quick coffee at the Café Verdun," Verlaque said. "And I'll explain why I wanted you to come this morning, and what our friend in Melbourne had to say, and why I called London. And then we can go to Marine's apartment. Sigisbert Valets will be there, and his accomplice, Mamadou Zouma."

The duke was kneeling on a board to which Manuel had nailed a small rectangular cushion. He was furiously weeding. Sweat ran down the back of his neck and into his shirt, as it was a warm morning. But he didn't care. He knew he should have stopped minutes ago and had some water, but he couldn't stop. Haydn's German national anthem was playing in his head; he had heard it on Radio France that morning and now couldn't get it out of his head. It did not remind him of the Nazis, who had claimed the song as their own anthem, but rather all the good things in Germany: the fine white wines of the Mosel, Albrecht Dürer's portraits, the English garden in Munich, buttery pastries made with walnuts and apples and nutmeg, and of course Marguerite. He had been thinking a lot about Marguerite.

"*Bonjour, mon ami,*" said a voice behind him.

The duke looked up and smiled. "It's so nice to see you," he said. Frère Joël helped him to his feet. "Let me ask Manuel to bring us some water and coffee. And cake."

Frère Joël beamed. "Are you sure?"

"Absolutely," the duke answered. "I've been working too

hard and need a break. Plus, I'd like to talk to you. I'll go in and wash my hands. I won't be a minute."

Frère Joël sat down and admired the garden. The priests had their own small garden, between the church and the Musée Granet, but the minute he went into it, another priest or brother would appear, wanting to talk about the next mass or the organ fund-raiser or the youth group. In this garden he could do what he wanted.

A few minutes later the duke came back out, followed by Manuel, who carried a tray with coffee, water, and cake. "Thank you, Manuel," the duke said. "It's spice cake," the duke told Frère Joël, pointing to the cake. "I know it's not Christmas, but I had a sudden urge for one. And Manuel follows Marguerite's recipe to the tee." He sat down and sliced them each a piece, setting them on blue-and-white Wedgwood plates.

"Josiah Wedgwood the abolitionist," Frère Joël said, picking up one of the plates and recognizing the pattern.

"Quite right," the duke said, now pouring the coffee. He enjoyed the brother's company, noting that he also had the same rich conversations with Gaëlle Dreyfus. And unlike the brother, Gaëlle was not homely and slightly overweight; she was still a very handsome woman. He handed Frère Joël a coffee and then sat back, smiling.

"I hope I'm not being indiscreet," Frère Joël said, "but do you have good news from your doctor?"

"Yes," the duke answered, turning to look at his friend. "The tumor is benign."

"Excellent news!" Frère Joël said, lifting his demitasse in the air. "I'll drink to that."

"We will, some evening soon if you like. If you appreciate old Armagnacs."

"Oh, indeed!"

The duke smiled. He admired the brother, his calmness and his modesty. "Frère Joël," he began, "one of the reasons I like you so much, other than our conversations, is your temperate and moderate nature."

The brother smiled, knowing the duke was once again quoting Montaigne. "Montaigne was unpopular with the Romantics over that," he said, biting into the spice cake.

"I know," the duke answered. "He wasn't hot-blooded enough for them."

"I can see why they thought that," Frère Joël said. "Take, for instance, Montaigne's visit to Torquato Tasso in Ferrara . . ."

The duke nodded. He spoke quickly, wanting to make up for his earlier mistake in confusing Euripides for Sophocles. "An excellent example. By the time our essayist visited his poet friend in Ferrara, Tasso had lost his mind and was living in a madhouse. Montaigne was horrified by the conditions and irritated that Tasso had driven himself mad by spending too long in states of poetic ecstasy. Montaigne knew that writing poetry required a particular kind of frenzy, but what was the point if it drove you mad, and you could never write again?"

Frère Joël said, "George Sand thought that Montaigne was too indifferent to suffering, so she stopped reading him."

"But that's misunderstanding him," the duke said. "Montaigne was very saddened by Tasso's condition, but what the Romantics couldn't forgive was his irritation. They bought into all that frenzy, that blinding brilliance, creating until one collapsed . . ."

"Give me peace and calm any day," Frère Joël said, crossing his legs and putting his hands behind his head.

"My late wife, Marguerite, was full of the same frenzy," the duke said. "She wasn't mad like the poet Tasso, but toward the end of her life I couldn't understand her anymore."

Frère Joël, although he loved calm and quiet, brought his hands back down onto his lap and looked at the duke. He nodded very slightly, encouraging the duke to go on. But instead of speaking of Marguerite, he said another name.

"Delphine was like sunshine to me," the duke said, looking up at the blue sky. "I hadn't been able to communicate properly with Marguerite for years, and Delphine's husband was dead."

Frère Joël leaned forward. He had been expecting some sort of confession, perhaps linking Marguerite to Grégory de Castelbajac's murder. He had not expected the duke to confess to a love affair.

"Do you remember when we spoke of Freud's house in Hampstead?"

Frère Joël nodded.

"I went there with Delphine," the duke said. "'It is the hour of feeling,' Delphine liked to say. She was quoting Wordsworth, her favorite poet."

"All about slowing down," Frère Joël said. "Appreciating the moment."

"Yes, but alas . . . we didn't have much time together, because I wouldn't leave Marguerite, and I think that Delphine knew that she was sick and didn't have much time left, and she wanted to spend it with her grandchildren. But what a wonderful time it was."

"You shouldn't feel guilty."

"Oh, I don't feel guilty over the affair," the duke said, reaching over and patting the brother's shoulder. "I feel guilty because I wouldn't . . . couldn't . . . leave my wife."

"You were married, under God's—"

"Don't give me that malarkey," the duke said. "I couldn't leave Marguerite because I needed her family money."

Chapter Twenty-three

⚜

Suspicion of Murder

Verlaque and Paulik arrived at Marine's apartment just before 10:00 a.m. Bear, Florian, and Mamadou were there, all of them working in the kitchen. Loud music was playing, unbearably bad to Paulik's opera-loving ears, and he winced.

"Sorry," Bear said, reaching over to his iPad and turning off the music.

"Can we go into the other room to talk?" Verlaque said.

"All of us?" Bear asked, looking at his coworkers.

"Just you and Mamadou."

Florian said, "I'll keep working on the stock, Chef."

The four of them sat down in what used to be Marine's living room and Verlaque, putting his hands on the table, began speaking. "I should have asked you more questions about your friendship with Grégory de Castelbajac," he said, looking at Bear. "But I was lax. Probably too caught up in your good food."

Bear tried to smile, but his nervousness showed. "I told you—"

"No, you didn't," Paulik said.

"This morning I had a phone conversation with Jean-Baptiste Dellaney," Verlaque said. "Did you think I wouldn't get ahold of him?"

Bear looked down at the table and Mamadou asked, "What's going on, Chef?"

Verlaque, tired of the charade, said, "You know what's going on, Mamadou."

"What—" Bear said. Mamadou looked genuinely shocked.

"Why don't you tell us what went on between you three?"

"I was in London," Bear said.

Verlaque sat back and crossed his arms.

Bear looked at Paulik and Verlaque and then continued. "Okay, I went to London to school not because I thought the French school system was shit, which is what I told everyone, but because Grégory had become crazy. He was hounding me all the time . . ."

"Were you lovers?" Verlaque asked. He had been thinking more about the photograph of Grégory in the Castelbajacs' library and how much he looked like Bruce Chatwin, whose travel books Verlaque had devoured when he was in his twenties. He knew that gay men came in all shapes and sizes, but the fact that Chatwin, who was gay, looked so much like Grégory, had led him down that path of logic.

"No," Bear said. "That was part of the problem. Grégory loved me, but I couldn't love him . . . in the way he wanted."

Verlaque said, "Dellaney told me that when you left Aix, Grégory was devastated. He even went to London a few times to try to get you back."

Bear nodded, his head hanging low.

"What was Grégory involved in that made you leave Aix? You can tell me, or I can tell you what Dellaney told me this morning."

Bear clutched the edge of the table. "Grégory had become more and more fanatic. He was always against the nobility and the rich, always a champion of the poor and impoverished. But he was under the sway of someone new—"

"A lover?" Verlaque asked.

"No, no," Bear said. "I don't think so. It was an older person, someone who was an anarchist. I don't even know if that person was male or female. Grégory wanted me to help them—"

"Because of your science background?" Paulik asked.

"Yes," Bear said, his voice cracking. "We had been radicals in junior high." He paused to laugh. "Ridiculous, to be radicals at fourteen. Jean-Baptiste had been very political, like Grégory and I, but had slowly been losing his edge, and in high school all but abandoned Grégory. After university he suddenly split to Australia, helped by his parents. I think they were worried he was a druggie or something." Bear then smirked. "He became worse than that; he became an advertising man. But he knew enough of the plan—"

Verlaque nodded. "The plan to set off a bomb at the next royalist meeting? Here in Aix?"

"I refused to help them!" Bear said. "I told Grégory to tell his mentor that they were both insane."

"Grégory's parents could have been present," Paulik said. "Or his brothers."

"He said he'd make sure they were out of the room," Bear

said. "I don't know how. They were after one person in particular. I don't know whom, either."

"Why didn't you report them?" Verlaque asked.

Bear looked across the room at one of Sylvie's photographs. "I should have, but I was terrified I'd lose my job. I had put so much on the line to become a cook. And I suppose I hoped they would lose their courage and not go through with it. It seemed so unreal at the time."

"As it turns out," Verlaque said, "it never happened, right?"

"Technical problems," Bear said. "Thank God. The bomb never went off."

"Did Grégory threaten to reveal you as a fellow anarchist?" Verlaque asked. "To ruin you?"

"Yes, that's when I blew up," Bear answered. "I even phoned Jean-Baptiste in Melbourne to complain about it."

"Jean-Baptiste told me so," Verlaque said.

"But that doesn't mean I killed Grégory!"

"You had a good life in London," Verlaque said. "That could have been ruined. I called your ex-bosses in London."

"You did what?" Bear exclaimed, rising from his chair.

Paulik immediately got up from his and Bear sat back down, burying his head in his hands.

"I can't believe you called them . . ."

Verlaque then looked at Mamadou. "I asked them about you, too."

Mamadou let out a gasp.

Verlaque said, "You didn't tell us you worked in London and knew Bear years ago."

"I didn't want to get him into trouble," Mamadou whispered.

"You must have found it a great coincidence while chatting on break at Cavalo Nero that you both knew the same family in Aix," Verlaque said. "And so you, Sigisbert, unable to leave the London restaurant, knew that your old coworker from Cavalo Nero was now in Aix, working at the Flunch. Quite a downslide"—he now looked at the dishwasher—"from London's hippest restaurant to a cafeteria chain."

"It was the only thing I could find," Mamadou said.

"What do you know about our kind of work?" Bear shouted.

Verlaque ignored his comment and went on. "So you told Mamadou to kill Grégory for you."

"Bullshit!" Bear said.

"And Mamadou had a perfect motive," Verlaque said. "Revenge."

"I would never kill anyone!" Mamadou said, his voice rising for the first time. "That's why I left Africa! That's all I saw . . . violence and death."

"You see? You've got it so wrong!" Bear yelled, pounding on the table. "Once again! The newspapers are right about you!"

"We're taking you both to the Palais de Justice," Paulik said, getting up. "Suspicion of murder. There's a van waiting downstairs."

Chapter Twenty-four

❧

Suzette's Ginger Shrimp

Verlaque had the beginnings of a headache by the time he got home from work. He and Paulik had questioned Bear and Mamadou for hours. Bear had an alibi thanks to Cavalo Nero's careful record keeping, although Grégory de Castelbajac could have been murdered any time that August, eight years ago. But it would have been difficult for Bear to leave work, fly from London to Marseille, murder Grégory, and then fly back. Sophie Goulin was checking with the airlines, just in case. Jane Clark had been the one speaking to Verlaque, until Judith grabbed the receiver out of her hand and verbally attacked him with a string of cuss words that had probably made even Jane blush. Verlaque put the receiver down, wishing he hadn't played so many rugby tournaments in the UK. He actually knew what some of the words meant.

Mamadou couldn't remember what he had been doing eight

years ago other than working at Flunch. He did remember the name of his former boss, who had now been promoted to a Flunch in Paris. Paulik found the restaurant's number and called the manager, who had only good things to say about his former employee. "I was freaked out by the scar, I'll admit that," the manager said, "but Mamadou was a great employee, and a real teddy bear." He lowered his voice and added, "I would have promoted him had we not been inspected."

Walking through the door of his apartment, Verlaque emptied his pockets out on the marble kitchen counter. He set his phone down and looked at the time; it was just before 7:00 p.m. He stopped himself from going to his club chair, taking off his tie and shoes, and lighting a cigar. Instead he opened the refrigerator to see if he could help Marine prepare dinner. A bag of jumbo shrimp that Marine had taken out of the freezer that morning was thawing on a plate. He remembered a dish they had eaten in Marseille, prepared by a female chef who had since retired, which she called, simply, Suzette's Ginger Shrimp. He opened the vegetable crisper and saw that there was a large piece of knobby fresh ginger and plenty of garlic. There had been something green, too, and he thought it might have been basil. Marine had just bought a small basil plant; she had set it on the terrace as the days and nights were now warm. White wine was the next ingredient he needed; two bottles. The chef had told them she put "liberal" amounts of wine in the shrimp, probably about two cups, he guessed, to make a reduction, and he'd need another bottle for them to have with the meal. In fact, making the rice would take longer than the shrimp, so he'd probably even have time for a cigar on the terrace.

He grabbed his keys and headed to the stairs toward the cellar to fetch two bottles of his current obsession, a small-batch Chardonnay made by Jean-Pierre Michel from vines scattered over the hills west of Mâcon. They had a few bottles left, Verlaque was certain. He walked quickly down the stairs, looking forward to cooking a simple meal, listening to some music, and sharing a fabulous wine with his wife.

Once down on the ground-floor landing he put the long antique key into the cellar's door and turned on the light at the top of the stairs. He tried to ignore the rat traps and walked quickly down the stone steps to the dirt floor. There were four small separate *caves*, one for each tenant, each one with a wooden door. He turned on the light for his *cave*, which was just to the right of the door, and put a small key into the keyhole to open it. Jean-Pierre Michel's wine was right in front of him, on a middle shelf; its oversize "M" was easy to spot. He had opened the cardboard box and gotten out a bottle when he heard the cellar door at the top of the stairs close. "*Merde!*" he called out. "Don't close the bloody door on me!" He picked out another bottle and turned around to leave when he saw Yannis Malongo pointing a small gun at him. "I'll trade you," Verlaque said, holding up the bottles and gesturing to the gun.

"Keep quiet and step back inside," Malongo said, his hand shaking. He closed the door behind him. "I finally have you in a place where it can be just the two of us."

"You've been following me, Yannis." Verlaque thought how lucky he had been that night when fate had put the drunken students between him and Yannis Malongo.

"Yeah, well, let's just say I became a little obsessed."

"It's not my fault that your brother—"

Yannis hissed. "Don't you dare say anything about Kévin. He's dead because of you!"

Verlaque closed his eyes, carefully picking out his words. He decided to be honest. "I may have been wrong about Kévin—" The ache in his head was now pressing against his forehead.

Malongo's hand was now shaking more than ever. His eyes filled with tears. "I knew it!"

"I've instructed an independent judge, in Marseille, to reexamine the witness who claimed she saw Kévin—"

"How do I know you're not lying?"

"It will be in the papers tomorrow," Verlaque said. "If you let me out of here, we can call the judge and you can ask her yourself."

Malongo's shoulders collapsed and he slid down and sat on the floor. "Sit down," he ordered.

Verlaque looked around, wishing he had something he could sit on. He sighed and sat down across from Malongo, his legs bent at the knee. He set the wine bottles down on the earth floor beside him. "There's a guy in the Palais de Justice right now, being held on suspicion of murder," he said.

"So what?"

"He may have killed someone, an innocent, to revenge his brother's death," Verlaque said. "Do you think that a second death rights the first one?"

"What?"

"Fixes the first one. Or erases it."

Malongo stayed silent, the gun still in his hand but now dangling between his knees. They stayed like that for about thirty minutes. Verlaque looked at the gun and saw that Malongo's right hand was firmly holding the gun's grip. Malongo saw him looking and waved the gun. "Don't get any ideas."

"You should let me out so that we can call that judge in Marseille," Verlaque said. "You're in a bit of *merde* now, but it will get worse if you keep me in here or—" He stopped himself and Malongo smirked, but he could see that Malongo was just as tired as he was and was having a hard time concentrating.

They were both startled by the cellar door opening. Marine called down the stairs, "Antoine? Are you down there? Are you in the *cave*?" She had come home twenty minutes earlier and seen Verlaque's phone on the counter and the garlic and ginger sitting out. At first she thought that he had gone out to the convenience store around the corner to buy a missing ingredient for this mysterious meal he was preparing, but he always took his cell phone. But he wouldn't have when going down to select some wine—there was no cell reception down there. She waited a few minutes longer then began to worry. Arnaud had installed a few hooks inside the kitchen cabinets and she remembered that Verlaque had hung a spare set of cellar keys there. She grabbed them and a flashlight, in case something was wrong with the lights and he had fallen. She ran out of the apartment and down the stairs, then pounded on Arnaud's apartment door on the second floor. She waited two seconds, swore under her breath, and ran down the rest of the stairs, fumbling with the antique key as she opened the cellar door.

"Tell her you're picking a wine and you'll be right up," Malongo whispered. "I want her out of here."

Marine ran down the cellar steps and they could hear her

breathing on the other side of the *cave*'s wooden door. "I'm picking out a wine!" Verlaque said, trying to sound cheery. "Go back upstairs!"

"Antoine, what are you doing?"

"Go away, Marine! I'm getting a nice oaky white wine for dinner!"

Marine's heart pounded. She knew that Verlaque hated overly oaked wines, red or white.

"Go away," Verlaque called out again. "I'll be up in a minute with the Castello Spegnere de Luci!" He hoped his Italian was good enough that she would understand his command.

Marine reached over, turned off the lights, and stood aside. Verlaque kicked the gun out of Malongo's hand and they struggled on the floor. Marine turned the lights back on and, her hand shaking, put the smaller key in the lock and opened the door. Arnaud was now at her side; he had heard the banging on his apartment door but hadn't answered it in time. He threw Marine aside, mumbled "Sorry!" and grabbed Yannis Malongo by the shoulders, dragging him up. "Don't you move," he said, pinning Malongo against the stone wall. "Sorry about that, Marine!" he called over to Marine, not taking his eyes off Malongo.

Verlaque reached down and took the gun, which had slid beside an old suitcase. He ran out of the *cave* to Marine, who was leaning against the wall, panting. He quickly hugged her.

"I'm okay," she insisted.

"Could you run upstairs and call the police?" Verlaque asked her. "I'll stay down here."

"Of course," she said, brushing off the back of her skirt. "Are *you* all right?"

Verlaque nodded, quickly closed his eyes, and then opened them.

Marine smiled and caressed her husband's cheek. When she was at the first step she turned her head around and said, "*Spegni la luce*. You used the infinitive back there."

Chapter Twenty-five

❧

Goldman

Verlaque and Marine slept in the next morning. They'd been so tired the night before that they had both forgotten to set an alarm. They had stayed up late talking about Yannis, trying to figure out how he managed to hide himself from Verlaque. The most probable explanation they came up with was that Yannis heard Verlaque coming down the stairs—he was humming—and had hidden behind the back door that led to the apartment's back courtyard.

After they dressed and showered they stood side by side in the kitchen, drinking coffee and eating toast off the same plate. Verlaque looked at Marine and saw that she was smiling. He wiped the toast crumbs off his mouth and said, "What's up?"

"I wanted to tell you last night," she began, "but we were both too tired and in that weird state of shock. But I have good news—"

Verlaque felt a lump in his throat and his stomach tightened. "Go on."

"I heard from the publishers yesterday," she began.

"Oh!" he exclaimed, relieved that the news had to do with her book and not an announcement that they were about to become parents.

"They're going to publish my book. They say that although dozens of books have been written about Sartre and Beauvoir, none have concentrated on their relationship as a couple."

He wrapped his arms around Marine. "Congratulations!" he said.

Marine said, "They want to meet me in Paris next week."

"I'll go with you," Verlaque said. "We can stay at my father's."

"That would be great. Will everything be finished here?"

"With Grégory de Castelbajac's murder?" Verlaque asked. "Yes . . ."

"You're hesitating."

"There are still a few uncertainties," he said.

"You're second-guessing yourself now, because of Kévin Malongo."

"I just don't know . . ."

Marine patted his rear and told him to get to work. "I'll clear up the breakfast, then I'm off to the university library to check bibliographical references. After that I'm having lunch with colleagues . . . the ones who don't hate me."

"The ones who aren't jealous," he said, putting his cell phone and keys in his jacket pocket.

"You're not wearing a tie," Marine observed.

Verlaque looked down at his chest. "That's right."

He decided to walk to work the long way, down Gaston de Saporta, and cut through the Place Hôtel de Ville, always one of his favorite squares in Aix. He realized that he had purposely avoided the rue Esquicho-Coude, opting instead for a big open square, a bubbling fountain, tourists taking photos of the eighteenth-century Halle aux Grains, and waiters serving coffee at outdoor tables. He cut across the Place Richelme, where the daily market was in full swing. He took his time, strolling past tables loaded high with artichokes, salads, asparagus, and strawberries that he could smell from meters away. He bought a small barquette of *fraises des bois*, sneaking two or three and saving the rest for Mme Girard.

He was on the steps of the Palais de Justice when his cell phone rang. He took it out of his pocket and didn't recognize the number, but it was another cell phone exchange, and since he didn't often give his number out, he answered it. "Verlaque."

"Judge Verlaque?" A woman's voice sounded on the other end.

"Yes."

He walked back down the stairs to find a quiet place to speak. He recognized the voice.

"It's me, Juliette de Castelbajac."

"Are you all right?" he quickly asked.

"Yes, yes," she answered. "I left in a hurry."

"I know. Why? Where are you?"

"I'm in a family cottage in Finistère."

"Brittany?" he asked. "Why are you up there?"

"I was afraid," she answered. "I drove all night and part of the next day."

"Who are you afraid of?" he asked.

"I don't know," she answered. "That's part of the problem. Grégory warned me just before he disappeared that this might happen."

"Was he worried about his own safety?"

"Yes . . ."

Verlaque said, "You should have told me."

"I know, but I wanted to get away."

"Did you send those anonymous letters to Sigisbert Valets?"

"Yes, Grégory made me promise," she said. "He told me that if anything ever happened to him, I was to warn Sigisbert. When they found Grégory's body, I began sending letters to the restaurant."

"You're not afraid of Bear?" he asked.

She laughed. "No, of course not! Why?"

Verlaque didn't answer, thinking of his conversation that morning with Marine.

"What are you getting at?" she asked, her voice sounding breathy. "They loved each other. Okay, Grégory wanted more out of the relationship, and he was too heartsick to accept the fact that Sigisbert wasn't gay, but they would never hurt each other. Do you understand me? Bear would never have hurt Grégory."

"Who would have?" he asked.

"Grégory's mentor," she said. "I don't know who it was. But Grégory told me on the day of our grandmother's funeral that the mentor was threatening to expose him."

"Expose his homosexuality?"

"That, yes, which you can imagine wouldn't go down too well with our family."

"In this day and age?"

"You don't know my aunt and uncle, or my cousins, especially Ludovic and Philippe. But this person also told Grégory that he or she would reveal who he was selling pot to, and he freaked out. It was a side business of his, let's just say. Then Grégory, in all his wisdom, threatened back, saying he would expose their stupid plan to try to blow up the next ANF meeting. Thank God that plan didn't work, but the mentor was furious at Grégory's threat. The last time I saw him he gave me an envelope and told me that if anything ever happened to him, I should take it to the police."

"Why didn't you?" Verlaque asked, trying to control his temper.

"I freaked out," she said. "It took me two days to find it again, and the morning that you came to Avignon I finally had enough courage to look inside."

"And?"

"They're negatives," she answered. "I held them up to the light. I can't really make them out."

"Are they of people?" he asked. He thought that perhaps Grégory had been bribing someone.

"No, some kind of landscapes."

"Landscapes? We need to see those negatives," he replied. "As soon as possible."

"I want to stay here—"

Verlaque tried to remain calm. "Then mail them special delivery to me. I'll pay at this end when I receive them. Do you have any idea who this mysterious mentor was?"

"No, but Grégory accidentally once mumbled a nickname,

or a code name, or whatever you want to call it. He was a bit stoned."

"And?"

Her voice became muffled on the other end.

"I didn't make that out," Verlaque said, trying to stay calm.

"Sorry, I'm walking on the bluffs," she replied. "Goldman, Grégory said. At least that's what it sounded like. Goldman."

Verlaque thanked Juliette and hung up, but his phone rang again before he had the chance to put it back in his pocket. He saw that it was Jean-Marc. "*Salut,* Jean-Marc," he said. "Is it quick? I don't mean to be rude."

"Free for lunch tomorrow?" Jean-Marc asked.

"Yes, thanks. Where?"

"At my apartment," Jean-Marc answered. "I've invited my mother over; I thought it was about time you two met. You'll like her. My dad's off with some old dentist friends, hiking, reliving their medical-school days."

"Sounds perfect," Verlaque said.

"Good, come at noon."

Verlaque hung up and ran up the stairs. When he got to his floor, Mme Girard wasn't around, so he put the basket of strawberries on her desk. He saw Bruno Paulik and Jules Schoelcher in a corner, talking, and he called them over. "Juliette de Castelbajac just called me. Goldman is who we're looking for," he said. "I don't think Bear or Mamadou were involved in Grégory's death."

"We don't, either," Paulik said.

"Goldman?" Jules asked.

"Yeah," Verlaque said. "What does it mean to you?"

"In English, it could be a rich man," Jules suggested. "A man of gold."

Paulik looked puzzled.

"*Un homme d'or*," Jules explained.

"Who is Goldman exactly?" Paulik asked.

"Grégory de Castelbajac's partner in crime," Verlaque said. "Goldman was his code name. A rich man . . ."

Paulik snapped his fingers. "The Duke de Pradet."

"Motive?" Jules asked.

"Juliette said that Grégory was threatening to expose Goldman and their plan to blow up the next royalist meeting," Verlaque said.

"The duke a radical?" Jules asked.

"Maybe he's good at hiding his real beliefs," Paulik said. "Besides, he wouldn't be the first noble or rich man to become radicalized, to give it all up."

Verlaque ran his hand through his hair. "He seems so thoroughly old-fashioned and decent to me," he said.

"I thought you didn't entirely trust the answers he gave you the first time you met."

"I know him better now. Besides, if he were a radical, we would have seen signs of that. He still lives in relative opulence and has properties in Paris and Burgundy. He doesn't belong to the ANF anymore, okay, but he's hardly an anarchist."

"Then he could be protecting his late wife," Jules said. "Did she kill Grégory?"

"Now that sounds more plausible," Verlaque said. "She was an extreme royalist. She could have overheard their plan. And then she and Grégory would have argued. The duke would want to cover up the murder to protect her good name. Plus Grégory was buried in a shallow grave. That's always suggested two things to me: a woman or an old man."

"In this case, perhaps both of them," Paulik said. "We'll do a background check on Marguerite and the ANF. Jules, can you do a search for us?"

"No problem," Jules said, sitting down at his desk and pulling the computer's mouse toward him.

"Juliette has a bunch of negatives that Grégory left in her care," Verlaque said.

"What are they of?" Paulik asked.

"She can't quite make them out. Landscapes, she thought."

Paulik narrowed his eyes. "Was Grégory going to blackmail Goldman? What could landscapes have to do with it?"

"A real estate deal gone sour?" Jules asked, looking up from the computer.

"Pot plants," Verlaque suggested. "Was Grégory's dope on Goldman's property?" Could the duke have fields of pot behind his Burgundian manor house? It seemed very unlikely. "Let's go into my office, Bruno," he said. "We need to figure out what to do with Mamadou and Bear. Gracefully."

"And quietly," Paulik added, having seen the headline on the front page of *La Provence* that morning: JUDGE ANTOINE VERLAQUE ADMITS MISTAKE IN KÉVIN MALONGO VERDICT.

"Gather around me as close as you can," Gaëlle hollered over the wind. "Because of the traffic we'll look at that fountain in front of us from the safety of this sidewalk." The tourists turned their heads toward the Cours Mirabeau—save for one, who had, from the beginning of the tour, been playing with his camera. These thirteen retirees had come on a hired bus from their small market town in the interior of Brittany; the other half of their group was now somewhere near Aix's cathedral, guided by Anthony Sauze. Gaëlle liked doing the historical walking tours. She closed her shop earlier than usual—in the late morning—and carried on the tours over her lunch break when the shop was closed. She sometimes earned more money from the tours than she did from selling knickknacks or table-cloths.

"It's called Nine Cannons," she explained, "not because there were ever any cannons here, but after its nine water spouts. As you can see the fountain has an especially low basin compared to the other fountains we've seen in Aix. Any reason why?"

A white-haired, bespectacled woman whom Gaëlle had pegged as a retired nurse or schoolteacher politely raised her hand. "For horses?" she asked. "To drink from."

"Ah, very close," Gaëlle answered, smiling. "For sheep, ac-tually. The sheep were led here in late spring all the way from Arles, to begin their summer transhumance in the mountains around Aix. The right for the Arlesian shepherds to use Nine Cannons dates back to the twelfth century."

The cameraman busily snapped photographs and Gaëlle continued. "I like to begin this section of the tour, focused on World War II in Aix, with the Nine Cannons. If you look at the road, you will see two rows of embedded stones around the fountain." The group strained their heads and some nodded in confirmation. "Good," she said. "The stones mark the position of the original basin, which for years had been chipped away by passing cars and trucks because of its low height. The final damage was done one glorious day in Aix, the sixteenth of August 1944, and after that the basin was permanently remodified." She looked at her tour group and waited.

"The Allies coming into town!" shouted an elderly man who wore a striped bow tie.

"Exactly!" Gaëlle said. "One of their tanks plowed right over one of the wings of the basin. But nobody minded."

"I should think not," a woman said. "The fountain must have seen worse."

"Yes, indeed," Gaëlle confirmed, thinking of her own nameless fountain. If only it could speak. It had seen so much; she hoped more joy than sorrow. "Let's walk up to the *hôtel particulier* at number 38." She led the group up the Cours, careful to point out interesting architectural features or warning when there were loose cobblestones or dog feces. She found herself thinking of Grégory de Castelbajac, as she had been doing more and more of lately. The fountain knew who Grégory's murderer was. She shuddered and tightened the silk scarf around her neck. Did they really need to know who was responsible, eight years later? Would that change anything?

"Here we are," Gaëlle said, stopping at the front doors, above which was a balcony that appeared to be held up by two bearded men. "Any ideas what these stone male sculptures are called?"

"Atlantes," the schoolteacher/nurse answered.

"Exactly," Gaëlle said. "Some people say that these two guys are the only people in Aix doing any work."

Her group loved the joke and a man hollered, "*C'est le sud!*"

"The *hôtel* was built in 1650 for Pierre Maurel, and thanks to the Atlantes is one of the most photographed buildings in Aix." Her photographer began clicking, on cue. She continued. "Maurel began life as a humble cloth trader, but after three marriages, each one increasing his wealth, he was able to buy one of these empty plots on the newly constructed and very desirable avenue. Not only did he build a beautiful house and garden, he also gave himself a title, making himself Pierre Maurel de Pontèves, and Pontèves is how the building is now known. Pierre Maurel was still alive during Louis XIV's visit to Aix in 1660, and must have been over the moon to host the king's cousin, Anne-Marie de Montpensier." A few of her group caught her sarcasm and snorted. "When Maurel died in 1672 he left more than two million pounds to his eight children. You can imagine how much money that would be today. A century later the house was taken over during the French Revolution, when it was used as the district's Criminal Tribunal. These statues behind me must have inspired dread upon those unlucky people getting dragged in here during that time. At least the revolutionaries didn't deface the façade's sculptures, as they so stupidly did in so many other places in France." Gaëlle paused, realizing her pro-monarchy, pro-nobility stance was probably a little too obvious. She should have said "thoughtlessly" instead of "stupidly." She quickly went on. "But our story doesn't end here, as the house once again had . . . unwelcomed inhabitants . . . the Gestapo, who used it from 1942 to 1944 as their headquarters."

"Were there many Germans here?" a woman asked.

Gaëlle nodded. She liked that some people were curious and paying attention. "German and Italian soldiers; more than ten thousand were stationed here. The Hotel du Roi René was used for the top ranks, this one for the Gestapo, the former Office of Tourisme for the police . . . good thing there weren't any tourists! . . . and the Lycée Mignet, the high school of both Cézanne and Zola, was used for storing munitions."

"*Et les soldats Aixois?*" the old man with the bow tie asked.

"Before the invasion there were almost two thousand French officers stationed here, who either joined the Resistance or the forces gathering in Africa. Of them, three hundred and eighty-five died in battle, including eleven of their teachers from the École Militaire. Two of the Resistance fighters, brothers, were killed in the garden behind my shop. Let's head that way now."

Chapter Twenty-six

❧

Gabriella de La Serna

V erlaque paused on the steps leading down out of the Palais de Justice and speed-dialed Marine's number. "*Oui*, Antoine?" she answered, whispering.

"I'm sorry," he said, letting himself out the front door. "Are you at lunch?"

"Actually, I'm in the restaurant restroom," Marine replied. "So go ahead."

"Goldman. Is there any historical importance to that name?"

"Radical philosopher," Marine answered.

"He was?" Verlaque asked, now running down the steps.

"*She* was," Marine replied. "Emma Goldman."

"You're a genuis."

Marine laughed. "Because I know of Emma Goldman? She was an anarchist, but also an early champion of women's rights. It's a name everyone should be familiar with. She also—"

"Thank you, my dear," Verlaque said, in too much of a hurry for one of Marine's lectures.

"Why are you asking me this?"

"Goldman is the code name of someone highly influential in Grégory de Castelbajac's life. They were going to try to assassinate someone at an ANF meeting and then they had a falling-out, threatening to expose each other for various reasons. Good motive for murder."

"That's interesting, because Emma Goldman once tried—"

"Thank you!"

"Antoine! If you hang up you'll be sorry!"

He walked toward the Passage Agard, not sure where he was going, only thinking he would look for somewhere to eat. "What, then?"

"Emma Goldman, and her longtime partner, whose name I've forgotten . . ."

Verlaque smiled. He knew how much it irriated Marine to forget a name or date.

She went on. "There's a connection here. They also tried to assassinate someone. Frick. I think his full name was Henry Clay Frick."

"Frick? As in the museum?" Verlaque asked.

"Yes, as in your favorite New York museum."

"Thank you once again," Verlaque said. He stopped in the passage and looked at some color real estate listings that were posted behind glass. The country houses were large and luxurious, with pools and formal gardens. He had been thinking more and more about their two apartments, and more and more about the upcoming hot weather and how nice it would be to have a swimming pool, some olive trees, and even a couple of rows of vines. "I'll see you tonight." He hung up, thinking of the assassination connection. Who was their Henry Clay Frick? He called Marine back.

"*Merde*, Antoine!" Marine answered.

"One last question," Verlaque said. "Who do you see at the ANF as being a potential bomb target? Someone hated . . ."

"I was only there once," she answered, leaning against the sinks. "I won't ask you who you have in mind as Goldman."

"Thank you." He frowned, realizing that the duke was the furthest thing from a revolutionary he could imagine, as his noble status was still very much intact. This made Marguerite more likely the murderer. A crime of passion, after an argument with the radical Grégory.

Marine continued. "If *I* were angry at someone at the ANF, it would be the member who researches the validity of families' claims to nobility. That's a nasty task. And for the recipient . . . Can you imagine waking up one day and your familiy is no longer titled? So Goldman might be someone who was disgraced and is looking for vengeance."

"Of course," Verlaque quickly said. This was another track that he would have to follow. "When you were at the ANF meeting, you mentioned that they went through a list of families who had recently had their status taken away."

"Yes."

"Who announced it?" he asked. "Does someone in particular do the research?"

"At that meeting it was Charles de Saint-Félix."

Verlaque ate some tempura and sushi on the rue d'Italie, not because he was in the mood for Japanese food but because from the restaurant's window he had a view of the Duke de Pradet's front door. He had only partly agreed with Marine's opinion; after all, she'd been to only one meeting. Perhaps the members fought all the time among themselves, and the duke, or even Marguerite, hated one of them. But no one came or went from the duke's home as Verlaque ate. He wasn't surprised; it would have been a long shot had he seen some kind of sign of the duke's guilt, and Marguerite was long dead. He only saw Père Jean-Luc, hurrying up the street carrying a gym bag, looking around as if he had just robbed a bank. Verlaque chuckled; perhaps the overweight priest was embarrassed to be seen coming back from the gym? Verlaque paid the bill and left. As he walked up the street, he dialed Paulik. "I got your message as I was finishing lunch," he said when Paulik answered. "Where should I be going?"

"*Ici*," Paulik replied. "*Palais de Justice. Vite.*"

Verlaque walked quickly. When he got there, he once again ran up the stairs to his office. "I'm going to eat a huge steak tonight," he said as he stuck his head in Paulik's office. "All I've been doing today is walking and running, and I had Japanese for lunch."

Paulik laughed. "Let's go to your office," he said. "You have the espresso maker."

"What's up? You said it was urgent."

"That Italian photographer called back. His Argentinean girlfriend wants to talk to us, but she wants to speak in English."

"Doesn't anyone here speak Spanish? What's the urgency?"

Paulik said, "She wanted to speak to you or me, and I don't speak either language. I always knew I should have paid attention in English class. She's a supermodel. Are you ready? Gabriella de la Serna."

Verlaque stopped. "Gabriella de la Serna?" He opened his office door and let Paulik pass in before him. "Wow. Well, then, sorry, I'll have to speak to her. But why didn't she call earlier?"

"She was away on a shoot. In Alaska."

"As one would be," Verlaque said. He sat down and Paulik handed him a piece of paper. Verlaque put on his reading glasses and dialed the phone number that Paulik had written down, putting the phone on speaker. She answered in three rings.

"This is Gabriella."

"Um, hello, this is Antoine Verlaque," he began, clearing his throat. "I'm the examining magistrate in Aix-en-Provence. Can you hear me all right?"

Paulik grinned, seeing that his boss was nervous, and Verlaque waved the back of his hand at the commissioner.

"Yes, of course," she replied. "My name is Gabriella de la Serna. I'm Federico Renzi's girlfriend."

"Yes, we spoke to Monsieur Renzi. Do you have information on Grégory de Castelbajac?"

"Oh, poor dear Grégo," she began. "Yes, I may be of some help. He was so sweet. We're all devastated here."

"Go on," he said.

"Just before Grégory went back to France, I think for a funeral . . . he spoke to me about his family. He was excitd to go back to Provence and said that he had some . . . how do you say it? . . . unfinished business with one of his brothers."

Verlaque's back went rigid and he picked up a pencil and a pad of paper.

"I don't know his name, but he was a ship captain," she continued. "And Grégory, being the ecologist that he was, had information about the brother's ship . . . things they were doing on board . . ."

"Do you remember the name of the ship?"

"Oh yes. The *Esmérelda*," she replied. "I'm a big Victor Hugo fan."

"What were they doing on board?"

"Grégo didn't go into details," she said, "but he did say they were doing inhumane things, including dumping oil sludge into the sea. Grégory said that all the big freighters did that, but Grégory had proof of the *Esmérelda*'s bad deeds. He was going to see his brother and challenge him on it. I told him it was a mistake, that he should talk to the . . . I forget the name . . ."

"*Les douanes*," Verlaque said. "Sorry. Coast Guard."

"Exactly," Gabriella replied. "Federico thought so, too."

"You were right to say so," Verlaque said.

"I'm afraid that's all," Gabriella said. "But Federico and I thought it might be important."

"I can't thank you enough. I know how busy you are—"

Paulik smirked and Verlaque smiled, waving his hand again. "One last question." He stopped himself from saying "I've always wanted to know." "Are you by any chance related to Che Guevara?"

"Third cousins," she replied. "Not many people know that Ernesto was a de la Serna."

"Well, thank you once again," Verlaque said. "Would you be willing to testify and tell a court what you've just told us?"

She hesitated. "Yes, if it helps catch whoever killed Grégo. Yes."

Verlaque hung up and Paulik said, "If she comes to Aix she can stay at my place."

"Shut up," Verlaque said, laughing.

Gaëlle looked at her watch and tried to speed things up. They were late for their lunch, booked at a mediocre but friendly restaurant on the rue Fernand Dol that was used to hosting big groups. "This is Aix's oldest free-standing statue, which was built in 1667 by the Archbishop Michel Mazarin," she said. "Orignally, this spot was to have a statue of the archbishop's brother, but luckily the priest died before the statue was begun and we were instead given this wonderfully playful Baroque fountain, called, for obvious reasons, Les Quatre Dauphins." She paused so the tourists could take photographs of one another in front of the four fat dolphins spewing water. "This is quintessential Aix," she continued. "It's my favorite part of the city, and why I chose to live and work here. In the fall the square's four giant trees drop their chestnuts, children come and go from the local schools, and in summer there are impromptu concerts. And the vistas in each direction are fabulous. If you look up the rue Cardinale, you'll see the early Gothic church Saint-Jean de Malte, which was already here when Archbishop Mazarin hired the architect Jean Lombard to redesign this former church land into a new chic neighborhood, one that he hoped would rival Paris."

"It's nicer than Paris," someone said. Gaëlle smiled, all too aware of the provincial dislike of the capital. She loved Paris.

"Is the water good?" another asked.

"Oh yes," Gaëlle answered. "Although a new fountain in this neighborhood wasn't entirely necessary as most of the homes had fountains in their gardens, or even one in the entrance hall, which was the latest in chic design."

"Will we see your fountain?" the same woman asked. "Where the *résistants* were killed by the Germans?"

"By the Nazis," Gaëlle corrected. "No, we can't, as the garden is private and shared among many neighbors. And besides, the police have the area around the fountain cordoned off . . ."

The group leaned forward, and even the photographer stopped looking at the photographs he had taken that day. Gaëlle regretted her slip of the tongue, but in minutes they would be walking by La Fontaine on their way to lunch and then the group would surely see the police crime-scene tape that closed off the restaurant. Gaëlle motioned for them to come closer. "A skeleton was recently discovered in the garden," she quickly said. She might as well give them good value. "It was buried eight years ago and sadly has been identified as a local young man. And now the fountain has stopped running."

A few of the tourists gasped. "Did it stop running during the war?" the schoolteacher asked. "When the *résistants* were murdered?"

Gaëlle did not speak but simply nodded up and down for extra-dramatic effect.

"It's cursed!" the old man cried.

"*Exactement*," Gaëlle said.

"Did you know the young man?" one of the younger men—at least a few years under sixty—asked.

Gaëlle nodded. "I did." The tourists blinked, and a few whispered their condolences. She thought of Grégory, and of Béatrice Germain's brothers, and of Valère the peasant who had refused to bow before Louis XIV. Four young men, their lives cut short, in the same garden, and all were violent deaths. She saw the old man with the bow tie rub his stomach and look at his watch. "Oh my, we're late for lunch," she said, relieved to be interrupted. "The restaurant is just around the corner; let's move on."

"What in the world was she thinking?" Verlaque asked. He and Paulik were walking side by side down a hall on the way to the room where Ludovic de Castelbajac sat waiting. "Calling Castelbajac and accusing him of who knows what. So naïve."

"We're so lucky he didn't skip town," Paulik replied.

"And lucky he didn't go after her," Verlaque said. "I had specifically asked Juliette to courier me the negatives."

"It figures that one-hour photo places still exist in Brittany. I understand her shock when she saw that the photographs were not of landscapes but seascapes, but still—"

"Here we are," Verlaque said as they stopped in front of a door. "After you."

Ludovic de Castelbajac sat at a table with his arms crossed across his chest. He looked out of the window, but Verlaque wasn't entirely sure if he was taking in the view across the rooftops of Aix. He turned his head as the judge and the commissioner said hello. "Most people go gaga for these red-tile roofs," Castelbajac said. "Apartment owners do anything to build terraces on their rooftops, just to get a view of them. But it's nothing compared to the view of the water and sky when you've been out at sea for days or weeks."

Verlaque and Paulik sat down and let the sea captain continue speaking. "I knew after Juliette called me that you would find out about the *Esmérelda*," he said. "I almost came here on my own."

"But we still had to pick you up at your apartment," Paulik said. "So it's a little hard to believe you."

"Grégory threatened to reveal what was going on on the *Esmérelda*," Verlaque said. He didn't point out the irony that Ludovic had been illegally polluting the beautiful sea that he had just been waxing on about, never mind tossing stowaways out to sea. "What happened between you the last time you saw each other?"

Castelbajac looked surprised. "Now wait a minute—"

"You were in Aix, and not out at sea, when Grégory died," Verlaque began. "For your grandmother's funeral."

"Of course. I saw Grégo the night before her funeral," Castelbajac said. "Then the next morning at the funeral, but not after. The last time I saw him was outside the church on August eighth."

"Then the night before the funeral," Verlaque said. "What went on between you two?"

"Grégory was stoned, and laughing," Castelbajac began. "We were upstairs at my place, and he told me some photographer friend of his had photographs of my ship out at sea—"

"Dumping oil?" Paulik asked.

Castelbajac nodded.

"Why is Juliette so upset?" Verlaque asked. "She took a big risk in calling you."

Ludovic de Castelbajac threw his hands up in the air. "Juliette's a nut and always has been! She actually accused me of murdering Grégo! Can you imagine such a thing?" His eyes watered and reddened and he looked from Verlaque to Paulik.

"Does the name Goldman mean anything to you?" Paulik asked.

Castelbajac tilted his head back and laughed. "Not that again! Grégory mentioned him once or twice. His mentor. What a farce. I think that Grégory actually believed at times that he was some kind of revolutionary."

"Do you know who Goldman could be?" Verlaque asked.

"Of course not. Goldman may not even exist," Castelbajac said. He pointed to his forehead. "Grégory had a very vivid imagination."

Verlaque resisted the temptation to look over at Paulik. The fact that Goldman might be an invented character had never entered his head.

"Did Grégory mention Goldman that night before the funeral?" Verlaque asked.

"No, I don't think so," Castelbajac replied. "He was in better spirits than usual, before he started taunting me with the photographs and what he thought were the rules at sea."

"Let's talk about what happened out at sea," Verlaque said. "And Mamadou Zouma."

Castelbajac hung his head. "I'm guilty of everything he

probably told you." He looked up and said, "I'm not the only sea captain who puts stowaways out at sea. We don't have many options—"

"Why did you accuse him of murdering Grégory?" Paulik asked.

"It seems logical to me!" Castelbajac said, his voice rising. "He thought that I was responsible for the death of his brother. So he kills mine!"

"Do you really think that's possible?" Verlaque asked.

"Oh, I don't know!"

"So who did kill Grégory?" Verlaque went on.

"I would never kill my own brother, if that's what you're getting at!" the ship captain yelled. He took a breath and tried to calm himself down. "I was in Sanary immediately after the funeral. You can ask my brothers. We all waited for Grégo to show up, but he didn't, of course. I stayed there with them for two days, and on the third day we gave up, assuming that Grégo had split. We went on a sailing trip to Italy that we had planned as a family. Grand-mère had left us money for it. I didn't even need to go back to Aix; I had brought everything with me for the sailing trip."

Verlaque stayed silent. Castelbajac could have snuck out in the middle of the night and driven back to Aix. It was only an hour's drive.

"We'll check your story with your brothers and parents," Paulik said. "In the meantime, some members of the International Oceanographic Commission will be coming here, and they want you to answer some questions."

Castelbajac hung his head again and rubbed his eyes. "I

figured so, and I'm willing to cooperate. But you must believe me that I never touched my brother. Ever."

The next day at 12:30 Verlaque arrived on the rue Papassaudi. He ran up the stairs, disconcerted that he was late for lunch as his morning meetings had all gone overtime. When he walked into the living room, an older female version of Jean-Marc Sauvat was sitting in an armchair with a glass of white wine in her hand. She got up and Verlaque saw that the woman was tall and slim like Jean-Marc, with his broad shoulders. She had puffy eyelids that, like her son's, were not ugly but dramatic. Her high cheekbones were what his grandmother Emmeline always referred to as aristocratic. She smiled as she shook his hand. "Antoine," she said, "I'm so pleased to finally meet you. I'm Anne Sauvat."

"Lovely to meet you," Verlaque answered. He liked her deep, husky voice.

"Antoine, help yourself to a glass of wine," Jean-Marc called from the kitchen. "The first course is almost up! Asparagus in vinaigrette. I hope you aren't tired of asparagus!"

"Definitely not," Verlaque replied.

"When we were children we'd pick wild asparagus on the side of the road," Mme Sauvat said. "My mother would scold us. She didn't like the neighbors seeing us gathering food like that."

"Nobles didn't do such things?" Jean-Marc asked, coming into the room carrying an antique oblong platter full of bundles of asparagus that were tied together with thin strips of blanched leek leaves. "*À table!*" he said.

"Certainly not," Mme Sauvat replied, walking toward the table. "She didn't mind us foraging in the fields behind the house, but it was the roadside that had the most asparagus."

"Maman, you can sit at the head of the table," Jean-Marc said, "and we'll be on either side of you."

Verlaque took the white wine off the coffee table and topped up their glasses. It was comforting to him that he could be so relaxed at Jean-Marc's and, much to his own surprise, he said so. Jean-Marc looked at Verlaque with a look of shock but quickly wiped that expression off his face.

"What a nice reflection, Antoine," Mme Sauvat said, sitting down and putting the ironed white napkin on her lap. "Friends are hard to make and hard to keep," she went on. "I don't mean difficult as in tricky, but more in the sense of it being time-consuming. It takes work and effort."

"And it's so worth it," Jean-Marc said. "Take a bundle of asparagus, Maman."

"I lost friends when I married your father," she said, putting a bundle on her plate then passing the asparagus to Verlaque.

"That's a shame," Verlaque said.

"Well, if that was the case, they weren't worth keeping," Jean-Marc said.

"All the same, it hurt." Mme Sauvat looked at Verlaque and said, "I was born Anne d'Estève de Bosch."

"Yes, Jean-Marc only recently told me."

"But what I did was a choice," she continued, setting her elbows on the table and her chin in her hands. "For some nobles, it can be much harder."

"What do you mean, Maman?" Jean-Marc asked. He

motioned for Antoine to begin eating, seeing that his mother was now reminiscing.

"The families who had their nobility taken away," she said, picking up her knife and fork, only to set them down again.

"Nineteenth-century forgers?" Jean-Marc asked. "You can't feel that sorry for them."

"But imagine finding out that your whole way of life is a sham," she said. "It drove one of our local counts to the mad-house. His wife died penniless, after having to sell off pieces of their property. It's happened to many families . . . a family here, too. The father committed suicide and his wife died soon after. Their children never recovered, and the daughter in particular is still very bitter to this day. I've heard she's a radical—at least she was. There, I've said too much."

Verlaque thought of the conversation he had had with Ma-rine, when he had been drooling over real estate ads posted in the Passage Agard. Marine's words came back to him: Can you imagine waking up one day and your familiy is no longer titled?

Jean-Marc laughed, winking at Verlaque. "Don't worry, Maman, that's not our circle."

"Oh, you wouldn't know her, you're right," Mme Sauvat said, taking a sip of wine. "Neither of you have children."

"I meant posh nobles. Where does having children come into it? Is this person a nanny?" Jean-Marc teased. "Or a kin-dergarten teacher?"

"No, she teaches teenagers, I believe," she answered, cutting her asparagus. "High school."

"Excuse me," Verlaque said, getting up from the table. "I have to go. I'm so sorry."

He walked down the rue du 4 Septembre until he got to the dolphin fountain and then turned left on Cardinale. At rue Mistral he turned left again and rang the bell at number 22. While he waited, he texted Paulik.

Bénédicte Tivolle opened the door. "Hello," she said. "I'm just about to leave to teach this afternoon. Will it be quick?"

"I'm afraid not," Verlaque said. "I need to question you further regarding your part in the murder of Grégory de Castelbajac." He saw some of the color drain from her face.

"You'd better come in, then," she said, standing aside.

"You've got it all wrong," Bénédicte Tivolle said as she sat across from Verlaque in her surprisingly small kitchen. She called her school to cancel classes and had made them coffee.

Verlaque said, "You must know why I'm here. You're Goldman."

"Ah," she said, turning around from the espresso maker. "How did you find out?"

"It doesn't matter," he answered. "You didn't teach Grégory, but you tutored him, right?"

Bénédicte nodded.

"Both his brothers and friends told me he had tutors, but I didn't make the connection at first, until I found out that your code name when with Grégory was Goldman."

Bénédicte sat down, handing him a coffee, the sugar bowl, and a spoon. "Emma Goldman was an underrated political thinker."

"So I've heard."

She went on. "Goldman was ahead of her time. She wrote and

lectured on such a wide variety of issues, ones that we take for granted today, at least in the West. She wrote in favor of prison reform, atheism, freedom of speech, free love, women's suffrage, and homosexuality. She encouraged American men not to sign up for war in 1917 and was deported back to her native Russia for it."

"In 1917?"

"Yes, not a convenient time to be back in Russia."

"Did you threaten Grégory?" Verlaque asked.

Bénédicte stirred sugar into her coffee. "Yes, and I regret it. I was so angry . . ."

"At Charles de Saint-Félix?"

"You've done your research," she said, her eyebrows raised. "Yes, Saint-Félix did the poking around in records that allowed the ANF to take away my family's title. He's a little weasel, and for years I held him responsible for my father's suicide. Are your parents still alive, Judge?"

"My father is," Verlaque replied. "But my mother is dead. She, too, committed suicide."

"With a hunting rifle like my father?"

"No," he replied. "She starved herself. Anorexia."

"I'm sorry," she said with earnestness, much to his surprise.

"So you and Grégory planned to kill Saint-Félix?" he said, changing the subject.

"Yes," she said clearly and even a little loudly. "As you know it didn't work. You can arrest me for that, if you have the proof, which you don't. But you can't arrest me for Grégory's murder. He disappointed me at the time, and I was so angry that I threatened to expose him—"

"For his homosexuality," Verlaque said. "Which your Emma

Goldman defended, at the turn of the last century. And you threatened to expose his drug selling as well. Whom did he sell to?"

"He would never tell me," she said. "I pretended that I found out, but I was bluffing. He did say it was for a good cause." She laughed slightly and rubbed her eyes.

"Did you have an argument eight years ago?" Verlaque asked. "Here? Or outside, in the garden? It was summer; you must have been out there. Grégory threatened to expose you and you pushed him."

She looked at him and her eyes narrowed. She leaned over the kitchen table and said, "You have no proof. There was a skeleton found in the garden and that's all—"

A door opened on the floor above, and Bénédicte turned her head slightly, but they both ignored it. Verlaque answered, "Our pathologist has made a new discovery." He tried staring down the philosophy teacher, in the hopes that his lie would have some effect. He, too, could bluff.

Instead she laughed. "A discovery, with bones buried eight years ago?"

Her comment made Verlaque think of the Paulik boys and their search for the farmer's bones in the Luberon woods. Like magic, a text came in from Paulik, causing Verlaque's cell phone to vibrate against the wooden table. He picked it up, read the message, and then said aloud, "The pathologist with more news."

"You liar!" Bénédicte hissed. "You can't link me to Grégory's murder."

"But *I* can." A tall man stood in the doorway of the kitchen, his hands grasping each side of the doorframe. Bénédicte swung around and looked at him. "Don't be a fool, Serge," she said.

"We can't lie anymore," Serge Tivolle said. He stayed in the doorway as if he were unable to walk into the kitchen.

Verlaque looked at him, surprised by his movie-star good looks—thick graying hair and a wide smile with perfect teeth, and tall. He had imagined Bénédicte's husband to be a small, somewhat ugly man.

Bénédicte got up from the table and Verlaque quickly did the same. "Serge, there's no proof, and you know that," she said, moving toward him.

"I'm the proof, Bénédicte," he answered, moving slightly back into the dining room. "I came home early . . ." He looked at Verlaque, his eyes pleading and apologetic. "I was supposed to return the next day from dropping the kids off at their grandparents', but I had some drawings to finish."

"Yes, and of course you had to race home to do them in the middle of the night, you—" Bénédicte said, raising her arms.

"Mme Tivolle," Verlaque said, reaching for her. "Please, let's sit back down."

She swung around and Verlaque felt a sting across his left cheek. Stunned, he reached up and felt the heat on his face. Lurching toward her, Serge Tivolle picked his wife up by the shoulders and set her down in a chair. Verlaque grabbed his cell phone and sent a text message to Paulik: "Come ASAP."

"I'm not afraid of you anymore," Serge said as he stared into his wife's eyes. "We have to tell the truth now. You killed Grégory de Castelbajac and buried him, and I said nothing."

"He fell!" she cried out.

Serge said, "Yes, but then he died in front of you and you did nothing—"

Bénédicte's head dropped toward the table and at the last minute Serge protected her fall with his right forearm. "It's over," he said, putting his left arm around her back. "It wasn't your fault that Grégory hit his head on the fountain, but you should have called an ambulance."

Verlaque watched Serge Tivolle, trying to fill in the blanks. It seemed from what he had just heard that Dr. Cohen's hyphosis that the murderer watched Grégory die had been correct. Minutes later the doorbell rang and Verlaque got up to answer it. Bénédicte was now weeping, repeating "I'm sorry, I'm sorry" over and over again.

Chapter Twenty-seven

❧

The Curse of La Fontaine

I was hoping for meat and potatoes," Verlaque said, staring at his plate. Marine set her knife and fork down and he smiled. "I'm joking. I'm grateful for this, even if it's fish."

"Salmon is good for us," Marine said, pouring her husband a glass of wine, "and you went to all that trouble the other night to get Jean-Pierre Michel's wine out of the cellar."

"You're teasing me," Verlaque said, swirling Michel's golden-colored Chardonnay around in his glass. He smelled it, then took a sip and closed his eyes. "Burgundy."

"The problem with us is that we love too many places," Marine said, putting her glass to her nose. "Italy, Burgundy . . ."

"Lisbon."

"Dublin."

"We need a hundred lives so that we can live in each place," he said.

"Or different jobs," Marine said. "How are you feeling, anyway? You must be so relieved to have the Castelbajac murder wrapped up."

"I am," Verlaque replied. "Bénédicte Tivolle was formally arrested today."

"And her husband?" she asked, taking a bite of the salmon that she had steamed and then sauced with a warm vinaigrette made from olive oil, lemon juice, capers, and olives.

"He'll get a lesser sentence, but yes, he, too, was arrested."

Marine shuddered. "The children——"

"I suppose they'll live with grandparents, or cousins. I have a hard time thinking of that."

Marine's eyes watered and he reached across the table and took her hand. She asked, "What happened? Did Serge Tivolle come home in the middle of the night?"

"Yes," Verlaque answered. "Grégory was already dead, and Bénédicte had just finished burying him."

"Why didn't he help her dig a deeper grave?"

"You're gruesome," he answered, smiling. "They were both panicked, but I would imagine especially him. He said he couldn't go near the body . . . If they had called an ambulance or the police, even after Grégory had died, they would be in better shape right now. But they lost their heads."

"We should eat before it gets cold," Marine suddenly said.

Verlaque nodded. The fish tasted bland to him, and he washed each forkful of salmon down with a swallow of M Michel's Chardonnay.

She smiled and poured out more wine. "What kind of proof did Grégory have on the *Esmérelda*'s illegal practices?" she asked. "You mentioned something to me on the phone after you spoke to that supermodel."

Verlaque felt himself blushing and hoped that Marine didn't notice. She did. "Grégory had photographs taken by a friend—the supermodel's boyfriend—who was on board the Green Party ship. He took it with a powerful zoom lens. Paulik spoke today with the *Esmérelda*'s owner, a Greek guy."

"Greek? What a surprise," she said.

"Well, this guy is an honest shipping magnate. He had been giving Ludovic de Castelbajac money to dispose of the excess oil and sludge legally, in processing plants, but Castelbajac pocketed the money."

"Polluting the sea instead."

"Castelbajac told the arresting officers that he burned the photographs. Grégory had stupidly showed him the photos on the night he died."

"What about the negatives?"

"On my desk."

"What?"

"Juliette de Castelbajac had them," he replied. "She'd only just looked closely at them. She told me they were landscapes, but the sea can look like land on a tiny negative. Grégory told Ludovic that the negatives had been lost."

"So Ludovic is in trouble," Marine said.

"Yes, although not for murder. The Greek tycoon told Paulik he would testify, and we have Mamadou's testimony as well."

"The poor family," she said. "The more I heard about Grégory, the more I liked him. His heart was in the right place."

"I agree. The Duke de Pradet phoned me this afternoon," Verlaque said. "He's invited me to tea tomorrow morning."

"How proper."

"I feel guilty," Verlaque said. "I suspected him for a while, and his late wife."

"At least you didn't take him in for questioning," Marine said, laughing. She coughed and then added, "Sorry. Bad joke."

"And I didn't accuse him outright," he said, "like I did with Bear and Mamadou, and then Ludovic."

"We all make mistakes."

"Those are big mistakes, mistakes that can ruin people."

"Don't exaggerate." Marine poured them what was left of the wine. "Well," she said, "you can make it up to Bear and Mamadou by apologizing. Neither of them seem like the kind of person who would hold a grudge. Hell, they don't have time for that kind of nonsense. You can tell them tomorrow; we're invited to have lunch at La Fontaine. Bear would like to thank us for the loan of my apartment."

"Oh, so he's treating us," Verlaque said. "I should be doing something for him."

"Saying sorry is enough. Are you free?"

"Yes, of course," he said, finishing the rest of his salmon. He wiped his mouth with a linen napkin. "This was particularly good salmon. Very fine. Thank you."

"You'll sleep better tonight than you would have after eating a steak."

Verlaque grunted and managed a smile. "Is there a cheese course?"

The duke had paced around all morning, unable to drink his usual morning coffee. He ate a bit of toast. He tried losing himself in a book and jumped when the front doorbell rang. He heard Manuel speaking with the judge and showing him into the living room. The duke put down his book, carefully using a photograph for a bookmark—he always used photographs to mark the pages he wanted to come back to. He left the library and walked across the tiled hall to the salon.

"Good morning, Judge Verlaque," he said, shaking Verlaque's hand.

"Good morning," Verlaque said. "Thank you for the invitation."

"It was the least I could do. Manuel has made us some Earl Grey tea, which goes so well with lemon cake," the duke said, gesturing to the Spode teapot and the cake.

"My grandmother always said the same thing," Verlaque said.

The duke gestured for Verlaque to sit down. Verlaque said to him, "I spoke to you too harshly the last time I was here. I'm sorry. I thought that you were protecting your late wife, that perhaps she had something to do with Grégory de Castelbajac's death."

"I understand why you had your doubts about me and Marguerite," the duke said. "I should explain a bit. Marguerite and I had grown apart, but we were still living in the same house. She had become so radical . . . the monarchy group, you know. She didn't understand why I couldn't be bothered to attend their meetings. Incestuous little bunch." He set down his teacup and brooded.

"What was Marguerite planning eight years ago?"

"Oh, you heard about that?" the duke asked. "Nothing vicious, don't worry. But it would have been embarrassing for me. For us. We weren't as well off financially as we appeared to be. Running this place, and the house in Burgundy and the apartment in Paris, was a drain. There were months when we couldn't pay the co-owner fees on the Paris apartment or the gardener to keep up the lawn in Burgundy." He leaned forward and whispered, "I could never have fired Manuel. Can you imagine? He's been with me since he was a teen. One or two of the residences would have to be sold, after having been in the family for generations. I never really figured out how to make money."

Verlaque nodded, and the duke continued. "We weren't the only nobles experiencing this sort of problem. And so Marguerite came up with an option that I completely disagreed with: to open this and the Burgundy house up for public visits."

Verlaque realized that Marguerite had probably discussed the issue with Charles de Saint-Félix. In that morning's *La Provence* the Saint-Félix château had been on the front page with the caption "Open for visits, starting Saturday." He had shown Marine the headline and she had replied, "That's what he and Louis were arguing about, at the ANF meeting."

"That makes sense," he said to the duke. "The National Trust in England does the same thing."

The duke shuddered. "*Quelle horreur.*"

"So you didn't have to open any of your homes to visitors?"

"No," the duke replied. "Marguerite had an aunt in Germany who died, leaving us more than enough money to get by. And I did compromise with the Paris apartment; when I'm not using it, it's rented out to wealthy American tourists. The agent who takes care of it for me tells me I could rent it out year-round, without a problem. In Paris there's never a low season, she tells me."

"My brother says the same thing," Verlaque said. He looked at the book beside him—a volume of Louis Racine's poems from the eighteenth century—and picked it up. "Racine . . . ," he said, not knowing what to say next.

"Not your cup of tea, I take it," the duke said. "You probably like those drunk sarcastic English poets."

Verlaque laughed. "Yes, and the Polish ones, too." He set the book back down and a photograph fell out onto the carpet. "I'm so sorry," he said, quickly leaning down and picking it up, handing it to the duke.

"That's Delphine, a friend, when we were once in London," the duke said, looking at the photograph. "She's dead now." He handed it back to Verlaque.

Verlaque looked at the photograph and tried to smile. He wasn't sure why the duke was sharing this information with him. The woman was smiling, her hands held behind her back. In the background was a flat-roofed apartment building, with artists' studio–size living room windows and an open parking garage beneath. "Is this really London? Looks more like L.A."

"Hampstead, believe it or not. I still remember the address, Two Willow Road. That was Delphine, ever the adventurer. She was a retired architect from Paris and had read about the houses in the newspaper. They had been built by a modernist architect, to the dismay of all the neighbors, including that fellow who wrote the James Bond books."

"Ian Fleming."

"That's him," the duke said. "They are now protected, listed buildings. They were giving tours that weekend . . . I think it was the National Trust you just mentioned."

Verlaque smiled and handed the duke the photograph.

"We were very happy that day," the duke said, slipping it back in the book. "You like Wordsworth?"

"Huge fan."

"Delphine was, too. When I first met you I didn't think you were that kind of a man," the duke said, smiling. "And I'm sorry for what I said about you and your wife one day growing apart. I suppose I was grieving a bit; over Delphine and Marguerite. I even told my good friend Frère Joël the other day that church weddings were malarkey. I need to apologize to him, too."

"Take him out for lunch," Verlaque said, smiling. "La Fontaine has reopened."

"I know," the duke said. "Mme Dreyfus telephoned me late last night to tell me that the old fountain is running once again. She could hear it from her apartment windows."

By the time Verlaque got to La Fontaine, Marine was already there, sitting in her preferred seat by the window. She waved and held up her glass of champagne. Verlaque walked in and leaned down to give her a kiss. He looked up and Bear waved from the open kitchen, then bent down and got back to work.

"I'll be right back," he whispered. He walked to the back of the restaurant and looked out of the windows at the sixteenth-century fountain, water flowing from its weathered brass spout. *There's joy in the mountains; There's life in the fountains*, he silently recited. Wordsworth, he thought, smiling.

He turned around when he heard Gaëlle Dreyfus's voice. "Hello, Judge," she said. "I'd like you to meet two of my esteemed colleagues on the historical society, Robert San Martin and Anthony Sauze."

The men quickly got up and shook hands with Verlaque, and he motioned to Marine to come over. "Admiring the fountain?" Gaëlle asked.

"Yes," Verlaque said. "I was promised that it would run again."

"You mean when the murder was solved?"

"Well, I'm not normally superstitious," Verlaque said.

Marine appeared at his side and handed him a glass of champagne. "Compliments of Bear," she whispered.

"Oh, I'm superstitious," Gaëlle said.

"Me, too," Marine agreed with her. Verlaque looked at his wife, surprised.

"None of you should be susperstitious," Robert San Martin said, scooping up the last bit of tapenade that Bear always put on the tables before the first dishes arrived. He spread it on a piece of bread and crumbs fell into his beard and shirt. Verlaque winced.

"And why is that?" Gaëlle asked.

San Martin brushed the crumbs off his shirt and let out a tiny belch. "It has nothing to do with a curse," he said. He took the tapenade bowl and peered into it, as if wishing for more. Jacques Oller quickly and silently appeared with more tapenade and another basket of bread. San Martin smiled and rubbed his hands together.

"Focus, Robert," Gaëlle said, rolling her eyes.

"Oh, right," he said. "There's no curse. I've been studying

earth movements over the past few months and how they affect our canals."

This time it was Anthony Sauze who spoke. "Robert works for the SCP."

"Société du Canal de Provence," Gaëlle said, sighing.

"Oh, I see," Verlaque said. "And what do the canals have to do with the fountain?"

"Nothing," San Martin said, biting into another tartine with tapenade. "But the tiny earthquakes that we have every week in Provence affect the thermal waters, cutting the flow off sometimes and at other times triggering it back into action. A week ago we had a small tremor and the fountain's water source stopped. Yesterday we had another one and the water came back out. It's all there on my spreadsheet at the office. Quite simple, really."

"That's fascinating, Robert," Gaëlle said, putting her elbows on the table and her chin in her folded hands.

"I'm a bit disappointed," Marine said. "I liked the idea of the curse."

"So did I," Verlaque agreed.

The front door opened and the Duke de Pradet walked in with Frère Joël. Gaëlle smiled, comfortable in the fact that she was to dine with the duke that evening, at his home. Jacques Oller directed the duke and the brother to the last available table.

"Have a good lunch," Verlaque said, looking at Gaëlle and her friends.

"Thank you," they replied in unison.

Marine smiled and linked her arm through Verlaque's as

they walked back to their table. She whispered that she was surprised to see members of Aix's historical committee at Bear's restaurant, and Verlaque agreed. "They must have come to a truce," he suggested.

At 2:30 p.m. Bear came out from behind the counter that separated the kitchen from the dining area to shake hands with his remaining diners. "Jacques will be giving you all a little grappa or nocino," Bear said. "To thank you all for your support." Frère Joël beamed; he had just eaten one of the best meals of his life. Père Jean-Luc was an experienced gourmet, and he couldn't wait to tell him about the spicy mussel soup he had eaten as an appetizer and the veal loin roasted with sage that had followed it.

"Sigisbert, I'm so glad we've been able to come to an understanding regarding the outdoor seating," Gaëlle said.

"I won't have outdoor seating here ever," Bear promised. "But I will have outdoor seating in my new restaurant on the Place des Fontêtes on the other side of town. It will be called Les Fontêtes."

Marine clapped and leaned over to Verlaque. "I love that square!"

"So do I," he said. One of the things he loved about it was its run-down shabbiness, and he hoped that a trendy restaurant wouldn't kill that charm. It probably would. "How will you cook in two places?" Verlaque asked.

"I'm staying here," Bear said. "And I'll go back and forth until Florian feels ready enough to take the helm at the new place."

Everyone clapped, and Florian, knife in hand, bowed from behind the counter. "And he'll have Mamadou as his sous chef," Bear announced.

More cheers came from the dining room, and Mamadou, bent over his washing, smiled from ear to ear.

"Congratulations, Bear," Marine said when he came over to their table.

"It's a good compromise," Bear said. "And don't worry; I'll try to keep the Place des Fontêtes' charm intact."

Marine began, "I never thought—"

"No," Bear said, laughing. "Your husband did. I could see the look of dread on his face."

"I have faith in you, my friend," Verlaque said.

"I thought he was going to bring us grappa," Robert San Martin said to Gaëlle in a whisper loud enough for everyone in the tiny restaurant to hear.

Chapter Twenty-eight

Trailblazers

The next day Verlaque woke up early, and after he showered and dressed, he read *Le Monde*. He had slept well, but he still wasn't entirely comfortable with the outcome of the investigation of Grégory de Castelbajac's death. But despite his conversation with Paulik, he couldn't put his finger on what was missing.

Marine was already upstairs working; he could hear her tapping the keys on her laptop. They had talked of their plan to sell her apartment and buy a house in the country, keeping Verlaque's smaller apartment for nights when they needed to sleep in town. They didn't discuss Marine quitting her job, but he knew that was around the corner. Making the decision to sell one apartment had been enough for now.

"I'm off," Verlaque said, getting up. "I'm going to leave a bit early so I can swing by Michaud's." He also planned to stroll by some real estate offices and look at their listings.

"Fine!" Marine called down. "Have a nice day!"

He walked out of their apartment and down the stairs, stopping by Arnaud's apartment to push an envelope under the door to pay for the shopping and odd jobs the student had done for them over the past month. Out on the street he walked toward the Place de la Mairie and when he got to the town hall his cell phone rang. He didn't recognize the number but answered it anyway. "Antoine Verlaque," he said.

"Judge Verlaque?"

"Yes," Verlaque said. "You're speaking to him."

"I'm sorry it took me over a week to call you," the man said, clearing his throat. "I only just got word two days ago, from Frère Joël at Saint-Jean de Malte, that you had questions regarding Grégory de Castelbajac. Apparently Père Jean-Luc forgot to call me. I'm sorry."

"That's all right," Verlaque said. "And you are?"

"Dreadfully sorry," he answered. "Père Etienne Fronton. I worked at Saint-Jean de Malte many years ago, when I was still a brother."

"Oh yes," Verlaque said. "With the youth group?"

"Exactly."

"The murderer has been arrested," Verlaque said. "But if you have any other information regarding Grégory—"

"I hardly think so," the priest answered. "I won't keep you any longer, and I can phone the church to find out what happened to poor Grégory. Such a shame, he was a good boy. A bit of a dreamer, but such a spirit whenever he did come to the youth group. We loved having him there, with his fine voice."

Verlaque stopped walking. He could see the Cours Mirabeau

up ahead, with the market stalls up and crowds already gathered around them, looking at the cheap clothes and toys. He almost swore under his breath. On Tuesdays and Thursdays he tried to avoid the Cours in the morning. "Singer?" he asked.

"Oh yes, kept the choir director busy, Grégory did," Père Etienne replied. "I'll let you go now. Goodbye."

"Goodbye," Verlaque said. He ran across the Cours and down the rue Mistral and kept running until he got to the Quatre Dauphins. He turned left on Cardinale and kept running to the rue d'Italie. He saw Manuel Arruda strolling up the street with a market basket in his hand. Verlaque nodded to Arruda and carried on until he saw the bicycle locked to a lamppost by the red door. The door was open, and he walked in. Philomène Joubert was working at the desk, humming and putting stamps on envelopes.

"The organ drive," she said, holding up an envelope. "But you've already generously donated, Judge Verlaque."

He sat down across from her and stayed silent.

"Cat has your tongue this morning," Philomène said, stuffing an envelope.

"I'm just trying to understand why you said you didn't know Grégory de Castelbajac. You're the choir director, and Grégory was a member and a fine singer, I'm told."

Philomène licked another stamp, put it on the envelope, and then set it aside. "Oh, I see." She folded her short thick arms on the desk and played with her wedding ring.

"Or why Père Jean-Luc promised he would have Frère, now Père, Etienne Fronton call me regarding Grégory but then never did. Frère Joël had to do it. Père Etienne just called."

Père Jean-Luc had been in the hall when Verlaque came in. He stepped into the office and approached the desk. "What should we do?" Philomène asked him.

Verlaque looked over and saw Philomène's bicycle paniers sitting at the side of the desk, covered by a red-and-white-checked tea towel. "Your bakery deliveries," he said. "Did Grégory assist in any way?"

Père Jean-Luc nodded, and Philomène wrung her hands.

"Do you visit cancer patients, Mme Joubert?" Verlaque asked.

She nodded.

"I can't believe I'm the one who has to ask all the questions," Verlaque said. "Getting information out of you two is like—"

He waited for Philomène to give him a Provençal expression, preferably from Menpenti in Marseille, but she stayed silent.

Père Jean-Luc walked over and locked the red door that gave onto the rue d'Italie. "Grégory, bless him, sold us marijuana," he whispered.

"Lower than street price," Philomène said, and Verlaque had to force his mouth not to grin.

He nodded, trying to look stern. "And you, Mme Joubert, put it into the cakes."

"And cookies," Philomène said. "Just tiny amounts."

"May I ask where you get the marijuana now?"

"Best not," Père Jean-Luc replied. "But I can tell you it's organic, and locally grown."

"You can try a piece of cake," Philomène said, gesturing to the basket.

"No thank you," Verlaque said. He rubbed his eyes, wishing he had headed straight for Michaud's and never answered his telephone.

"It gives the patients so much comfort," Père Jean-Luc said. "I even have part of a brownie now and again—"

Verlaque looked up, surprised.

"Chronic back pain," the priest explained, rubbing his lower back for effect.

"We know it's against the law," Philomène explained. "But it's becoming legal, for medicinal purposes, in so many places, and soon that will happen here, too. We were just jumping the gun a bit. Trailblazers. I think that's the word. Trailblazers."

Epilogue

The Last Photograph

*F*lorence Bonnet put on her reading glasses and looked at the photograph, smiling. A crowd of about sixty people, most of them dressed in their finest, including a few women wearing very large hats, filled the tiny rue Clemenceau. Some passersby smiled and gestured at the crowd, while others stopped and stared, as if trying to decide whether to pretend to be a guest and help themselves to a glass of champagne. Even if Florence would never, ever have thought of having a party in a café, out in the street, she had had a good time, and she decided that she would frame this photograph. Florence had been half relieved when Marine and Antoine had suggested a civil ceremony in Aix and a church wedding and grand lunch in Italy. She had never been one of those mothers able to organize perfect birthday parties and had dreaded Marine's wedding reception. She had friends who dove into the preparations of their daughters' weddings with glee, sometimes spending more than a year, clipping out pictures from magazines and trading addresses of caterers, flower shops, and châteaux in the Aix region that rented out their buildings and gardens. The party in the street ended up being fun and casual, and Florence had been able to invite colleagues from the university, neighbors, and some of the choir friends without the hassle or worry about logistics or the food and drink.

She loved this picture: Her daughter and husband were in the middle of the crowd, looking at each other and smiling; Anatole was saying something excitedly and Marine was smiling, holding her champagne in one hand, the other hand posing on her father's shoulder. They stood out in the middle of the photograph and the guests around them seemed blurry, as if moving in slow motion. Florence wasn't sure if the photographer had done that on purpose; she knew photographers could do tricks with the focusing. She wasn't in the photograph, but that didn't matter; she hated having her picture taken. The important thing was that it was of Marine and her father, who were very close. Perhaps if they had had a son—if baby Thomas had lived—she would have bonded with the son, sharing the same relationship with him that Marine and Anatole had. To the right of Marine was Antoine's brother—Sébastien, she thought his name was—sneaking a look at his cell phone. She snorted. She had tried to talk to him when they were all in Italy, over the long extended lunch, but he only seemed interested in staring at Sylvie. On the other hand, Florence had had a fascinating conversation with the senior Verlaque, Gabriel, having cornered him when his too-young girlfriend had been busy speaking to Marine. They spoke of their love of the paintings of Ghirlandaio, especially the seldom-visited *Last Supper* in Florence's Ognissanti refectory. Perhaps Antoine Verlaque had this same knowledge, and love, of Renaissance painting, but she had never had a conversation like that with him. She knew she was partly to blame, as she was too busy sizing him up; trying to figure out if he was good enough for her daughter. She still hadn't decided.

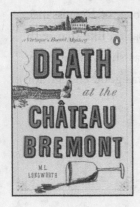 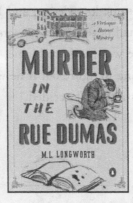 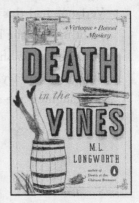